CAPTURED!

As she pushed her way through the snow-laden bushes, becoming wetter and wetter in the process, she felt a surge of pleasure. The first snare in the line held the body of a small ground-foraging bird. Evanlyn smiled grimly as she thought how once she might have objected to the cruelty of the bird's death. Now, all she felt was a sense of satisfaction as she realized that they would eat well today.

Amazing how an empty belly could change your perspective, she thought, removing the noose from the bird's neck and stuffing the small carcass in her makeshift game bag. She reset the snare, sprinkling a few seeds of corn on the ground beyond it, then rose to her feet, frowning in annoyance as she realized that the melting snow had left two wet patches on her knees as she'd crouched.

Evanlyn sensed, rather than heard, the movement in the trees behind her and began to turn.

Before she could move, she felt an iron grip around her throat, and as she gasped in fright, a fur-gloved hand, smelling vilely of smoke, clapped over her mouth and nose, cutting off her cry for help.

Read all of the adventures of

RANGER'S APPRENTICE

RANGER'S APPRENTICE

BOOK FOUR: THE BATTLE FOR SKANDIA

JOHN FLANAGAN

PUFFIN BOOKS

PUFFIN BOOKS
Published by the Penguin Group
Penguin Young Readers Group, 345 Hudson Street, New York, New York 10014, U.S.A.
Penguin Group (Canada), 90 Eglinton Avenue East, Suite 700, Toronto, Ontario, Canada M4P 2Y3
(a division of Pearson Penguin Canada Inc.)
Penguin Books Ltd, 80 Strand, London WC2R 0RL, England
Penguin Ireland, 25 St Stephen's Green, Dublin 2, Ireland (a division of Penguin Books Ltd)
Penguin Group (Australia), 250 Camberwell Road, Camberwell, Victoria 3124, Australia
(a division of Pearson Australia Group Pty Ltd)
Penguin Books India Pvt Ltd, 11 Community Centre, Panchsheel Park, New Delhi - 110 017, India
Penguin Group (NZ), 67 Apollo Drive, Rosedale, North Shore 0632, New Zealand
(a division of Pearson New Zealand Ltd)
Penguin Books (South Africa) (Pty) Ltd, 24 Sturdee Avenue,
Rosebank, Johannesburg 2196, South Africa

Registered Offices: Penguin Books Ltd, 80 Strand, London WC2R 0RL, England

Published in Australia by Random House Australia Children's Books
First American Edition published by Philomel Books,
a division of Penguin Young Readers Group, 2008
Published by Puffin Books, a division of Penguin Young Readers Group, 2009

13 15 17 19 20 18 16 14 12

THE LIBRARY OF CONGRESS HAS CATALOGED THE PHILOMEL BOOKS EDITION AS FOLLOWS:
Flanagan, John (John Anthony).
The battle for Skandia / John Flanagan.—1st American ed.
p. cm. — (Ranger's apprentice ; bk. 4)
Summary: After Ranger's apprentice Will battles Temujai warriors to rescue Evanlyn, Will's kingdom
of Araluen joins forces with rival kingdom Skandia to defeat a common enemy.
ISBN 978-0-399-24457-5 (hc)
[1. Heroes—Fiction. 2. War—Fiction. 3. Fantasy.]
I. Title.
PZ7.F598284Bat 2008 [Fic]—dc22 2007023646

Puffin Books ISBN 978-0-14-241340-1

Designed by Marikka Tamura. Text set in Adobe Jensen.

Printed in the United States of America

To Leonie, for always believing.

1

IT WAS A CONSTANT TAPPING SOUND THAT ROUSED WILL FROM his deep, untroubled sleep. He had no clear idea at what point he first became aware of it. It seemed to slide unobtrusively into his sleeping mind, magnified and amplified inside his subconscious, until it crossed over into the conscious world and he realized he was awake, and wondering what it might be.

Tap-tap-tap-tap . . . It was still there, but not as loud now that he was awake and aware of other sounds in the small cabin.

From the corner, behind a small curtain of sacking that gave her a modicum of privacy, he could hear Evanlyn's even breathing. Obviously, the tapping hadn't woken her. There was a muted crackle from the heaped coals in the fireplace at the end of the room and, as he became more fully awake, he heard them settle with a slight rustling sound.

Tap-tap-tap . . .

It seemed to come from nearby. He stretched and yawned, sitting up on the rough couch he'd fashioned from wood and canvas. He shook his head to clear it and, for a moment, the sound was obscured. Then it was back once more and he realized it was coming from outside the window. The oiled cloth panes were translucent—they would admit the gray light of the pre-dawn, but he couldn't see anything more than a blur through them. Will knelt on the couch and unlatched the frame, pushing it up and craning his head through the opening to study the small porch of the cabin.

A gust of chill entered the room and he heard Evanlyn stir as it eddied around, causing the sacking curtain to billow inward and the embers in the fireplace to glow more fiercely, until a small tongue of yellow flame was released from them.

Somewhere in the trees, a bird was greeting the first light of a new day, and the tapping sound was obscured once more.

Then he had it. It was water, dripping from the end of a long icicle that depended from the porch roof and falling onto an upturned bucket that had been left on the edge of the porch.

Tap-tap-tap . . . tap-tap-tap.

Will frowned to himself. There was something significant in this, he knew, but his mind, still fuddled with sleep, couldn't quite grasp what it was. He stood, still stretching, and shivered slightly as he left the last warmth of his blanket and made his way to the door.

Hoping not to wake Evanlyn, he eased the latch upward and slowly opened the door, holding it up so that the sagging leather hinges wouldn't allow the bottom edge to scrape the floor of the cabin.

Closing the door behind him, he stepped out onto the rough boards of the porch, feeling them strike icy cold against his bare feet. He moved to the spot where the water dripped endlessly onto the bucket, realizing as he went that other icicles hanging from the roof were also dripping water. He hadn't seen this before. He was sure they usually didn't do this.

He glanced out at the trees, where the first rays of the sun were beginning to filter through.

In the forest, there was a slithering thump as a load of snow finally slid clear of the pine branches that had supported it for months and fell in a heap to the ground below.

And it was then that Will realized the significance of the endless tap-tap-tap that had woken him.

Behind him, he heard the door creak and he turned to see Evanlyn, her hair wildly tousled, her blanket wrapped tight around her against the cold.

"What is it?" she asked him. "Is something wrong?"

He hesitated a second, glancing at the growing puddle of water beside the bucket.

"It's the thaw," he said finally.

After their meager breakfast, Will and Evanlyn sat in the early morning sun as it streamed across the porch. Neither of them had wanted to discuss the significance of Will's earlier discovery, although they had since found more signs of the thaw.

Small patches of soaked brown grass were showing through the snow cover on the ground surrounding the cabin, and the sound of wet snow sliding from the trees to hit the ground was becoming increasingly common.

The snow was still thick on the ground and in the trees, of course. But the signs were there that the thaw had begun and that, inexorably, it would continue.

"I suppose we'll have to think about moving on," Will said, finally voicing the thought that had been in both their minds.

"You're not strong enough yet," Evanlyn told him. It had been barely three weeks since he had thrown off the mind-numbing effects of the warmweed given to him as a yard slave in Ragnak's Lodge. Will had been weakened by inadequate food and clothing and a regimen of punishing physical work before they had made their escape. Since then, their meager diet in the cabin had been enough to sustain life, but not to restore his strength or endurance. They had lived on the cornmeal and flour that had been stored in the cabin, along with a small stock of vegetables and the stringy meat from whatever game Evanlyn and he had been able to snare.

There was little enough of that in winter, and what game they had managed to catch had been in poor condition itself, providing little in the way of nourishment.

Will shrugged. "I'll manage," he said simply. "I'll have to."

And that, of course, was the heart of the problem. They both knew that once the snow in the high passes had melted, hunters would again begin to visit the high country where they found themselves. Already, Evanlyn had seen one such—the mysterious rider in the forest on the day when Will's senses had returned to him. Fortunately, since that day, there had been no further sign of him. But it was a warning. Others would come, and before they did, Will and Evanlyn would have to be long gone, heading down the far side of the mountain passes and across the border into Teutlandt.

Evanlyn shook her head doubtfully. For a moment, she said nothing. Then she realized that Will was right. Once the thaw was well and truly under way, they would have to leave whether she felt he was strong enough to travel or not.

"Anyway," she said at last, "we have a few weeks yet. The thaw's only just started, and who knows? We may even get another cold snap."

It was possible, she thought. Perhaps not probable, but at least it was possible. Will nodded agreement.

"There's always that," he said.

The silence fell over them once more like a blanket. Abruptly, Evanlyn stood, dusting off her breeches. "I'll go and check the snares," she said, and when Will began to rise to accompany her, she stopped him.

"You stay here," she said gently. "From now on, you're going to have to conserve your strength as much as possible."

Will hesitated, then nodded. He recognized that she was right.

She collected the hessian sack they used as a game bag and slung it over her shoulder. Then, with a small smile in his direction, the girl headed off into the trees.

Feeling useless and dispirited, Will slowly began to gather up the wooden platters they had used for their meal. All he was good for, he thought bitterly, was washing up.

The snare line had moved farther and farther from the cabin over the past three weeks. As small animals, rabbits, squirrels and the occasional snow hare had fallen prey to the snares that Will had built, the other animals in that area had become wary. As a consequence, they had been compelled to move the snares into new locations every few days—each one a little farther away from the cabin than the one before.

Evanlyn estimated that she had a good forty minutes' walking on the narrow uphill track before she would reach the first snare. Of course, if she'd been able to move straight to it, the walk would have been considerably shorter. But the track wound and wandered through the trees, more than doubling the distance she had to cover.

The signs of the thaw were all around her, now that she was aware of it. The snow no longer squeaked dryly underfoot as she walked. It was heavier, wetter and her steps sank deeply into it. The leather of her boots was already soaked from contact with the melting snow. The last time she had walked this way, she reflected, the snow had simply coated her boots as a fine, dry powder.

She also began to notice more activity among the wildlife in the area. Birds flitted through the trees in greater numbers than she'd previously seen, and she startled a rabbit on the track, sending it scurrying back into the protection of a snow-covered thicket of blackberries.

At least, she thought, all this extra activity might increase the chances of finding some worthwhile game in the snares.

Evanlyn saw the discreet sign that Will had cut into the bark of a pine and turned off the track to find the spot where she and Will had laid the first of the snares. She recalled how gratefully she had greeted his recovery from the warmweed drug. Her own survival skills were negligible and Will had provided welcome expertise in devising and setting snares to supplement their diet. It was all part of his Ranger training under Halt, he had told her.

She remembered how, when he had mentioned the older Ranger's name, his eyes had misted for a few moments and his voice had choked slightly. Not for the first time, the two young people had felt very, very far from home.

As she pushed her way through the snow-laden bushes, becoming wetter and wetter in the process, she felt a surge of pleasure. The first snare in the line held the body of a small ground-foraging bird. They had caught a few of these previously and the bird's flesh made excellent eating. About the size of a small chicken, it had carelessly poked its neck through the wire noose of the snare, then become entangled. Evanlyn smiled grimly as she thought how once she might have objected to the cruelty of the bird's death. Now, all she felt was a sense of satisfaction as she realized that they would eat well today.

Amazing how an empty belly could change your perspective,

she thought, removing the noose from the bird's neck and stuffing the small carcass in her makeshift game bag. She reset the snare, sprinkling a few seeds of corn on the ground beyond it, then rose to her feet, frowning in annoyance as she realized that the melting snow had left two wet patches on her knees as she'd crouched.

Evanlyn sensed, rather than heard, the movement in the trees behind her and began to turn.

Before she could move, she felt an iron grip around her throat, and as she gasped in fright, a fur-gloved hand, smelling vilely of smoke, sweat and dirt, clapped over her mouth and nose, cutting off her cry for help.

2

THE TWO RIDERS EMERGED FROM THE TREES AND INTO A CLEAR meadow. Down here in the foothills of Teutlandt, the coming spring was more apparent than in the high mountains that reared ahead of them. The meadow grasses were already showing green and there were only isolated patches of snow, in spots that usually remained shaded for the greater part of the day.

A casual onlooker might have been interested to notice the horses that followed behind the two mounted men. They might even have mistaken the men, at a distance, for traders who were hoping to take advantage of the first opportunity to cross through the mountain passes into Skandia, and so benefit from the high prices that the season's first trade goods would enjoy.

But a closer inspection would have shown that these men were not traders. They were armed warriors. The smaller of the two, a bearded man clad in a strange gray and green dappled cloak that seemed to shift and waver as he moved, had a longbow slung over his shoulders and a quiver of arrows at his saddle bow.

His companion was a larger, younger man. He wore a simple brown cloak, but the early spring sunshine glinted off the chain mail armor at his neck and arms, and the scabbard of a long sword showed under the hem of the cloak. Completing the picture, a round buckler was slung over his back, emblazoned with a slightly crude effigy of an oakleaf.

Their horses were as mismatched as the men themselves. The younger man sat astride a tall bay—long-legged, with powerful haunches and shoulders, it was the epitome of a battlehorse. A second battlehorse, this one a black, trotted behind him on a lead rope. His companion's mount was considerably smaller, a shaggy barrel-chested horse, more a pony really. But it was sturdy, and had a look of endurance to it. Another horse, similar to the first, trotted behind, lightly laden with the bare essentials for camping and traveling. There was no lead rein on this horse. It followed obediently and willingly.

Horace craned his neck up at the tallest of the mountains towering above them. His eyes squinted slightly in the glare of the snow that still lay thickly on the mountain's upper half and now reflected the light of the sun.

"You mean to tell me we're going over that?" he asked, his eyes widening.

Halt looked sidelong at him, with the barest suggestion of a smile. Horace, however, intent on studying the massive mountain formations facing them, failed to see it.

"Not over," said the Ranger. "Through."

Horace frowned thoughtfully at that. "Is there a tunnel of some kind?"

"A pass," Halt told him. "A narrow defile that twists and winds through the lower reaches of the mountains and brings us into Skandia itself."

Horace digested that piece of information for a moment or two. Then Halt saw his shoulders rise to an intake of breath and knew that the movement presaged yet another question. He closed his eyes, remembering a time that seemed years ago when he was alone and when life was not an endless series of questions.

Then he admitted to himself that, strangely, he preferred things the way they were now. However, he must have made some unintentional noise as he awaited the question, for he noticed that Horace had sealed his lips firmly and determinedly. Obviously, Horace had sensed the reaction and had decided that he would not bother Halt with another question. Not yet, anyway.

Which left Halt in a strange quandary. Because now that the question was unasked, he couldn't help wondering what it would have been. All of a sudden, there was a nagging sense of incompletion about the morning. He tried to ignore the feeling but it would not be pushed aside. And for once, Horace seemed to have conquered his almost irresistible need to ask the question that had occurred to him.

Halt waited a minute or two but there was no sound except for the jingling of harness and the creaking of leather from their saddles. Finally, the former Ranger could bear it no longer.

"What?"

The question seemed to explode out of him, with a greater degree of violence than he had intended. Taken by surprise, Horace's bay shied in fright and danced several paces sideways.

Horace turned an aggrieved look on his mentor as he calmed the horse and brought it back under control.

"What?" he asked Halt, and the smaller man made a gesture of exasperation.

"That's what I want to know," he said irritably. "*What?*"

Horace peered at him. The look was all too obviously the sort of look that you give to someone who seems to have taken leave of his senses. It did little to improve Halt's rapidly rising temper.

"What?" said Horace, now totally puzzled.

"Don't keep parroting at me!" Halt fumed. "Stop repeating what I say! I asked you 'what,' so don't ask me 'what' back, understand?"

Horace considered the question for a second or two, then, in his deliberate way, he replied: "No."

Halt took a deep breath, his eyebrows contracted into a deep V, and beneath them his eyes sparked with anger. But before he could speak, Horace forestalled him.

"What 'what' are you asking me?" he said. Then, thinking how to make his question clearer, he added, "Or to put it another way, why are you asking 'what'?"

Controlling himself with enormous restraint, and making no secret of the fact, Halt said, very precisely: "You were about to ask a question."

Horace frowned. "I was?"

Halt nodded. "You were. I saw you take a breath to ask it."

"I see," said Horace. "And what was it about?"

For just a second or two, Halt was speechless. He opened his mouth, closed it again, then finally found the strength to speak.

"That is what I was asking you," he said. "When I said 'what,' I was asking you what you were about to ask me."

"I wasn't about to ask you 'what,'" Horace replied, and Halt glared at him suspiciously. It occurred to him that Horace could be indulging himself in a gigantic leg pull, that he was secretly laughing at Halt. This, Halt could have told him, was not a good career move. Rangers were not people who took kindly to being laughed at. He studied the boy's open face and guileless blue eyes and decided that his suspicion was ill-founded.

"Then what, if I may use that word once more, were you about to ask me?"

Horace drew breath once more, then hesitated. "I forget," he said. "What were we talking about?"

"Never mind," Halt muttered, and nudged Abelard into a canter for a few strides to draw ahead of his companion.

Sometimes the Ranger could be confusing, and Horace thought it best to forget the whole conversation. Yet, as happens so often, the moment he stopped trying to consciously remember the thought that had prompted his question, it popped back into his mind again.

"Are there many passes?" he called to Halt.

The Ranger twisted in his saddle to look back at him. "What?" he asked.

Horace wisely chose to ignore the fact that they were heading for dangerous territory with that word again. He gestured to the mountains frowning down upon them.

"Through the mountains. Are there many passes into Skandia through the mountains?"

Halt checked Abelard's stride momentarily, allowing the bay to catch up with them, then resumed his pace.

"Three or four," he said.

"Then don't the Skandians guard them?" Horace asked. It seemed logical to him that they would.

"Of course they do," Halt replied. "The mountains form their principal line of defense."

"So how did you plan for us to get past them?"

The Ranger hesitated. It was a question that had been taxing his mind since they had taken the road from Chateau Montsombre. If he were by himself, he would have no trouble slipping past unseen. With Horace in company, and riding a big, spirited battlehorse, it might be a more difficult matter. He had a few ideas but had yet to settle on any one of them.

"I'll think of something," he temporized, and Horace nodded wisely, satisfied that Halt would indeed think of something. In

Horace's world, that was what Rangers did best, and the best thing a warrior apprentice could do was let the Ranger get on with thinking while a warrior took care of walloping anyone who needed to be walloped along the way. He settled back in his saddle, contented with his lot in life.

3

ERAK STARFOLLOWER, WOLFSHIP CAPTAIN AND ONE OF THE
senior war jarls of the Skandians, made his way through the low-
ceilinged, wood-paneled lodge to the Great Hall. His face was
marked with a frown as he went. He had plenty to do, with the
spring raiding season coming on. His ship needed repairs and refit-
ting. Most of all, it needed the fine-tuning that only a few days at
sea could bring.

Now this summons from Ragnak boded ill for his plans.
Particularly since the summons had come through the medium of
Borsa, the Oberjarl's hilfmann, or administrator. If Borsa were involved, it usually meant that Ragnak had some little task for Erak to
look after. Or some not-so-little task, the wolfship skipper thought
wryly.

Breakfast was long since finished, so there were only a few servants cleaning up the Hall when he arrived. At the far end, seated at
a rough pine table off to one side of Ragnak's High Seat—a massive
pinewood chair that served in place of a throne for the Skandian
ruler—sat Ragnak and Borsa, their heads bowed over a pile of
parchment scrolls. Erak recognized those scrolls. They were the
tax returns for the various towns and shires throughout Skandia.

Ragnak was obsessed with them. As for Borsa, his life was totally dominated by them. He breathed, slept and dreamed the tax returns, and woe betide any local jarl who might try to shortchange Ragnak or claim any deduction that wouldn't pass Borsa's fine-tooth comb inspection.

Erak put two and two together and sighed quietly. The most likely conclusion that he could draw from the two facts of his summoning and the pile of tax returns on the table was that he was about to be sent off on another tax-collecting mission.

Tax collecting was not something that Erak enjoyed. He was a raider and a sea wolf, a pirate and a fighter. As such, his inclination was to be more on the side of the tax evaders than the Oberjarl and his eager-fingered hilfmann. Unfortunately, on those previous occasions when Erak had been sent out to collect overdue or unpaid taxes, he had been too successful for his own good. Now, whenever there was the slightest doubt about the amount of tax owing from a village or a shire, Borsa automatically thought of Erak as the solution to the problem.

To make matters worse, Erak's attitude and approach to the job only added to his desirability in Borsa's and Ragnak's eyes. Bored with the task and considering it embarrassing and belittling, he made sure he spent as little time on the job as possible. The tortuous arguments and recalculation of amounts owing after all deductions had been approved and agreed were not for him. Erak opted for a more direct course, which consisted of seizing the person under investigation, ramming a double-headed broadax up under his chin and threatening mayhem if all taxes, every single one of them, were not paid immediately.

Erak's reputation as a fighter was well known throughout Skandia. To his annoyance, he was never asked to make good on his threat. Those recalcitrants whom he visited invariably coughed up the due amount, and often a little extra that had never been in contention, without the slightest argument or hesitation.

The two men at the table looked up as he made his way through the benches toward the end of the room. The Great Hall served more than one purpose. It was where Ragnak and his close followers took their meals. It was also the site of all banquets and official gatherings in Skandia's rough and ready social calendar. And the small, open annex where Ragnak and Borsa were currently studying tax returns was also Ragnak's office. It wasn't particularly private, since any member of the inner or outer council of jarls had access to the hall at any time of day. But then, Ragnak wasn't the sort to need privacy. He ruled openly and made all his policy statements to the world at large.

"Ah, Erak, you're here," said Borsa, and Erak thought, not for the first time, that the hilfmann had a habit of stating the bleeding obvious.

"Who is it this time?" he asked in a resigned tone. He knew there was no use trying to argue his way out of the assignment, so he might as well just get on with it. With luck, it would be one of the small towns down the coast, and at least he might have a chance to work up his crew and wolfship at the same time.

"Ostkrag," the Oberjarl told him, and Erak's hopes of salvaging something useful from this assignment faded to nothing. Ostkrag lay far inland, to the east. It was a small settlement on the far side of the mountain range that formed the rugged spine of Skandia and was accessible only by going over the mountains themselves or through one of the half dozen tortuous passes that wound their way through.

At best, it meant an uncomfortable journey there and back by pony, a method of transport that Erak loathed. As he thought of the mountain range that reared above Hallasholm, he had a quick memory of the two Araluen slaves he had helped to escape several months ago. He wondered what had become of them, whether they had made it to the small hunting cabin high in the mountains and whether they had survived the last months of winter. He realized abruptly that Borsa and Ragnak were both waiting for his reaction.

"Ostkrag?" he repeated. Ragnak nodded impatiently.

"Their quarterly payment is overdue. I want you to go and shake them up," the Oberjarl said. Erak noticed that Ragnak couldn't quite hide the avaricious gleam that came into his eyes whenever he talked about tax and payments. Erak couldn't help giving vent to an exasperated sigh.

"They can't be overdue by more than a week or so," he temporized, but Ragnak was not to be swayed and shook his head violently.

"Ten days!" he snapped. "And it's not the first time! I've warned them before, haven't I, Borsa?" he said, turning to the hilfmann, who nodded.

"The jarl at Ostkrag is Sten Hammerhand," Borsa said, as if that were explanation enough. Erak stared blankly at him. "He should be called Sten Gluehand," he elaborated with heavy sarcasm. "The tax payments have stuck to his fingers before this, and even when they're paid in full, he always makes us wait long past the overdue date. It's time we taught him a lesson."

Erak smiled with some irony at the small, sparsely muscled hilfmann. Borsa could be an extremely threatening figure, he thought—when someone else was available to carry out the threats.

"You mean it's time I taught him a lesson?" he suggested, but Borsa didn't notice the sarcasm in his voice.

"Exactly!" he said, with some satisfaction. Ragnak, however, was a little more perceptive.

"It's my money, after all, Erak," he said, and there was an almost petulant note in his voice. Erak met his gaze steadily. For the first time, he realized that Ragnak was growing old. The once flaming red hair was duller and turning gray. It came as a surprise to Erak. He certainly didn't feel that he was growing older, yet Ragnak didn't have too many years on him. He could notice other changes in the Oberjarl now that he had become aware of the fact. His jowls were heavier and his waistline thickening. He wondered if he was changing too.

"It's been a severe winter," he suggested. "Perhaps the passes are still blocked. There was a lot of late snow."

He moved to the large scale map of Skandia that was displayed on the wall behind Ragnak's table. He found Ostkrag and, with one forefinger, traced the way to the closest pass.

"The Serpent Pass," he said, almost to himself. "It's not impossible that all that late-season snow and the sudden thaw could have led to landslides in there." He turned back to Ragnak and Borsa, indicating the position on the map to them.

"Maybe the couriers simply can't get through yet?" he suggested. Ragnak shook his head and again Erak sensed the irritability, the irrational annoyance that seemed to grip Ragnak these days whenever his will was thwarted or his judgment questioned.

"It's Sten, I know it," he said stubbornly. "If it were anyone else, I might agree with you, Erak." Erak nodded, knowing full well that the words were a lie. Ragnak rarely agreed with anyone if it meant changing his own position. "Get up there and get the money from him. If he argues, arrest him and bring him back. In fact, arrest him even if he doesn't argue. Take twenty men with you. I want him to see a real show of strength. I'm sick of being taken for a fool by these petty jarls."

Erak looked up in some surprise. Arresting a jarl in his own lodge was not something to be lightly contemplated—particularly for such a petty offense as a late tax payment. Among the Skandians, tax evasion was considered to be almost obligatory. It was a form of sport. If you were caught out, you paid up and that was the end of it. Erak could not remember anyone being submitted to the shame of arrest on that count.

"That might not be wise," he said quietly, and Ragnak glared up at him, his eyes searching for Erak's over the scattered accounts on the table before him.

"I'll decide what's wise," he grated. "I'm Oberjarl, not you."

The words were offensive. Erak was a senior jarl and by long-established custom he was entitled to air his opinion, even though it might be contrary to his leader's. He bit back the angry retort that sprang to his lips. There was no point provoking Ragnak any further when he was in this mood.

"I know you're the Oberjarl, Ragnak," he said quietly. "But Sten is a jarl in his own right and he may well have a perfectly valid reason for this late payment. To arrest him in those circumstances would be unnecessarily provocative."

"I'm telling you he won't have what you call a 'valid reason,' damn it!" Ragnak's eyes were narrowed now and his face was suffused with his anger. "He's a thief and a holdout and he needs to be made an example to others!"

"Ragnak . . . ," Erak began, trying to reason one last time. This time it was Borsa who interrupted.

"Jarl Erak, you have your instructions! Now do as you are ordered!" he shouted, and Erak turned angrily to face him.

"I follow the Oberjarl's orders, hilfmann. Not yours."

Borsa realized his mistake. He backed away a pace or two, making sure the substantial bulk of the table was between him and Erak. His eyes slid away from the other man's and there was an ugly silence. Finally, Ragnak seemed to realize that some form of back-down might be necessary—although not too much. He said, in an irritated tone: "Look, Erak, just go and get those taxes from Sten. And if he's been holding out on purpose, bring him back here for trial. All right?"

"And if he has a valid reason?" Erak insisted.

The Oberjarl waved a hand in surrender. "If he has a valid reason, you can leave him alone. Does that suit you?"

Erak nodded. "Under those conditions, all right," he agreed.

He had the loophole he'd been looking for. As far as he was concerned, the fact that Ragnak was an insufferable pain in the buttocks was a more than valid reason for not paying taxes on time. Mind you, he might have to find another way of phrasing it when he returned without arresting Sten.

4

Will came awake with a jerk. He had been sitting on the edge of the porch in the sun and he realized that he must have nodded off. Ruefully, he thought about how much of his time he spent sleeping these days. Evanlyn said it was only to be expected, as he was regaining his strength. He supposed she was right. But that didn't mean he had to like it.

There was also the fact that there was so little to do around the hut where they had spent their time since escaping from the Skandian stronghold. Today he had cleared away and washed their breakfast dishes, then made the beds and straightened the few pieces of furniture in the cabin. That had taken barely half an hour, so he had groomed the pony in the lean-to behind the cabin until its coat shone. The pony looked at him, and at itself, with mild surprise. He guessed nobody had ever spent so much care on its appearance in the past.

After that, Will had wandered aimlessly around the cabin and the small clearing, inspecting those patches where the damp brown grass was beginning to show through the snow cover. He had idly considered making some more snares, then discarded the idea. They had more than they needed already. Feeling bored and useless, he had sat down on the porch to wait for Evanlyn's return. At some stage, he must have nodded off, affected by the warmth of the sun.

That warmth was long gone now, he realized. The sun had traveled fully across the clearing and the pines were throwing long shadows across the cabin. It must be midafternoon, he estimated.

A frown creased his forehead. Evanlyn had left well before noon to check the snares. Even allowing for the fact that they had moved the trapline farther and farther away from the cabin, she should have had time to reach the line, check the snares and return by now. She must have been gone for at least three hours—possibly more.

Unless she had already returned and, seeing him sleeping, had decided not to wake him. He stood now, his stiff joints protesting, and checked inside the cabin. There was no sign that she had returned. The game bag and her thick woolen cloak were missing. Will's frown deepened and he began to pace the small clearing, wondering what he should do. He wished he knew exactly how long she had been gone and silently berated himself for falling asleep. Deep down in the pit of his stomach, a vague uneasiness stirred as he wondered what could have become of his companion. He reviewed the possibilities.

She could have lost her way, and be wandering through the thickly growing, snow-covered pines, trying to find her way back to the cabin. Possible, but unlikely. He had blazed the paths leading to their trapline with discreet marks and Evanlyn knew where to look for them.

Perhaps she had been injured? She could have fallen, or twisted an ankle. The paths were rough and steep in places and that was a definite possibility. She might be lying now, injured and unable to walk, stranded in the snow, with the afternoon drawing on toward night.

The third possibility was the worst: she had encountered someone. Anyone that she ran into on this mountain was likely to be an enemy. Perhaps she had been recaptured by the Skandians. His pulse raced for a moment as he considered the thought. He knew they would show little mercy to an escaped slave. And while Erak had helped them before, he would be unlikely to do so again—even if he had the opportunity.

As he had been considering these possibilities, he had begun moving around the cabin, collecting his things in preparation for setting out to look for her. He had filled one of their water skins from the bucket of creek water that he brought to the cabin each day, and crammed a few pieces of cold meat into a carry sack. He laced on his thick walking boots, winding the thongs rapidly around his legs, almost up to the knee, and unhooked his sheepskin vest from the peg behind the door.

On the whole, he thought, the second possibility was the most likely. The chances were that Evanlyn was injured somewhere, unable to walk. The chance that she might have been retaken by the Skandians was very slim indeed, he realized. It was still too early in the season for people to be moving around the mountain. The only reason for doing so would be to hunt game. And it was still too scarce to be worth the trouble of fighting through the thick drifts of snow that blocked the way in so many parts of the mountain. No, on the whole, it was most likely that Evanlyn was safe, but incapacitated.

Which meant his next logical move would be to put a bridle and saddle on the pony and lead him along as he tracked her, so that she could ride back to the cabin once he found her. He had no doubt that he *would* find her. He was already a skilled tracker, although nowhere near the standard of Halt or Gilan, and tracking the girl through snow-covered territory would be a relatively simple matter.

And yet . . . he was reluctant to take the pony with him. The little horse would make unnecessary noise and a nagging doubt told Will he should proceed with caution. It was unlikely that Evanlyn had encountered strangers, but it wasn't impossible.

It might be wiser to travel unobtrusively until he found out the real state of affairs. As he came to this decision, he stripped the beds of their blankets, tying them into a roll that he slung over his shoulder. It might prove necessary to spend the night in the open and it would be better to be prepared. He picked up a flint and steel from near the fireplace and dropped it into one of his pockets.

Finally, he was ready to go. He stood at the door, taking one last look around the cabin to see if there was anything else he might need. The small hunting bow and a quiver of arrows leaned by the doorjamb. On an impulse, he picked them up, slinging the quiver across his back with the roll of blankets. Then another thought struck him and he crossed back to the fireplace, selecting a half-burned stick from the ashes.

On the outside of the door, he printed in crude letters: "Looking for you. Wait here."

After all, it was possible that Evanlyn might turn up after he had left and he wanted to make sure she didn't go blundering off, trying to find him while he was trying to find her.

He took a few seconds to string the bow. Halt's voice echoed in his ears: "An unstrung bow is just something extra to carry. A strung bow is a weapon." He looked at it disdainfully. It wasn't much of a weapon, he thought. But that and the small knife in his belt were all that he had. He moved to the edge of the clearing, picking up the clear trail of Evanlyn's footprints in the snow. They were blurred after a morning of spring sunshine, but they still showed up. Maintaining a steady trot, he moved off into the forest.

◆   ◆   ◆

He followed her trail easily as it wound up into the higher reaches of the mountain. Before too long, his pace had dropped from the steady jog and he was walking, breathing hard as he went. He realized that he was in poor condition. There had been a time when he could have maintained that ground-eating lope for hours. Now, after barely twenty minutes, he was puffing and exhausted. He shook his head in disgust and continued to follow the footprints.

Of course, following the trail was made easier by the fact that he already had a good idea of the direction Evanlyn had been heading. He had helped her relocate the snares a few days earlier. At that time, he recalled, they had gone at an easier pace, resting frequently so as not to tire him out.

Evanlyn had been reluctant to allow him to walk so far, but had given in to the inevitable. She had no real idea how to place the snares where they might have the best chance of trapping small game. That was one of Will's areas of expertise. He knew how to look for and recognize the small signs that showed where the rabbits and birds moved, where they were most likely to poke their unsuspecting heads into the looped snares.

It had taken Evanlyn about forty minutes to reach the trapline that morning. Will covered the distance in an hour and a quarter, stopping more frequently as the time went on to rest and recover his breath. He resented the stops, knowing they were costing him daylight. But there would be no point pushing himself until he was utterly exhausted. He had to keep himself in condition to give Evanlyn any assistance she might need when he found her.

The sun had dropped over the crest of the mountain by the time he reached the blazed tree that marked the beginning of the trapline. He touched one hand to the cut bark, then turned to head off the track into the pines when he saw something out of the corner of his eye. Something that froze his heart in midbeat.

There was the clear imprint of a horse's hooves in the snow—and they overlay the tracks that Evanlyn had left. Someone had followed her.

Forgetting his weariness, Will ran, half crouching, through the thick pines to the spot where the first snare had been laid. The snow there was disturbed and scuffed. He fell to his knees, trying to read the story that was written there.

The empty snare first: he could see where Evanlyn had reset the noose, smoothing the snow around it and scattering a few grains of seed. So there had been an animal in the snare when she'd arrived.

Then he cast wider, seeing the other set of footprints moving into position behind her as she had knelt, engrossed in the task of resetting the snare and probably jubilant at the fact that they had caught something. The horse's tracks had stopped some twenty meters away. Obviously, the animal was trained to move silently—much as Ranger horses were. He felt an uneasy sense of misgiving at that. He didn't like the idea of an enemy who had those sorts of skills—and by now he knew he was dealing with an enemy of some kind. The signs of the struggle between Evanlyn and the enemy were all too clear to his trained eye. He could almost see the man—he assumed it was a man—moving quietly behind her, grabbing her and dragging her back through the snow.

The wild disturbance of the ground showed how Evanlyn had kicked and struggled. Then, suddenly, the struggling had stopped and two shallow furrows in the snow led back to where the horse waited. Her heels, he realized, as her unconscious body had been dragged away.

Unconscious? Or dead, he thought. And a chill hand seized his heart at the thought. Then he shook it away determinedly.

"No sense in carrying her away if he'd killed her," he told himself. And he almost believed it. But he still had that gnawing uncertainty in the pit of his belly as he followed the horse's tracks back to the main trail, and then in the opposite direction of the trail that led back to the cabin.

He was glad he'd thought to bring the blankets. It was going to be a cold night, he thought. He was also glad that he'd thought to bring the bow, although he found himself wishing that he still had the powerful recurve bow that he had lost at the bridge in Celtica. It was a far superior weapon to the low-powered Skandian hunting bow. And he had the uncomfortable certainty that he was going to need a weapon in the very near future.

5

THE WORLD WAS UPSIDE DOWN AND BOUNCING. GRADUALLY, AS Evanlyn's eyes came into focus, she realized that she was hanging, head down, her face only centimeters away from the front left shoulder of a horse. The inverted position made the blood pound painfully in her head, a pounding that was accentuated by the steady, bouncing trot that the horse was maintaining. He was a chestnut, she noted, and his coat was long and shaggy and badly in need of grooming. The small area she could see was matted with sweat and dried mud.

Something hard ground into the soft flesh of her belly with every lurching step the horse took. She tried to wriggle to relieve the pressure and was rewarded for her efforts with a sharp blow to the back of her head. She took the hint and stopped wriggling.

Turning her head to face toward the rear, she could make out her captor's left leg—clad in a long, skirt-like fur coat and soft hide boots. Below her, the churned snow of the trail passed rapidly by. She realized her unconscious body had been slung unceremoniously across the front of a saddle. That projection stabbing dully into her stomach must be the pommel.

She remembered now: the slight noise behind her, the blur of movement as she started to turn. A hand, stinking of sweat and smoke and fur, clamped over her mouth to prevent her screaming. Not that there had been anyone within earshot to hear, she thought regretfully.

The struggle had been brief, with her assailant dragging her backward to keep her off balance. She had tried to fight her way free, tried to kick and bite. But the man's thick glove made her attempts at biting useless, and her kicks were ineffective as she was dragged backward. Finally, there had been an instant of blinding pain, just behind her left ear, and then darkness.

As she thought of the blow, she became aware that the area behind her left ear was another source of throbbing, another source of pain. The discomfort of being carried along helplessly like this was bad enough. But the inability to see anything, to get a look at the man who had taken her prisoner, was, if anything, worse. From this doubled-over, facedown position, she couldn't even see any features of the land they were passing through. So if she did eventually escape, she would have no memory of any landmarks that might help her retrace her steps.

Unobtrusively, she tried to twist her head to the side, to get a look at the rider mounted behind her. But he obviously felt the movement, minimal as she tried to keep it, and she felt another blow on the back of her head. Just what she needed, she thought ruefully.

Realizing that there was no future in antagonizing her captor, Evanlyn slumped down, trying to relax her muscles and ride as comfortably as possible. It was a fairly unsuccessful attempt. But at least when she let her head hang down, her cramping neck and shoulder muscles felt some relief.

The ground went by below her: the snow churned up by the horse's front hooves, showing the sodden brown grass that lay underneath. They were making their way downhill, she realized, as the rider reined in the horse to negotiate a steeper than normal part of the trail at a walk. She felt the rider lean back away from her as she slid forward, saw his feet pushing forward against the stirrups as he leaned back to compensate and help the horse balance.

Just ahead of them, visible from her facedown position, was a patch of snow that had melted and refrozen. It was slick and icy and the horse's hooves went onto it before she could sound any warning. Legs braced, the horse slid downward, unable to check its progress. She heard a startled grunt from the rider and he leaned farther back, keeping the reins taut to still the horse's panic. They slid, scrabbled, then checked. Then they were across the icy patch and the rider urged the horse back into its steady trot once more.

Evanlyn noted the moment. If it happened again, it might give her a chance to escape.

After all, she wasn't tied onto the horse, she realized. She was merely hanging either side like a bundle of old clothes. If the horse fell, she could be off and away before the rider regained his feet. Or so she thought.

Perhaps fortunately for her—for she couldn't see the bow slung over the rider's back, nor the quiver full of arrows that hung at his right side—the horse didn't fall. There were a few more steep sections, and a couple of other occasions when they slid, legs locked forward and rear hooves scrabbling for purchase, for several meters down the slope. But on none of those occasions did the rider lose control or the horse do more than whinny in alarm and concentration.

Finally, they reached their destination. The first she knew of it was when the horse slid to a stop and she felt a hand on her collar, heaving her up and over, to send her sprawling in the wet snow that covered the ground. She fell awkwardly, winding herself in the process, and it was several seconds before she could regain her presence of mind and take the time to look around her.

They were in a clearing where a small camp had been set up. Now she could see her captor as he swung down from the saddle. He was a short, stocky man, dressed in furs—a long, wide-skirted fur coat covered most of his body. On his head he wore a strange, conical fur hat. Beneath the skirts of the coat he wore shapeless trousers made from a thin kind of felt, with soft hide boots pulled up over them, about knee high.

He walked toward her now, rolling slightly with the bowlegged walk of a man who spent most of his time in the saddle. His features were sharp—almond-shaped eyes that slitted to almost nothing from years of looking across long distances into the wind and the glare of a hard land. His skin was dark, almost nut brown from exposure to the sun, and the cheekbones were high. The nose was short and wide, and the lips were thin. Her first impression was that it was a cruel face. Then she amended the thought. It was simply an uncaring face. The eyes showed no signs of compassion or even interest in her as the rider reached down and grabbed her collar, forcing her to her feet.

"Stand," he said. The voice was thick and the accent guttural, but she recognized the single word in the Skandian tongue. It was basically similar to the Araluen language and she had spent months with the Skandians in any event. She allowed herself to be raised to her feet. She was nearly as tall as the man, she noticed, with a slight feeling of surprise. But, small as he was, the strength in the arm that dragged her upright was all too obvious.

Now she noticed the bow and the quiver, and was instinctively glad that no chance had arisen for her to try to escape. She had no doubt that the man shoving her forward was an expert shot. There was something totally capable about him, she realized. He seemed so confident, so much in control. The bow might have simply marked him as a hunter. The long, curved sword in a brass-mounted scabbard on his left hip said that he was a warrior.

Her study of the man was interrupted by a chorus of voices from the camp. Now that she had the time to look, she saw another five warriors, similarly dressed and armed. Their horses, small and shaggy-coated, were tethered to a rope slung between two trees, and there were three small tents placed around the clearing, made from a material that appeared to be felt. A fire crackled in a small circle of stones set in the center of the clearing and the other men were grouped around it. They rose to their feet in surprise as she was pushed toward them.

One of them stepped forward, a little apart from the others. That fact, and the commanding tone in his voice, marked him as the leader of the small group. He spoke rapidly to the man who had captured her. She couldn't understand the words, but the tone was unmistakable. He was angry.

While he was obviously the leader of the small party, it was equally obvious that the man who had brought her here was also relatively senior. He refused to be cowed by the other man's angry words, replying in equally strident tones and gesturing toward her. The two of them stood, nose to nose, becoming louder and louder in their disagreement.

She stole a quick glance at the other four men. They had resumed their seats around the fire now, their initial interest in the captive having subsided. They watched the argument with interest, but with no apparent concern. One of them went back to turning a few green twigs with fresh meat spitted on them over the fire. The fat and juices ran off the meat and sizzled in the coals, sending up a cloud of fragrant smoke.

Evanlyn's stomach growled softly. She hadn't eaten since the meager breakfast she had shared with Will. From the position of the sun, it must be late afternoon by now. She calculated that they had been traveling some three hours at least.

Finally, the argument seemed to be resolved—and in favor of her captor. The leader threw his hands in the air angrily and turned away, walking back to his place by the fire and dropping to a cross-legged position. He looked at her, then waved dismissively to the other man. Her fate, it appeared, was in his hands.

The horseman took a length of rawhide rope from his saddle bow and quickly ran two loops around her neck. Then he dragged her toward a large pine at the edge of the clearing and fastened the rope to it. She had room to move, but not too far in any direction. He turned her around, shoving her roughly, and grabbed her hands, forcing them behind her back and crossing the wrists over each other. She resisted. But the result was another stinging blow across the back of her head. After that, she allowed her hands to be roughly tied behind her, with a shorter piece of rawhide. She winced and muttered a protest as the knots were drawn painfully tight. It was a mistake. Another blow across the back of her head taught her to remain silent.

She stood uncertainly, hands bound and tied by her neck to the tree. She was considering the best way to sit down when the problem was solved for her. The horseman kicked her feet out from under her and sent her sprawling in the snow. That, at least, brought a couple of low chuckles from the men around the fire.

For the next few hours she sat awkwardly, her hands gradually growing numb from the pressure of the bonds. The six men now seemed content to ignore her. They ate and drank, swigging what was obviously a strong spirit from leather bottles. The more they drank, the more boisterous they became. Yet she noticed that, even though they seemed to be drunk, their vigilance didn't relax for a second. One of them was always on guard, standing outside the glare of the small fire and moving constantly to monitor the approaches to the camp from all directions. The guard changed at regular intervals, she noticed, without any dissension or need for persuasion. All of them seemed to take an equal turn too.

As it grew to full night, the men began to retire into the small felt tents. They were dome shaped and barely waist high, so their occupants had to crawl into them through a low entrance. But, she thought enviously, they were probably a lot warmer than she would be, sitting out here.

The fire died down and one of the men—not the one who had captured her—walked in that same bandy-legged stride toward Evanlyn and tossed a heavy blanket over her. It was rough and carried the rank smell of their horses, but she was grateful for the warmth. Even so, it was not really enough for comfort. She huddled against the tree, shrugging the blanket higher around her shoulders, and prepared for a supremely uncomfortable night.

6

Halt leaned back and surveyed his handiwork with a satisfied sigh.

"There," he said. "That should do the trick."

Horace looked at him doubtfully, his eyes moving from Halt's pleased expression to the official-looking document that he had just completed forging.

"Whose seal is that at the bottom?" he asked finally, indicating the impression of a rampant bull that was set in a large splodge of wax in the bottom right-hand corner of the parchment. Halt touched the wax gently, checking to see if it had hardened completely.

"Well, I suppose if it's anyone's it's mine," he admitted. "But I'm hoping that our Skandian friends will think it belongs to King Henri of Gallica."

"Is that what his royal seal looks like?" Horace asked, and Halt studied the symbol impressed in the wax a little more critically.

"Pretty much," he replied. "I think the real one may be a trifle leaner in the body, but the forger I bought it from had a pretty indistinct impression to work from."

"But . . ." Horace began unhappily, then stopped.

Halt looked at him, one eyebrow raised quizzically. "But?" he repeated, making the word into a question.

Horace merely shook his head. He knew Halt would probably laugh at his objection if he voiced it. "Oh, never mind," he said at last. Then, realizing that the former Ranger was still waiting for him to speak, he changed the subject.

"I thought you said there was no ruling court in Gallica," he said. Halt shook his head.

"There's no effective ruling court," he told the young man. "King Henri is the hereditary king of the Gallicans, but he has no real power. He maintains a court in the southern part of the country and lets the local warlords do as they please."

"Yes. I noticed some of that," Horace said meaningfully, thinking about the encounter with the warlord Deparnieux that had delayed their progress through Gallica.

"So old King Henri is something of a paper tiger," Halt continued. "But he has been known to send envoys into other countries from time to time. Hence this." He gestured at the sheet of parchment that he was waving gently in the air so that the ink might dry and the wax seal might harden. The sight of the seal brought back all of Horace's misgivings.

"It just doesn't seem right!" he blurted out, before he could stop himself. Halt smiled patiently at him, blowing gently on some damp patches of ink.

"It's as right as I can get it," he said mildly. "And I doubt that the average border guard in Skandia will see the difference—particularly if you're dressed in that fine suit of Gallican armor you took from Deparnieux."

But Horace shook his head doggedly. Now that his concern was out in the open, he was determined to plow on.

"That's not what I meant," he said, then added, "and well you know it."

Halt grinned easily at the young man's troubled expression. "Sometimes your sense of morality amazes me," he said gently. "You do understand that we have to get past the border guards if we're to have any chance of finding Will and the princess?"

"Evanlyn," Horace corrected him automatically. Halt waved the comment aside.

"Whoever." He knew that Horace tended to refer to Princess Cassandra, the daughter of the Araluen King, by the name she had assumed when Will and Horace had first encountered her. He continued: "You do realize that, don't you?"

Horace heaved a deep sigh. "Yes, I suppose so, it's just that it seems so . . . dishonest, somehow."

Halt's eyebrows rose in a perfect arch. "Dishonest?"

Horace went on, awkwardly. "Well, I was always taught that people's seals and crests were sort of . . . I don't know, sacrosanct. I mean . . ." He gestured toward the figure of the bull impressed in red wax. "That's a *king's* signature."

Halt pursed his lips thoughtfully. "He's not much of a king," he replied.

"That's not the point. It's a principle, don't you see? It's like . . ." He paused, trying to think of a reasonable parallel, and finally came up with: "It's like tampering with the mail."

In Araluen, the mail was a service controlled by the Crown and there were dire penalties proscribed for anyone who tried to interfere with it. Not that such penalties had ever stopped Halt in the past when he'd needed to do a little tampering in that direction. He decided that it wouldn't be wise to mention that to Horace right now. Obviously, the morality code taught in Castle Redmont's

Battleschool was a good deal more rigid than the behavior embraced by the Ranger Corps. Of course, the knights of the realm were entrusted with the protection of the Royal Mail, so it was logical that they should have such an attitude ingrained in them from an early part of their training.

"So how would you suggest that we deal with the problem?" he asked at last. "How would you get us past the border?"

Horace preferred simple solutions. "We could fight our way in," he suggested with a shrug. Halt raised his eyes to heaven at the thought.

"So it's immoral to bluff our way past with an official document—" he began.

"A false document," Horace corrected. "With a forged seal at the bottom."

Halt conceded the point.

"All right—a forged document if you like. That's reprehensible. But it would be perfectly all right for us to go through the border post hacking and shooting down everyone in sight? Is that the way you see it?"

Now that Halt put it that way, Horace had to admit there was an anomaly in his thinking. "I didn't say we should kill everyone in sight," he objected. "We could just fight our way through, that's all. It's more honest and above board, and I thought that's what knights were supposed to be."

"Knights may be, but Rangers aren't," Halt muttered. But he said it below his breath so that Horace couldn't hear him. He reminded himself that Horace was very young and idealistic. Knights *did* live by a strict code of honor and ethics and those factors were emphasized in the first few years of an apprentice knight's training. It was only later in life that they learned to temper their ideals with a little expediency.

"Look," he said, in a conciliatory tone. "Think about it this way: if we just barged on through and headed for Hallasholm, the border guards would send word after us. The element of surprise would be totally lost and we could find ourselves in big trouble. If we decide to fight our way in, the only way to do it is by leaving nobody alive to spread the word. Understand?"

Horace nodded, unhappily. He could see the logic in what Halt was saying. The Ranger continued in the same reasoning tone. "This way, nobody gets hurt. You pose as an emissary from the Gallican court, with a dispatch from King Henri. You wear Deparnieux's black armor—it's obviously Gallican in style—and you keep your nose stuck in the air and leave the talking to me, your servant. That's the sort of behavior they'd expect from a self-important Gallican noble. There's no reason for any word to be sent informing Ragnak that two outlanders have crossed the border—after all, we're supposed to be going to see him anyway."

"And what's in the dispatch that I'm supposed to be taking?" Horace asked.

Halt couldn't resist a grin. "Sorry, that's confidential. You don't expect me to breach the secrecy of the mail system, do you?" Horace gave him a pained look and he relented. "All right. It's a simple business matter, actually. King Henri is negotiating for the hire of three wolfships from the Skandians, that's all."

Horace looked surprised. "Isn't that a little unusual?" he asked, and Halt shook his head.

"Not a bit. Skandians are mercenaries. They're always hiring out to one side or another. We're just pretending that Henri wants to subcontract a few ships and crews for a raiding expedition against the Arridi."

"The Arridi?" Horace said, frowning uncertainly.

Halt shook his head in mock despair. "You know, it might be

more useful if Rodney spent less time teaching you people ethics and a little more time on geography. The Arridi are the desert people to the south." He paused and saw that this made no impression on the young man. Horace continued to look at him with a blank expression. "On the other side of the Constant Sea?" he added, and now Horace showed signs of recognition.

"Oh, them," he said dismissively.

"Yes, them," Halt replied, mimicking the tone. "But I wouldn't expect you to think about them too much. There are only millions of them."

"But they never bother us, do they?" Horace said comfortably. Halt gave a short laugh.

"Not so far," he agreed. "And just pray they don't decide to."

Horace could sense that Halt was on the verge of delivering a lecture on international strategy and diplomacy.

That sort of thing usually left Horace's head spinning after the first few minutes, while he tried to keep up with who was aligned with whom and who was conspiring against their neighbors and what they hoped to gain from it. He preferred Sir Rodney's type of lecture: right, wrong, black, white, out swords, hack and bash. He thought it might be expedient to head off Halt's incipient harangue. The best way to do that, he had learned from past experience, was to agree with him.

"Well, I suppose you're right about the forgery," he admitted. "After all, it's only the Gallican's seal we're forging, isn't it? It's not as if you're forging a document from King Duncan. Even you wouldn't go as far as that, would you?"

"Of course not," Halt replied smoothly. He began to pack away his pens and ink and his other forger's tools. He was glad he'd laid hands on the forged Gallican seal in his pack so easily. It was as well that he hadn't had to tip them all out and risk Horace's seeing the near-perfect copy of King Duncan's seal that he carried, among others. "Now may I suggest that you climb into your elegant tin suit and we'll go and sweet-talk the Skandian border guards."

Horace snorted indignantly and turned away. But another thought had occurred to Halt—something that had been on his mind for some time.

"Horace . . ." he began, and Horace turned back. The Ranger's voice had lost its former light tone and he sensed that Halt was about to say something important.

"Yes, Halt?"

"When we find Will, don't tell him about the . . . unpleasantry between me and the King, all right?"

Months ago, denied permission to leave Araluen in search of Will, Halt had devised a desperate plan. He had publicly insulted the King and, as a result, was banished for a period of one year. The subterfuge had caused Halt a great deal of mental anguish in the past months. As a banished person, he was automatically expelled from the Ranger Corps. The loss of his silver oakleaf was possibly the worst punishment of all, yet he bore it willingly for the sake of his missing apprentice.

"Whatever you say, Halt," Horace agreed. But Halt seemed to think, for once, that further explanation was necessary.

"It's just that I'd prefer to find my own way to tell him—and the right time. All right?"

Horace shrugged. "Whatever you say," he repeated. "Now let's go and talk to these Skandians."

But there was to be no talking. The two riders, trailed by their small string of horses, rode through the pass that zigzagged between the high mountains until the border post finally came into sight. Halt expected to be hailed from the small wooden stockade and tower at any moment, as the guards demanded that they dismount and approach on foot. That would have been normal procedure. But there was no sign of life in the small fortified outpost as they drew nearer.

"Gate's open," Halt muttered as they came closer and could make out more detail.

"How many men usually garrison a place like this?" Horace asked.

The Ranger shrugged. "Half a dozen. A dozen maybe."

"There don't seem to be any of them around," Horace observed, and Halt glanced sideways at him.

"I'd noticed that part myself," he replied, then added, "What's that?"

There was an indistinct shape apparent now in the shadows just inside the open gate. Acting on the same instinct, they both urged their horses into a canter and closed the distance between them and the fort. Halt already felt certain what the shape was.

It was a dead Skandian, lying in a pool of blood that had soaked into the snow.

Inside there were ten others, all of them killed the same way, with multiple wounds to their torsos and limbs. The two travelers dismounted carefully and moved among the bodies, studying the awful scene.

"Who could have done this?" said Horace in a horrified voice. "They've been stabbed over and over again."

"Not stabbed," Halt told him. "Shot. These are arrow wounds. And then the killers collected their arrows from the bodies. Except for this one." He held up the broken half of an arrow that had been lying concealed under one of the bodies. The Skandian had probably broken it off in an attempt to remove it from the wound. The other half was still buried deeply in his thigh. Halt studied the fletching style and the identification marks painted at the nock end of the arrow. Archers usually identified their own shafts in such ways.

"Can you tell who did this?" Horace asked quietly, and Halt looked up to meet his gaze. Horace saw an expression of deep concern in the Ranger's eyes. That fact alone, more than the carnage around them, sent a wave of uneasiness through him. He knew it took a lot to worry Halt.

"I think so," said the Ranger. "And I don't like it. It looks like the Temujai are on the move again."

7

THE TRACKS LED TO THE EAST. AT LEAST, THAT WAS THE general direction Will had discerned from them. As the unknown horseman had made his way down the mountain, the track wound and twisted on itself, of necessity, as he followed the narrow, circuitous trails through the thick pine. But always, whenever there was a fork in the trail, the horseman chose the one that would eventually take him eastward once more.

Exhausted before the first hour was out, Will kept doggedly on, stumbling in the snow from time to time and, on occasions too numerous to count, falling full length to lie groaning.

It would be so easy, he thought, to just stay here. To let the aches in his unfit muscles slowly ease, to let the pounding of the pulse in his temples calm down and to just . . . rest.

But each time the temptation seized him, he thought of Evanlyn: how she had hauled him up the mountain. How she had helped him escape from the stockade where the yard slaves waited for their eventual death. How she had nursed him and cured him of the mind-numbing addiction to warmweed. And as he thought of her and what she'd done for him, somehow, each time, he found a tiny, hidden reservoir of strength and purpose. And somehow he dragged himself to his feet again and staggered on in pursuit of the tracks in the snow.

Will kept dragging one foot after another, his eyes cast down to the tracks. He saw nothing else, noticed nothing else. Just the impressions of the hooves in the snow.

The sun dropped behind the mountain and the instant chill that accompanied its disappearance ate through his clothes, damp with the sweat of his exertions, and gnawed deep into his flesh. Dully, he reflected that he was lucky he had thought to bring the blankets with him. When he finally stopped for the night, the damp clothes would become a potential death trap. Without the warmth and dryness of the blankets to cocoon him, he could freeze to death in his damp clothes.

The shadows deepened and he knew nightfall wasn't far away. Still he kept on, keeping going as long as he could distinguish the scuffed hoofmarks in the trail. He was too exhausted to notice the variations in the tracks—the deep troughs dug by the horse's locked-up front legs as it had slid down the steeper sections of the path. Those areas were only remarkable to him for the fact that he fell down them himself, more often than not. He could read none of the subtleties and secret messages that he had been trained to see. It was enough that there was a clear trail to follow.

It was all he was capable of.

It was long after dark and he was beginning to lose sight of the tracks now. But he continued as long as there was no possible deviation, no fork in the trail where he might have to choose one direction over another. When he came to a place where he must choose, he told himself, he would stop and camp for the night. He would wrap himself in the blankets. Perhaps he might even risk a small, well-shielded fire where he could dry his clothes. A fire would bring warmth. And comfort.

And smoke.

Smoke? He could smell it, even as he thought of a fire. Pine smoke—the all-pervading smell of life in Skandia, the scented fragrance of the burning pine gum as it oozed from the wood and crackled in the flames. He stopped, swaying on his feet. He had thought of fire and, instantly, he could smell smoke. His tired mind tried to correlate the two facts, then realized there was no correlation, only coincidence. He could smell smoke because, somewhere near at hand, there was a fire burning.

He tried to think. A fire meant a camp. And that almost certainly meant that he had caught up with Evanlyn and whoever it was who had abducted her. They were somewhere close by, stopped for the night. Now all he had to do was find them and . . .

"And what?" he asked himself in a voice thickened by fatigue. He took a long swallow from the water skin that he'd hung from his belt. He shook his head to clear it. For hours now, his entire being had been focused on one task—to catch up with the unseen horseman. Now that he had almost accomplished that, he realized he had no plan as to what to do next. One thing was certain: he wouldn't be able to rescue Evanlyn by brute force. Swaying with fatigue, almost unconscious, he barely had the strength to challenge a sparrow.

"What would Halt do?" he wondered. It had become his mantra over the past months whenever he found himself uncertain over a course of action. He would try to imagine his old mentor beside him, eyeing him quizzically, prompting him to solve the problem at hand by himself. To think it through, then to take action. The well-remembered voice seemed to sound in his ear.

Look first, Halt had been fond of saying. *Then act.*

Will nodded, content that he had solved the problem for the time being.

"Look first," he repeated thickly. "Then act."

He gave himself a few minutes' rest, hunkered down and leaning against the rough bole of a pine, then he stood erect once more, his muscles groaning with stiffness. He continued on the track, moving now with extra caution.

The smell of smoke grew stronger. Now it was mixed with something else and he recognized the smell of meat roasting. A few minutes later, moving carefully, he could discern an orange glow up ahead. The firelight reflected from the whiteness of the snow all around him, bouncing and magnifying in intensity. He realized that it was still some way ahead and continued along the trail. When he judged he was within fifty meters of the source of light, he moved silently off into the trees, fighting his way through the thick snow that came knee deep or higher.

The trees began to thin out, revealing a small clearing and the camp set around the fire. He lowered himself to his belly and inched forward, staying concealed in the deep shadows under the pines. He could make out dome-shaped tents now, three of them, arranged in a semicircle around the fire. He could see no sign of movement. The smell of roasting meat must have hung in the still, clear air long after the meal had been eaten, he realized. He started to edge forward when a movement behind the tents stopped him. He froze, absolutely still, as a man stepped forward into the fringe of the firelight. Stocky, dressed in furs, his face was hidden in the shadow cast by the fur hat he wore. But he was armed. Will could see the curved sword hanging at his waist and the slender lance that he held in his right hand, its butt planted in the snow.

As Will looked, he made out more detail. Horses, six of them, tethered among the trees to one side. He supposed that meant six men. He frowned, wondering how he could possibly get Evanlyn away from here, then realized that, so far, he hadn't seen her. He cast his gaze around the camp, wondering if perhaps she was inside one of the tents. Then he saw her.

Huddled under a tree, a blanket pulled up to her shoulders. Peering more closely, he made out the bonds that kept her fastened in place. His eyes ached and he rubbed the back of one hand across them, then pinched the bridge of his nose between two fingers, trying to force his eyes to stay focused. It was a losing battle. He was exhausted.

He began to wriggle back into the forest, looking for a place where he could hide and rest. They weren't going anywhere this evening, he realized, and he needed to rest and recover his strength before he could accomplish anything. Tired as he was, he couldn't even begin to formulate a coherent plan.

He would rest, finding a spot far enough away to give him concealment, but not so far that he wouldn't hear the camp stirring in the morning. Ruefully, he realized that his earlier plans for a fire were now thwarted. Still, he had the blankets; that was something.

He found a hollow under the spreading branches of a massive pine and crawled into it. He hoped that the horsemen wouldn't patrol around their camp in the morning and find his tracks, then understood there was nothing he could do to prevent it. He untied the rolled-up blankets and hauled them tight around him, leaning against the bole of the massive tree.

He was never sure that he didn't fall asleep before his eyes actually closed. If not, it was certainly a close-run thing.

Sometime after midnight, Evanlyn woke, groaning in agony. The tight bonds were restricting blood flow and her shoulder muscles were badly cramped. The sentry, annoyed by the noise, loosened the bonds for a few minutes, then refastened her hands in front of her to take the strain off her shoulder muscles. It was a small improvement and she managed to sleep fitfully, until the sound of raised voices woke her.

Evanlyn had sensed the antagonism between the two warriors the night before. But in the morning, it reached crisis point.

She wasn't to know it, but this was just the latest in a series of arguments between the two men. The small scouting party was one of many that had crossed the border into Skandia. Some weeks previously, Evanlyn had actually seen a member of an earlier party, near the hut where she and Will had spent the winter.

The man who had captured her, Ch'ren, was the son of a high-ranking Temujai family. It was the Temujai custom to have their young nobles serve a year as common soldiers before they were promoted to the officer class. At'lan, the commander of the scouting party, was a long-term soldier, a sergeant with years of experience. But, as a commoner, he knew he would never rise above his present rank. It galled him that the arrogant, headstrong Ch'ren would soon outrank him, just as it galled Ch'ren to take orders from a man he considered to be his social inferior. The day before, he had ridden off into the mountains on his own to spite the sergeant.

He had taken Evanlyn prisoner on a whim, without any real thought of the consequences. It would have been better had he remained unseen and allowed her to go on her way. The scouting party was under strict orders to avoid discovery and they had no orders to take prisoners. Nor was there any provision for holding or guarding them.

The simplest solution, At'lan had decided, was that the girl must be killed. As long as she was alive, there was the chance that she would escape and spread the word of their presence. If that happened, At'lan knew he would pay with his own life. He felt no sympathy for the girl. Nor did he feel any antagonism. His feelings about her were neutral. She was not of the People and so barely qualified as a human being.

Now, he ordered Ch'ren to kill her. Ch'ren refused—not out of any regard for Evanlyn, but simply to infuriate the sergeant.

Evanlyn watched anxiously as they argued. Like the previous night, it was obvious to her that she was the reason for their disagreement. It was equally obvious, as their argument became more and more heated, that her position was becoming increasingly precarious. Finally, the older of the two drew back his hand and slapped the younger man across the face, sending him staggering a few paces. Then he turned and strode toward Evanlyn, drawing his curved saber as he came.

She looked from the sword in his hand to the totally matter-of-fact expression on his face. There was no malice, no anger, no expression of hatred there. Just the determined gaze of someone who, without the slightest qualm or hesitation, was about to end her life.

Evanlyn opened her mouth to scream. But the horror of the moment froze the sound in her throat and she crouched, openmouthed, as death approached her. It was odd, she thought, that they had dragged her here, left her overnight and then decided to kill her.

It seemed such a pointless way to die.

8

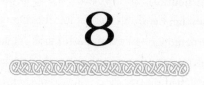

HALT CAST AROUND, EXAMINING THE CONFUSED MASS OF TRACKS in the soft snow, frowning to himself as he tried to make sense of the clues there. Horace waited, bursting with curiosity.

Finally, Halt stood up from where he had been kneeling, examining a particularly torn-up patch of ground.

"Thirty of them at least," he muttered. "Maybe more."

"Halt?" Horace asked experimentally. He didn't know if there were more details that Halt was about to reveal, but he couldn't wait any longer. The Ranger was moving away from the small stockade now, though, following another set of tracks that led into the mountains beyond the pass.

"A small party, maybe five or six, went on into Skandia. The rest of them went back the way they'd come."

He traced the directions with the tip of his longbow. He was speaking more to himself than to Horace, confirming in his own mind what the signs on the ground had told him.

"Who are they, Halt?" Horace asked quickly, hoping to break through the Ranger's single-minded concentration. Halt moved a few paces further in the direction taken by the smaller party.

"Temujai," he said briefly, over his shoulder.

Horace rolled his eyes in exasperation. "You already said that," he pointed out. "But who exactly are the Temujai?"

Halt stopped and turned to look back at him. For a moment, Horace was sure he was about to hear another comment on the sad state of his education. Then a thoughtful look crossed the Ranger's face and he said, in a milder tone than usual, "Yes, I suppose there's no reason why you should have ever heard of them, is there?"

Horace, loath to interrupt, merely shook his head.

"They're the Riders from the Eastern Steppes," the Ranger said. Horace frowned, not understanding.

"Steps?" he repeated, and Halt allowed a slight smile to show through.

"Not steps that you walk up and down," he told him. "Steppes—the plains and grasslands to the east. Nobody knows exactly where the Temujai originated. At one stage, they were simply a disorganized rabble of smaller tribes until Tem'gal welded them into one band and became the first Sha'shan."

"Sha'shan?" Horace interrupted hesitantly, totally unaware of what the word might mean. Halt nodded and went on to explain.

"The leader of each band was known as the Shan. When Tem'gal became the overlord, he created the title Sha'shan—the Shan of Shans, or the leader of leaders."

Horace nodded slowly. "But who was Tem'gal?" he asked, adding hastily, "I mean, where did he spring from?"

This time Halt shrugged. "Nobody really knows. Legend is that he was a simple herd boy. But somehow he became leader of one tribe, then united them with another, and another. The upshot was, he turned the Temujai into a nation of warriors—probably the best light cavalry in the world. They're fearless, highly organized and absolutely pitiless when it comes to battle. They've never been defeated, to my knowledge."

"So what are they doing here?" Horace asked, and Halt regarded him gravely, gnawing at his lower lip as he considered a possible answer.

"That's the question, isn't it?" he asked. "Perhaps we should follow this smaller group and see what we can find out. At least as long as they're heading in the direction we want to go."

And slinging his bow over his left shoulder, he walked to where Abelard stood patiently, reins trailing loosely on the ground. Horace hurried after him, swinging up astride the black battlehorse he had been riding to impress the border guards. All at once, the finery that he had donned to play the role of a Gallican courier seemed a little incongruous. He nudged the black with his heel and set out after Halt.

The other two horses followed, the battlehorse on its lead rein, and Tug trotting quietly along without any need for urging or direction.

Halt leaned down from the saddle, studying the ground.

"Look who's back," he said, indicating a trail in the snow. Horace nudged his horse closer and peered at the ground. To him there was nothing evident, other than a confusion of hoofprints, rapidly losing definition in the soft, wet snow.

"What is it?" he asked finally.

Halt replied without looking up from the track. "The single rider who went off on his own has come back."

Some way back, the trail had split, with one rider leaving the group and heading deeper into Skandia, while the main party had circled to the north, maintaining the same distance from the border. Now, apparently, that single rider had rejoined the group.

"Well, that makes it easier. Now we don't have to worry about his coming up behind us while we're trailing the others," Halt said. He started Abelard forward, then stopped, his eyes slitted in concentration.

"That's odd," he said, and slid down from the saddle to crouch on one knee in the snow. He studied the ground closely, then peered back in the direction from which the single rider had rejoined the group. He grunted, then straightened up, dusting wet snow from his knees.

"What is it?" Horace asked. Halt screwed his face into a grimace. He wasn't totally sure of what he was seeing, and that bothered him. He didn't like uncertainties in situations like this.

"The single rider didn't rejoin the group here. They went this way at least a day before he did," he eventually said. Horace shrugged. There was a logical reason for that, he thought.

"So he was heading after them to a rendezvous," he suggested. Halt nodded agreement.

"More than likely. They're obviously a reconnaissance group and he may have gone scouting by himself. The question is, who followed him when he came back?"

That raised Horace's eyebrows. "Someone followed him?" he asked. Halt let go a deep breath in frustration.

"Can't be sure," he said briefly. "But it looks that way. The snow's melting quickly and the tracks aren't totally clear. It's easy enough to read the horse's tracks, but this new player is on foot . . . if he's really there," he added uncertainly.

"So . . . ," Horace began. "What should we do?"

Halt came to a decision. "We'll follow them," he said, mounting once more. "I won't sleep comfortably until I find out what's going on here. I don't like puzzles."

The puzzle deepened an hour later when Tug, following quietly behind the two riders, suddenly threw back his head and let go a loud whinny. It was so unexpected that both Halt and Horace spun in their saddles and stared at the little horse in amazement. Tug whinnied again, a long, rising tone that had a note of anxiety in it. Horace's spare battlehorse jerked at its lead rope and whinnied in alarm as well. Horace was able to quell an incipient response from the black that he was riding, while Abelard, naturally, remained still.

Angrily, Halt made the Ranger hand signal for silence and Tug's whinny cut off in midnote. The others gradually quieted as well.

But Tug continued to stand in the trail, forelegs braced wide apart, head up and nostrils flaring as he sniffed the frigid air around them. His body trembled. He was on the brink of giving vent to another of those anguished cries and only the discipline and superb training of all Ranger horses was preventing him from doing so.

"What the devil . . . ," Halt began, then, sliding down from the saddle, he moved quietly back to the distressed horse, patting Tug's neck gently.

"Hush now, boy," he murmured. "Settle now. What's the trouble with you then?"

The quiet voice and the gentle hands seemed to soothe the little horse. He put his head down and rubbed his forehead against Halt's chest. The Ranger gently fondled the little horse's ears, still speaking to him in a soft croon.

"There you are . . . if only you could talk, eh? You know something. You sense something, isn't that right?"

Horace watched curiously as the trembling gradually eased. But he noticed the little horse's ears were still pricked and alert. He might have been quieted, but he wasn't at ease, the apprentice realized.

"I've never seen a Ranger horse behave like that before," he said softly, and Halt looked up at him, his eyes troubled.

"Neither have I," he admitted. "That's what has me worried."

Horace studied Tug carefully. "He seems to have calmed down a little now," he ventured, and Halt laid a hand across the horse's flank.

"He's still taut as a bowstring, but I think we can keep going. There's only an hour or so till dark and I want to see where our friends are camped for the night."

9

Deep in the shelter of the pine tree, wrapped in the inadequate warmth of the two blankets, Will spent a fitful night, dozing for short periods, then being woken by the cold and his racing thoughts.

Foremost in his mind was his sense of utter inadequacy. Faced with the need to rescue Evanlyn from her captors, he had absolutely no idea how he might accomplish the task. They were six men, well armed and capable-looking. He was a boy, armed only with a small hunting bow and a short dagger. His arrows were good only for small game—with points made by hardening the end of the wood in a fire and then sharpening them. They were nothing like the razor-sharp broadheads that he had carried in his quiver as an apprentice Ranger. "A Ranger wears the lives of two dozen men on his belt," went the old Araluen saying.

He racked his brain again and again throughout the long periods of sleeplessness. He thought bitterly that he was supposed to have a reputation as a thinker and a planner. He felt that he was letting Evanlyn down with his inability to come up with an idea. And letting down others too. In his mind's eye, half asleep and dozing, he saw Halt's bearded face, smiling at him and urging him to come up with a plan. Then the smile would fade, first to a look of anger, then, finally, of disappointment. He thought of Horace, his companion on the journey through Celtica to Morgarath's bridge. The heavily built warrior apprentice had always been content to let Will do the thinking for the two of them. Will sighed unhappily as he thought how misplaced that trust had become. Perhaps it was an aftereffect of the warmweed to which he had been addicted. Perhaps the drug rotted a user's brain, making him incapable of original thought.

Time and again through that unhappy night, he asked himself the question, "What would Halt do?" But the device, so useful in the past for providing an answer to his problems, was ineffectual. He heard no answering voice deep within his subconscious, bringing him counsel and advice.

The truth was, of course, that given the situation and the circumstance, there was no practical action that Will could take. Virtually unarmed, outnumbered, on unfamiliar ground and sadly out of condition, all he could do would be to keep watching the strangers' encampment and hope for some change in the circumstances, some eventuality that might provide him with an opportunity to reach Evanlyn and get her away into the trees.

Finally abandoning the attempt to rest, he crawled out from under the pine tree and gathered his meager equipment together. The position of the stars in the heavens told him that it was a little over an hour before he could expect to see the first light of dawn filtering through the treetops.

"At least that's one skill I've remembered," he said miserably, speaking the words aloud, as had become his custom during the night.

He hesitated, then came to a decision and moved off through the trees toward the campsite. There was always a chance that something might have changed. The sentry might have fallen asleep or gone off into the forest to investigate a suspicious noise, leaving the way clear to rescue Evanlyn.

It wasn't likely but it was possible. And if such an opportunity arose, it was essential that Will be present to take advantage of it. At least it was a definite course of action for him to follow, so he moved as quietly as possible, keeping one of the blankets draped around his shoulders as a cloak.

It took him ten minutes to find his way back to the small camp. When he did, his hopes were dashed. There was still a sentry patrolling and, as Will observed, the watch had changed, with a fresh man taking over the post, wide-awake and rested. He moved around the perimeter of the camp on a regular patrol, coming within twenty meters of the spot where the boy crouched hidden behind a tree. There was no sign of slackness or inattention. The man kept his point of vision moving, continually searching the surrounding forest for any sign of unusual movement.

Will looked enviously at the recurve bow slung, ready strung, over the man's right shoulder. It was very similar to the one Halt had given him when he had first taken up his apprenticeship with the grim-faced Ranger. Vaguely, he recalled Halt had said something about learning how to make such a bow from the warriors of the Eastern Steppes. He wondered now if these men were some of those warriors.

The sentry's bow was a real weapon, he thought, unlike the virtual toy that he carried. Now, if he had a bow like that in his hands, and a few of the arrows that showed their feathered tips in the sentry's back quiver, he might be able to accomplish something. For a while, he played with the idea of overpowering the sentry and taking his bow, but he was forced to reject the idea.

There was no way he would get within reach of the man without being seen or heard. And, even if he could accomplish that, there was little chance of his being able to overpower an armed warrior. Pitting the small dagger he carried against the man's saber would be suicide. He could chance a throw of the knife, of course, but it was a poorly balanced weapon and ill suited for throwing, without sufficient weight in the hilt to drive the blade home into the target.

And so he huddled in the snow at the base of the tree, watching and waiting for an opportunity that never came. He could see Evanlyn's crumpled shape to one side of the camp. The tree she was tied to was surrounded by clear space. There was no way he could approach her without the sentry seeing him. It all seemed hopeless.

He must have dozed off, lulled by the cold and by the restless night he had spent, for he was awoken by the sound of voices.

It was just after dawn and the early morning light struck obliquely through the gaps in the trees, throwing long shadows across the clearing. Two of the group of warriors were standing, a little apart from the others, arguing. The words were indecipherable to Will, but the subject of their debate was obvious, as one of them kept gesturing toward Evanlyn, still tied to the tree, huddled in the blanket she had been given, and now wide-awake and watchful.

As the discussion progressed, the men became increasingly angrier, their voices louder. Finally, the older man seemed goaded beyond restraint. He slapped the other man, sending him staggering. He nodded once, as if satisfied, then turned toward Evanlyn, his hand dropping to the hilt of his sword.

For a moment, Will remained frozen. The warrior's manner was so casual as he drew the sword and approached the girl that it seemed impossible to believe that he meant her any harm. There was a callousness about the entire scenario that seemed to belie any hostile intent. Yet it was that same callousness and casualness that created a growing sense of horror in Will. The man raised the sword above the girl. Evanlyn's mouth opened but no sound came and Will realized that killing her meant nothing, absolutely nothing at all, to the small, bowlegged warrior.

Acting under their own volition, Will's hands had drawn and nocked an arrow as the warrior dropped his hand to the sword hilt. The curved blade went up and Evanlyn crouched in the snow, one hand raised in a futile attempt to ward off the killing stroke. Will stepped out clear of the tree, bringing the bow to full draw as his mind rapidly weighed the situation.

His arrow wouldn't kill. It was little more than a pointed stick, even though that point had been hardened in a fire. The chances were that, if he aimed at the warrior's body, the thick furs and leather jerkin that he wore would stop the arrow before it even broke the skin. There was only one vulnerable point where the man was unprotected and that was, coincidentally, one that gave Will's shot the best chance of stopping the sword stroke. The man's wrist was exposed as his arm went up, the bare flesh showing at the end of the thick fur sleeve. All of this Will registered in the time it took him to bring the arrow's crude fletching back to touch his cheek. His aim shifted smoothly to the man's wrist, the tip of the arrow rising slightly to allow for drop. He checked his breath automatically, then released.

The bow gave a slight twang and the light arrow leapt away, arcing swiftly across the intervening space and burying its point into the soft flesh of the warrior's wrist.

Will heard the strangled shout of pain as his hands moved in the well-remembered sequence, nocking another arrow and sending it after the first. The sword had dropped from the man's grasp, falling noiselessly into the thick snow and causing Evanlyn to shrink back as its razor-sharp blade just missed her arm. The second arrow slapped against the man's thick sleeve and hung there harmlessly as he grasped his right wrist, blood pouring down over his hand.

Shocked and caught unaware as he was, the man had still turned instinctively in the direction from which the arrow had come and now, seeing the movement as Will fired the second time, he made out the small figure across the clearing. With a snarl of anger, he released his injured wrist and clawed a long dagger from his belt with his left hand. For a moment, Evanlyn was forgotten as he pointed in Will's direction to his men, shouting for them to follow him, then began to run toward his attacker.

Will's third arrow slowed the man down as it flashed past his face, causing him to jerk to one side to avoid it. But then he was coming again and two of his men were following. At the same time, Will saw a fourth man heading toward Evanlyn and his heart sank as he realized he had failed. He sent another shaft zipping toward him, knowing the effort was in vain. Turning to face the oncoming warrior, Will dropped the useless bow and reached for the knife in his own belt.

And then he heard a sound from the past, a sound eerily familiar from hours spent in the forest around Castle Redmont.

A deep thrum came from somewhere behind him, then the air-splitting hiss of a heavy shaft traveling at incredible speed, with enormous force behind it. Finally, Will heard the solid smack as it struck home.

The arrow, black-shafted, gray-feathered, seemed to appear in the center of the approaching warrior's chest. He fell backward in the snow. Another thrum-hiss-smack and the second man went down as well. The third turned and ran for the horses tethered on the far side of the camp. Galloping hoofbeats told Will that the remaining two men had already made their escape, unwilling to face the uncanny accuracy of the longbow.

Will hesitated, his mind in a turmoil. Instinctively, he knew what had happened. Logically, he had no idea how it had come about. He turned and saw the barely visible, gray-cloaked figure some thirty meters behind him, the huge longbow still held at the ready, another arrow already drawn.

"Halt?" he cried, his voice breaking. He started to run toward the figure, then remembered. Evanlyn! She was still in danger. As he turned, he heard the scrape of steel on steel and saw that she had managed to grab the fallen saber and ward off the first attack.

But it could only be a momentary respite as her hands were still tied in front of her and she was tethered firmly to the tree. He pointed toward her and yelled inarticulately, desperately urging Halt to shoot, then realized that the Ranger's view of the scene was blocked by the trees.

Then another figure was bounding toward the struggling girl and her attacker. A tall, well-built figure who looked strangely familiar, wearing chain mail and a white surcoat with a strange emblem that resembled a stylized oakleaf.

His long, straight sword intercepted the curved blade as it swung down. Then he had interposed himself between Evanlyn and the man who was trying to kill her and, in a series of flashing sword strokes that bewildered the eye, he drove the other man back away from the girl. He obviously had the better of the exchange and his opponent retreated before him, his parries and strokes growing more desperate as he realized that he was totally outmatched. The man lunged clumsily with his curved blade and it was deflected easily so that his momentum carried him forward, off balance, wide open to the retaliatory backhanded cut that was already on its way—

"Don't kill him!" Halt shouted, just in time, and Horace twisted his wrist so that the flat of his blade, not the razor edge, slammed into the side of the man's head. The man's eyes rolled up and he sagged to the ground, unconscious.

And very lucky.

"We want a prisoner," the Ranger finished mildly. Then he was driven back by the impact of a small body running headlong into him, and a pair of arms that wrapped around his waist, and Will was sobbing and babbling mindlessly as he embraced his teacher and mentor and friend. Halt patted his shoulder gently, and was surprised to find a single tear sliding down his own cheek.

Horace sliced through Evanlyn's bonds with the edge of his sword and gently assisted her to her feet.

"Are you all right?" he asked anxiously, then, satisfied that she was, he couldn't help a huge grin of relief breaking out across his face.

"Oh, Horace, thank God you're here!" the girl sobbed, and throwing her arms around his neck, she buried her face in his chest. For a moment, Horace was nonplussed. He went to embrace her in return, realized he was still holding his sword, and hesitated awkwardly. Then, coming to a decision, he planted it firmly, point first in the ground, and put his arms around her, feeling the softness of her and smelling the fragrance of her hair and skin.

His grin grew wider, which he wouldn't have thought was possible. He decided there were definite advantages to being a hero.

10

"YOU REALLY MEAN HORACE IS SOME KIND OF HERO IN GALLICA?" Will asked incredulously, not totally sure that Halt and Horace weren't pulling off some kind of enormous practical joke. But the grizzled Ranger was nodding his head emphatically.

"A regular figure of respect," he said. Evanlyn turned to the muscular young warrior and leaned forward to touch his hand lightly.

"I can believe it," she said. "Did you see the way he took care of that Temujai soldier who was trying to kill me?" Her eyes were alight with an unusual warmth and Will, noticing it, felt a sudden stab of jealousy for his old friend. Then he pushed the unworthy thought aside.

Halt had been unwilling to remain too close to the Temujai campsite. There was no telling how far away the main force might be and there was always the possibility that the two men who had escaped might lead others back to the spot.

They had retraced the path Halt and Horace had followed, moving back toward the border crossing where they had discovered the first evidence of the Temujai assault. Around the middle of the day, they found a spot on a hilltop with a good view of the surrounding terrain and a saucer-shaped depression that would keep them hidden from sight. Here, they could see without being seen, and Halt decided to camp there while he made up his mind as to their next move.

They had built a small fire, screened by a grove of young pines, and prepared a meal.

Evanlyn and Will fell ravenously on the savory stew that the Ranger had prepared and for a while there was silence, broken only by the sound of dedicated eating.

Then the old friends began to catch up on the events that had taken place since the final confrontation with the Wargal army on the Plains of Uthal. Will's jaw had dropped with amazement as Halt described how Horace had defeated the terrifying Lord Morgarath in single combat.

Horace looked suitably embarrassed and Halt, sensing this, described the combat in a lighthearted tone, jokingly implying that the boy had stumbled clumsily and fallen under the oncoming hooves of Morgarath's battlehorse, rather than choosing to do so as a deliberate last throw of the dice to unseat his opponent. The apprentice warrior blushed and pointed out that his final ploy—the double knife defense—had been taught to him by Gilan and that he and Will had spent hours practicing the skill on their trip through Celtica. He made it sound as if, somehow, Will deserved some share of the credit for his victory. As he spoke, Will leaned back comfortably against a log and thought how much Horace had changed. Once his sworn enemy when they were both growing up as castle wards, Horace had since become his closest friend.

Well, one of his closest friends, he thought, as he felt a shaggy head butt insistently against his shoulder. He twisted around, reaching out one hand to stroke Tug's ears and scratch the spot between them the way the little horse enjoyed. Tug let go a low snuffle of pleasure at the touch of his master's hand. Since they had been reunited, the horse had refused to stray more than a meter or two from Will's presence.

Halt looked at the two of them now, across the campfire, and smiled inwardly. He felt an enormous sense of relief now that he had finally found his apprentice. A weight of self-blame had lifted from him, for he had suffered greatly in the long months since he had watched the wolfship sailing away from the Araluen coast with Will on board. He felt he had failed the youngster, that he had somehow betrayed him. Now that the boy was safely back in his care, he was filled with a deep sense of well-being. Admittedly, the events of the past day had also left a new worry gnawing at the back of his mind, but for the moment, that could wait while he enjoyed the reunion.

"Do you think you could persuade that horse of yours to stay with the other horses for a minute or two?" he said with mock severity. "Otherwise he'll wind up believing that he's one of us."

"He's been driving Halt crazy since we first found your tracks," Horace put in. "He must have picked up your scent and known it was you we were following, although Halt didn't realize it."

At that, Halt raised an eyebrow. "Halt didn't realize it?" he repeated. "And I suppose you did?"

Horace shrugged. "I'm just a warrior," he replied. "I'm not supposed to be a thinker. I leave that to you Rangers."

"I must admit it had me puzzled," Halt said. "I've never seen a Ranger horse behave like that. Even when I ordered him to calm down and be silent, I could tell there was something on his mind. When you first stepped out of the trees to shoot, I thought he was going to take off after you."

Will continued to rub the shaggy head as it leaned down to him. He smiled broadly around the campsite. Now that Halt was here and he was surrounded by his closest friends, he felt safe and secure once more—a sensation he hadn't enjoyed in over a year. He smiled at the Ranger, relieved that Halt had been pleased with his actions. Evanlyn had described their journey across the Stormwhite Sea, and the series of events that had led to their arrival at Hallasholm.

Horace had looked at Will with open admiration as she described the way he had humbled the wolfship captain Slagor in the drafty, smoky cabin on the barren island where they had sheltered from the Stormwhite's worst excesses. Halt had merely studied his apprentice with a keen glance and nodded once. That single movement meant more to Will than volumes of praise from anyone else—particularly since he wasn't terribly proud of the way things had turned out at Hallasholm, and his subsequent addiction to warmweed. He had been fearful that Halt would disapprove, but when Evanlyn had spoken of her near despair when she had found him in the yard slaves' compound, mindless and unthinking, the Ranger had merely nodded once more and uttered a curse under his breath at people who would inflict such a substance on others. His eyes had met Will's anxious gaze across the fire and Will had seen a deep, deep sadness there.

"I'm sorry you had to go through that," his master said softly, and Will knew that everything would be all right.

Eventually, they had talked their fill. There would be details that could be filled in over the coming weeks, and there were items that they had forgotten. But in general terms, they were up to date with one another.

There was, however, one aspect of Halt's story that hadn't been revealed. Neither Will nor Evanlyn had learned of Halt's banishment, or his expulsion from the Ranger Corps.

As the shadows lengthened, Halt moved once more to the spot where their captive was tied hand and foot. He loosened the bonds for a few minutes, first the hands, then the feet, retying the hands before he released the second set of bonds. The Temujai warrior grunted a brief appreciation of the temporary relief. Halt had already done this several times during the afternoon, ensuring that the man wasn't permanently disabled by the restriction of the flow of blood to his hands and feet.

It also gave him an opportunity to make sure the man's bonds were tight and that he hadn't managed to loosen them or wriggle free. Knowing he would receive no reply, Halt asked the man for his name and his military unit. Although he spoke the Temujai tongue with reasonable fluency, having spent several years among the People, as they called themselves, he saw no reason to apprise the prisoner of that fact. As a consequence, Halt used the trader's language common to all the people of the Hemisphere—a mélange of Gallic, Teuton and Temujai words in a simple, pidgin-language structure that took no notice of grammar or syntax.

As he had expected, the Tem'uj simply ignored his overtures. Halt shrugged and moved away, deep in thought. Horace was sitting by the fireplace, carefully cleaning and oiling his sword. Evanlyn was in the sentry position at the brow of the hilltop, keeping watch over the hillside below them. She would be due to be relieved in another half hour, he thought idly. As Halt paced back and forth, turning over the problem that taxed his mind, he became aware of another presence beside him. He glanced around and smiled to see Will pacing with him, wrapped in the gray mottled Ranger cloak that Halt had carried with him, along with the bow he'd made and a saxe knife. The double-knife scabbards were a Ranger-issued item of equipment and Halt, expelled from the Corps, had been unable to find one for the boy. As yet, Will hadn't remarked on the fact.

"What's the problem, Halt?" the young man asked now.

Halt stopped pacing to face him, his eyebrow arcing in an expression that was familiar to Will.

"Problem?" he repeated. Will grinned at him, refusing to be put off, refusing to be diverted. He's grown up a lot in the past year, Halt thought, remembering how that response would once have left the boy confused and disconcerted.

"When you pace back and forth like a caged tiger, it usually means you're trying to think through a problem of some kind," Will said. Halt pursed his lips thoughtfully.

"And I suppose you've seen so many tigers in your time?" he asked. "Caged and otherwise?"

Will's grin widened a little. "And when you try to distract me from my question by asking a question back, I *know* you're thinking over some problem," he added. Halt finally gave in. He had no idea that his habits had become so easy to interpret. He made a mental note to change things, then wondered if he wasn't getting too old to do so.

"Well, yes," he replied. "I must admit I do have something on my mind. Nothing major. Don't let it worry you."

"What is it?" said his apprentice bluntly, and Halt cocked his head sideways.

"You see," he explained, "when I say 'don't let it worry you,' I mean, there's no real need for us to discuss it."

"I know that," said his apprentice. "But what is it anyway?"

Halt drew a deep breath, then let it out in a sigh. "I seem to remember that I once had much more authority than I seem to have these days," he said to no one in particular. Then, realizing that Will was still waiting expectantly, he relented.

"It's these Temujai," he said. "I'd like to know what they're up to." He glanced across their campsite to where the Tem'uj was sitting, securely bound. "And I've got a snowball's chance in a forest fire of finding out from our friend there."

Will shrugged. "Is it really any of our concern?" he asked. "After all, surely we can leave them and the Skandians to fight it out."

Halt considered this, scratching at his chin with forefinger and thumb. "I take it you're thinking along the lines of the old saying 'The enemy of my enemy is my friend'?" he said. Will shrugged once again.

"I wasn't thinking of it in those words exactly," he said. "But it does sum the situation up pretty well, don't you think? If the Skandians are kept busy fighting these Temujai, then they won't be able to bother us with their coastal raids, will they?"

"That's true, up to a point," Halt admitted. "But there is another old saying: 'Rather the devil you know.' Have you ever heard that one?"

"Yes. So you're saying that these Temujai could be a lot more of a problem than the Skandians?"

"Oh yes indeed. If they defeat the Skandians, there's nothing to stop them from moving on Teutlandt, Gallica, and finally Araluen."

"But they'd have to beat the Skandians first, wouldn't they?" Will said. He knew, from firsthand experience, that the Skandians were fierce, fearless warriors. He could see them forming an effective buffer between the invading Temujai and the other western nations, with both sides ending up severely weakened by the war and neither presenting a threat in the near future. It was a perfect strategic position, he told himself comfortably. Halt's next words made him feel considerably less comfortable.

"Oh, they'll defeat them, all right. Make no mistake about that. It will be a savage, bloody war, but the Temujai will win."

11

After the evening meal, Halt called the small group together. The wind had risen with the onset of night and it whistled eerily through the branches of the pines. It was a clear night, and the half-moon shone brilliantly above them as they huddled in their cloaks around the remnants of the fire.

"Will and I were talking earlier," he told them. "And I've decided that, since our discussion concerns all of us, it's only fair to tell you what I've been thinking."

Horace and Evanlyn exchanged puzzled looks. They had both simply assumed that the master and the apprentice were catching up on lost time together. Now, it appeared, there was something else to consider.

"First and foremost," Halt continued, seeing he had their undivided attention, "my aim is to get you, Will, and the Pr—" He hesitated, stopping before he used Evanlyn's title. They had all agreed that it would be safer for her to continue under her assumed name until they returned home. He corrected himself. "Will and Evanlyn, and Horace, of course, across the border and out of Skandia. As escaped prisoners, you're in considerable danger if the Skandians recapture you. And, as we all know, that danger is even greater for Evanlyn."

The three listeners nodded. Will had told Halt and Horace about the risk to Evanlyn should Ragnak ever discover her real identity as King Duncan's daughter. The Oberjarl had sworn a blood vow to the Vallas, the trio of savage gods who ruled the Skandian religion, in which he promised death to any relative of the Araluen King.

"On the other hand," Halt said, "I am deeply worried about the presence of the Temujai here on the borders of Skandia. They haven't come this far west in twenty years—and the last time they did, they put the entire western world at risk."

Now he really had their attention, he saw. Horace and Evanlyn sat up straighter and leaned a little closer to him. He saw the puzzled look on the young warrior's face in the firelight.

"Surely, Halt, you're exaggerating?" Horace asked.

Will looked sideways at his friend. "That's what I thought too," he said quietly, "but apparently not."

Halt shook his head firmly. "I wish I were," he said. "But if the Temujai are moving in force, it's a threat to all our countries, Araluen included."

"What happened last time, Halt?" It was Evanlyn who spoke now, her voice uncertain, the concern obvious in it. "Were you there? Did you fight them?"

"I fought with them and, eventually, against them," he said flatly. "There were things we wanted to learn from them and I was sent to do so."

Horace frowned. "Such as?" he asked. "What could the Rangers hope to learn from a bunch of wild horsemen?" Horace, it must be admitted, had a somewhat inflated idea of the extent of the Ranger

Corps' knowledge. To put it simply, he thought they knew just about everything that was worth knowing.

"You wanted to learn how they made their bows, didn't you?" said Will suddenly. He remembered seeing the bows carried by the horsemen and thinking how similar they were to his own. Halt looked at him and nodded.

"That was part of it. But there was something more important. I was sent to trade with them for some of their stallions and mares. The Ranger horses we ride today were originally bred from the Temujai herds," he explained. "We found their recurve bows interesting, but when you consider how difficult and time-consuming they are to make, they offered no significant improvement in performance over the longbow. But the horses were a different matter."

"And they were happy to trade?" asked Will. As he spoke, he turned to study the shaggy little horse standing a few paces behind him. Tug, seeing him turn to look, nickered a soft greeting. Now that Halt mentioned it, there was a distinct resemblance to the horses he had seen in the Temujai camp.

"They were not!" Halt replied with a heartfelt shake of the head. "They guarded their breeding stock jealously. I'm probably still wanted among the Temujai nation as a horse thief."

"You stole them?" Horace asked, in a mildly disapproving tone.

Halt hid a smile as he replied.

"I left what I considered a fair price," he told them. "The Temujai had other ideas about the matter. They weren't keen to sell at any price."

"Anyway," Will said impatiently, dismissing the matter of whether the horses had been bought or stolen, "what happened when their army invaded? How far did they come?"

Halt stirred the small pile of embers between them with the

end of a charred stick until a few tongues of flame flickered in the red coals. "They were heading farther south that time," he said. "They overran the Ursali nation and the Middle Kingdoms in no time at all. There was no stopping them. They were the ultimate warriors—fast moving, incredibly brave, but most of all, highly disciplined. They fought as a large unit, always, whereas the armies facing them almost always ended up fighting in small groups of perhaps a dozen at a time."

"How could they do that?" Evanlyn asked. She had been around her father's armies enough to know that the biggest problem facing any commander once battle started was staying in effective control and maintaining communication with the troops under him. Halt looked at her, sensing the professional interest behind her question.

"They've developed a signaling system that lets their central commander direct all his troops in concerted maneuvers," he told her. "It's a very complex system relying on colored flags in different combinations. They can even operate at night," he added. "They simply substitute colored lanterns for the flags. Quite frankly, there was no army capable of stopping them as they drove on toward the sea.

"They'd cut through the northeast corner of Teutlandt, then on through Gallica. Every army that faced them, they defeated. Their superior tactics and discipline made them unbeatable. They were only three days' riding from the Gallican coast when they finally stopped."

"What stopped them?" Will asked. A noticeable chill had fallen over the three young listeners as Halt had described the inexorable advance of the Temujai army. At the question, the Ranger gave a short laugh.

"Politics," he said. "And a dish of bad freshwater clams."

"Politics?" Horace snorted in disgust. As a warrior, he had a healthy contempt for politics and politicians.

"That's right. This was when Mat'lik was the Sha'shan, or supreme leader. Now, among people like the Temujai, that's a highly unstable position. It's taken by the strongest contender and very few Sha'shans have died in their beds. Although Mat'lik did, as it turned out," he added as an afterthought, before continuing.

"As a result, it's normal practice for anyone who might contest the position to be assigned tasks that keep them a long way from home. In this case, Mat'lik's brother, nephew and second cousin were the most likely candidates, so he made sure they were kept busy with the army. That way, not only could they not get up to mischief around him, but they could all keep an eye on one another as well. Naturally, they distrusted each other totally."

"Wasn't it dangerous to give them control over the army?" Will asked. Halt signified that the question was a good one.

"Normally, it might be. But the command structure was designed so that none of them had absolute control. Mat'lik's brother Twu'lik was the strategic commander. But his nephew was the paymaster and his cousin was the quartermaster. So, one led them, one fed them and one paid them. They all had pretty equal claims on the loyalty of the soldiers. That way, they could keep one another in check."

"So where did the clams come in?" Horace asked. Food was always a matter of interest to him. Halt resettled himself by the fire, leaning back against a log.

"Mat'lik was partial to freshwater clams," he told them. "So much so that he very unwisely had his wife prepare him a big dish when they were out of season. It seems that some of them were tainted and he was taken by a terrible fit while eating. He screamed, tore at his throat, fell down and went into a deep coma. It was obvious that he was very close to death.

"Naturally, when news reached the army, the three main contenders for the top job couldn't get back to the Sha'shan's court fast enough. The succession would be decided by an election among the senior Shans and they knew if they weren't back there to hand out the bribes and buy votes, someone else would get the prize."

"So they simply abandoned the invasion?" Will asked. "After they'd come so far?"

Halt made a dismissive gesture. "They were a pragmatic bunch," he said. "Gallica wasn't going to go away. They'd fought their way through there once, they could always do it again. But there was only going to be one chance to get the top job."

"So the western hemisphere was saved by a dish of bad clams?" Evanlyn said. The grizzled Ranger smiled grimly.

"It's surprising how often history is decided by something as trivial as bad shellfish," he told her.

"Where were you while this was all going on, Halt?" Will asked his master.

Halt smiled again at the memory. "I suppose it's one of those moments you never forget," he said. "I was hightailing it for the coast, with a small herd of . . ." He hesitated, glancing sidelong at Horace. ". . . fairly purchased horses, and a Temujai fighting patrol was right behind me. They were gaining on me too. Suddenly, one morning, they reined in and watched me gallop away. Then they simply turned around and started trotting back east—all the way to their homeland."

There was a brief silence as he finished the tale. Halt could have wagered that it would be Will who would come up with the next question, and he was not disappointed.

"So who became the Sha'shan?" he asked. "The brother, the nephew or the cousin?"

"None of them," Halt replied. "The election went to a dark horse candidate who had designs on the countries to the east of the Temujai homelands. The other three were executed for abandoning their mission in the west." He stirred the fire again, thinking back to that well-remembered day when the pursuing riders had suddenly given up the chase and left him to escape.

"And now they're back again," he said thoughtfully.

12

THEY BROKE CAMP EARLY THE FOLLOWING MORNING AND started down toward the pass that would take them across the border once more. Horace had offered Evanlyn the black battlehorse that had belonged to Deparnieux. When she had protested that this was a far superior animal to the bay he rode, he smiled shyly.

"Maybe so. But I'm used to Kicker. He knows my ways." And that was the end of the matter. The prisoner rode one of the horses they had taken from the Temujai camp. A second was carrying the packs and supplies that, up until now, had been carried by Tug. Naturally, the little Ranger horse was now the proud bearer of his long-lost master.

As they came closer to the treeline at the bottom of the hill, Tug showed his happiness once more, tossing his head and whinnying. Halt turned in the saddle and smiled.

"I'm glad he's happy," he said. "But I do hope he's not planning on keeping that up all the way home."

Will grinned in reply and leaned forward to pat the little horse's shaggy neck.

"He'll settle down soon enough," he said. At the touch, Tug

danced a few paces and tossed his head again. Surprisingly, Abelard
copied the actions.

"Now he's got my horse doing it too," Halt said, more than a
little surprised. He calmed Abelard with a quiet word, then turned
to Will again. "You seem to be popular among the horses of this
world, anyway. I thought . . ." His voice trailed away and he didn't
finish the sentence. Will saw his body stiffen to attention and the
gray-cloaked Ranger twisted in his saddle, peering into the trees,
which were now close on either side.

"Damn!" he muttered quietly. He turned to Horace and Evanlyn,
riding behind them and leading the prisoner's horse, but before he
could speak, there was a scuffle of movement in the trees and a party
of armed warriors stepped out into the open behind them, blocking
their retreat.

Halt swung quickly to the front once more, as a second group
emerged from the trees, fanning out to the sides and moving to cut
them off in all directions.

"Skandians!" exclaimed Will, as he recognized the horned hel-
mets and round wooden shields carried by the silent warriors. Halt's
shoulder slumped in a gesture of disgust with himself.

"Yes. The horses have been trying to warn us, only I didn't realize it."

A burly figure, wearing an enormous horned helmet and with
a double-bladed battle-ax laid negligently over his right shoulder,
stepped forward. Behind them, Halt heard the sinister whisper of
steel on leather as Horace drew his sword. Without turning, he
said:

"Put it away, Horace. I think there are too many of them, even
for you."

As Horace had moved, the huge ax had risen instantly to the

ready position. The Skandian wielded it as if it were a toy. Now he spoke, and Will started at the familiar voice.

"I think we'll have you down from those horses, if you don't mind."

Unable to stop himself, Will blurted out: "Erak!" and the man took a pace closer, peering at the second cloaked figure in front of him. The cowl had obscured Will's face so that the jarl hadn't recognized him. Now he could make out the boy's features and he frowned as he realized that there was something familiar about another of the riders. He hadn't recognized Evanlyn, swathed in a cloak against the cold. Now, however, he was sure that it must be she. He cursed quietly under his breath, then recovered.

"Down!" he commanded. "All of you."

He motioned the circle of men back as the four riders dismounted. The fifth, he noticed with some interest, was tied to his horse and couldn't comply. He gestured for two of his men to get the prisoner down from his saddle.

Halt threw back the hood on his cloak and Erak studied the grim, bearded face. Now that he was dismounted, the man looked surprisingly small, particularly measured against Erak's own burly form. Will went to throw back his own cowl, but Erak stopped him with a hand gesture.

"Leave it for the moment," he said in a lowered voice. He didn't know how many of his men might recognize the former slave who had escaped from Hallasholm months ago, but for now, something told him that the fewer who made the connection, the better it would be. He looked warningly at Evanlyn.

"You too," he ordered, and she inclined her head in agreement. Erak turned his gaze back to Halt.

"I've seen you before," he said. Halt nodded.

"If you're Jarl Erak, we saw each other briefly on the beach by the fens," he said, and recognition dawned in the jarl's eyes. It wasn't the man's face that had struck a chord of memory, rather his bearing—the way he held himself and the massive longbow that he carried still. Halt continued: "There was quite a distance between us, as I recall."

Erak grunted. "I seem to remember that we were well within bowshot," he said. Halt nodded, acknowledging the point. The Skandian's face darkened with anger as he looked once more at the bow and the quiver of arrows slung at Halt's belt.

"And now you've been up to the same foul business," he said. "Although what these two have to do with it is beyond me." He added the last in a puzzled tone, jerking a thumb at Will and Evanlyn.

Now it was Halt's turn to look puzzled. "What foul business?"

Erak gave a disgusted snort. "I've seen you with that bow, remember? I know what you can do. And I've just seen more of your handiwork at Serpent Pass."

Understanding dawned on Halt. He remembered the forlorn sight of the bodies at the small fort on the border. That must be the pass this Skandian was referring to. Since the garrison had been killed by archers and Erak knew Halt's skill with a bow, he had jumped to a rapid, if not too logical, conclusion.

"Not our work," he said, shaking his head. Erak stepped closer to him.

"No? I saw them there. All shot. And we followed your tracks from there."

"So you may have," Halt said calmly, "but if you're any sort of tracker, you'd know that there were only two of us. We found the garrison at the pass dead. And we followed the tracks of a larger party—the ones who killed them."

Erak hesitated. He wasn't a tracker. He was a sea captain. But one of the men who had come with him was an occasional hunter. While he didn't have the uncanny skills that the Rangers had developed in interpreting tracks, Erak now remembered that his man had said something about the possibility of there being two groups.

"Then," he said, bewildered by this turn of events, "if you didn't do it, who did?"

Halt jerked a thumb at the bound prisoner. "Him—and his friends," he said. "He was in a Temujai scouting party we ran into yesterday. There was a larger band who attacked the border garrison, then six of them came on into Skandia."

"Temujai, you say?" Erak asked him. He knew of the warlike people from the east, of course, but it had been decades since they had come this way in any numbers.

"We killed a couple of them," Halt told him. "Two got away and we captured this one."

Erak stepped to where the prisoner stood, hands tied in front of him, glaring fiercely at the big northerners who surrounded him. He studied the flat-featured, brown-skinned face and the furs the man wore.

"He's a Tem'uj, all right . . . but what were they doing here?" he asked, almost to himself.

"That's the question I was asking," Halt replied.

Erak glanced at him with a flash of anger. He hated being confused. He preferred a simple, straightforward problem—the kind he could solve with his broadax. "For that matter," he snapped, "what are you doing here?"

Halt faced him evenly, uncowed. "I came for the boy," he said quietly. Erak looked at him, then at the smaller figure beside him, his face still largely concealed by the gray mottled hood. His anger faded as quickly as it had flared.

"Yes," he said, in a calmer tone. "He said you would."

Like most Skandians, Erak valued loyalty and courage. Another thought struck him—something he'd wondered about for some time.

"At the beach," he said. "How did you know to find us there?"

"You left one of your men behind," Halt said. "He told me."

The disbelief was plain on Erak's face.

"Nordal? He'd have spat in your eye before he told you anything."

"I think he thought he owed me," Halt said quietly. "He was dying and he'd lost his sword, so I gave it back to him."

Erak went to speak, then hesitated. Skandians believed that if a man died without a weapon in his hand, his soul was lost forever. It seemed the Ranger knew about the belief.

"Then I'm in your debt," he said finally. Then, after another pause: "I'm not sure how that affects this current situation, however." He rubbed his beard thoughtfully, looking at the fierce little Temujai warrior, for all the world like a tethered hawk. "And I'd still like to know what this lad and his bunch are up to."

"That's what I had in mind," Halt told him. "I was planning to get my companions here across the border into Teutlandt. Then I thought I might come back with our friend here and find the rest of the Temujai—and see how many of them there are."

Erak snorted. "You think he'll tell you?" he asked. "I don't know too much about the Temujai, but I know this much: you can torture them to death and they'll never tell you anything they don't want to."

"Yes. I've heard that too," Halt said. "But there might be a way."

"Oh, might there?" the jarl asked scornfully. "And what might 'that way' be?"

Halt glanced at the horse warrior. He was following their discussion with some interest. Halt knew he spoke the trading language but he had no idea how much of the common tongue he might understand. As a member of a scouting party, it was probable that he had some command of the language. He took the jarl's arm and led him a few paces away, out of earshot.

"I rather thought I might let him escape," he said mildly.

13

THE TWO MEN STOOD OVER THE TANGLE OF DISCARDED ROPES lying in the snow. Erak pursed his lips, then turned to Halt. "Well, so far, you're right," he said. "The little beggar escaped once Olak pretended to fall asleep on guard duty." He glanced sideways at the large Skandian who had been assigned to the last watch. "You did pretend to fall asleep, didn't you?" he added, with a touch of sarcasm.

The warrior grinned easily at him. "I was wonderful, Jarl Erak," he said. "You've never seen such a lifelike impersonation of a sleeping man. I should have been a traveling player."

Erak grunted skeptically. "So what now?" he asked Halt.

"Now, I follow him while he leads me to the main body of Temujai," the Ranger said. "As we discussed last night."

"I've been thinking about that," Erak replied. "And I've decided we're going to make a change. I'm going with you."

Halt had been walking toward the spot where the horses were tethered. He stopped and turned to face the Skandian leader, a determined look on his face. "We discussed this last night. We agreed that I would be quicker and less noticeable if I went alone."

"No. We didn't agree that. You agreed that," Erak corrected

him. "And even if you're right, you're just going to have to settle for being slower and noisier, and make allowances for the fact."

Halt drew in breath to begin a protest, but Erak forestalled him.

"Be reasonable," he said. "We've agreed that circumstances seem to make us temporary allies—"

"Which is why you'll keep my three companions here as hostages," Halt put in sarcastically, and Erak simply shrugged.

"Of course. They're my surety that you'll come back. But put yourself in my shoes. If there is a Temujai army out there somewhere, I don't want to take a secondhand report to my Oberjarl. I want to see it for myself. So I'm coming with you. I may need you to track the prisoner, but I can do my own looking."

He paused, waiting to see Halt's reaction. The Ranger said nothing, so Erak continued: "After all, the hostages might ensure that you come back. But they're no guarantee that you'll give me an accurate report—or even an honest one."

Halt seemed to weigh the statement for a few seconds. Then he saw a possible advantage.

"All right," he agreed. "But if you're coming with me, there's no need to keep my companions as hostages to guarantee my return. Let them go back across the border while you and I go find the Temujai."

Erak smiled at him and shook his head slowly. "I don't think so," he replied. "I'd like to think that I can trust you, but there's really no reason why I should, is there? If you know my men are holding your friends, it might make you less likely to stick one of those knives in me the minute we're out of sight over the hill there."

Halt spread his hands in a an innocent gesture. "Do you really think an undersized little runt like me could get the better of a big, hulking sea wolf like you?"

Erak smiled grimly at him. "Not for a moment," he said. "But this way I'll be able to sleep nights and turn my back on you without worrying."

"Fair enough," Halt agreed. "Now, could we get going while these tracks are still fresh, or would you prefer to argue until the snow melts?"

Erak shrugged. "You're the one who's doing all the arguing," he told him. "Let's go."

Halt glanced over his shoulder as Abelard set his hooves more securely against the steep slope. Behind him, Erak was swaying insecurely on the back of the Temujai horse. The captive had made his escape on foot, and Halt had decided that the small, shaggy and sure-footed steppes pony would be a better mount for Erak than either of Horace's battlehorses. The Skandian warriors, as was their custom, had been traveling on foot.

"I thought you said you could ride," he challenged as the jarl grabbed nervously at his mount's shaggy mane, holding himself in the saddle more by brute strength than any inherent sense of balance.

"I did," Erak replied through gritted teeth. "I just didn't say I could ride well."

They had been following the escaped Temujai warrior's trail all day. After making their way through the Serpent Pass, their trail had swung back in an arc from the Teutlandt border and they were some thirty kilometers into Skandian territory once more. Halt shook his head, then went back to peering at the ground in front of them, looking for the faint traces that the fleeing Tem'uj had left behind him.

"He's very good," he said quietly.

"Who's that?" Erak asked, the last word being torn from him as his horse lurched and slid a few steps. Halt indicated the trail he was following. The Skandian looked but couldn't see a thing.

"The Tem'uj," Halt continued. "He's covering his tracks as he goes. I don't think your man would have been able to follow him."

Which was the crux of the matter. When Halt and Erak had agreed to join forces the previous night, it had been the result of their mutual need. Halt's natural inclination had been to see what the Temujai were up to. Erak had the same need. But he also had need of Halt's tracking skills. He was only too aware of his own men's limitations.

"Well," he said jerkily, "that's why you're here, isn't it?"

"Yes." Halt smiled grimly. "The question is, why are you?"

Erak wisely said nothing. He concentrated his efforts into staying astride the shaggy horse as it struggled up the steep slope, under the unaccustomed weight of the bulky Skandian sea captain.

They came to the crest with a sudden rush, their horses scrambling the last few meters through the wet snow. They found themselves looking down on a deep, wide valley, and beyond that, another range of hills.

Below them on the vast plain, a mass of campfires sent columns of smoke spiraling into the late-afternoon air, spreading as far as the eye could see—thousands of them, surrounded by more thousands of dome-shaped felt tents. The smell of the smoke reached them now. Not heady and scented, like pine smoke, but acrid and sour smelling. Erak wrinkled his nose in disgust.

"What are they burning?" he asked.

"Dried horse dung," Halt replied briefly. "They carry their fuel source with them. Look."

He pointed to where the Temujai horse herd could be seen, a

giant, amorphous mass that seemed to flow across the valley floor as the horses sought fresh grazing.

"Gorlog's teeth!" Erak exclaimed, stunned at the numbers. "How many are there?"

"Ten thousand, maybe twelve," Halt replied briefly. The Skandian let out a low whistle.

"Are you sure? How can you tell?" It wasn't a sensible question, but Erak was overwhelmed by the size of the horse herd and he asked the question more for something to say than for any other reason. Halt looked at him dryly.

"It's an old cavalry trick," he said. "You count the legs and divide by four."

Erak returned the look. "I was just making conversation, Ranger," he said. Halt seemed singularly unimpressed by the statement.

"Then don't," he replied shortly. There was silence as they studied the enemy camp.

"Are you saying there are ten to twelve thousand warriors down there?" Erak asked finally. The number was a daunting one. At best, Skandia could put a force of fifteen hundred warriors in the field to face them. Perhaps two thousand, at the outside. That meant odds of six or seven to one. But Halt was shaking his head.

"More like five to six thousand," he estimated. "Each warrior will have at least two horses. There are probably another four to five thousand personnel in the baggage train and supply columns, but they wouldn't be combatants."

That was a little better, thought Erak. The odds had reduced to around three or four to one. A little better, he thought. Not a lot.

Not a lot by a long way.

14

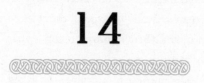

'WAIT HERE," HALT SAID BRIEFLY. "I'M GOING DOWN FOR A closer look."

"To hell with waiting here," Erak told him. "I'm coming with you."

Halt looked at the big Skandian, knowing it would be useless to argue. Still, he made the attempt. "I suppose it will make no difference if I point out I'm going to have to be as inconspicuous as possible?"

Erak shook his head. "Not in the slightest. I'm not taking back a secondhand report to my Oberjarl. I want to get a closer look at these people, get some idea of what we're up against."

"I can tell you what you're up against," Halt said grimly.

"I'll see for myself," the jarl said stubbornly, and Halt shrugged, finally giving in.

"All right. But move carefully, and try not to make too much noise. The Temujai aren't idiots, you know. They'll have pickets out in the trees around the camp, as well as sentries on the perimeter."

"Well, you just tell me where they are and I'll avoid them," Erak replied, with a little heat. "I can be inconspicuous when I need to."

"Just like you can ride, I suppose," Halt muttered to himself.

The Skandian ignored the comment, continuing to glare stubbornly at him. Halt shrugged. "Well, let's get on with it."

They tethered their horses on the reverse side of the crest, then began to work their way down through the trees to the valley below them. They had gone a few hundred meters when Halt turned to the Skandian.

"Are there bears in these mountains?" he asked.

His companion nodded. "Of course. But it's a bit early in the year for them to be moving around. Why?"

Halt let go a long breath. "Just a vague hope, really. There's a chance that when the Temujai hear you crashing around in the trees, they might think you're a bear."

Erak smiled, with his mouth only. His eyes were as cold as the snow.

"You're a very amusing fellow," he told Halt. "I'd like to brain you with my ax one of these days."

"If you could manage to do it quietly, I'd almost welcome it," Halt said. Then he turned away and continued to lead the way down the hill, ghosting between the trees, sliding from one patch of shadow to the next, barely disturbing a branch or a twig as he passed.

Erak tried, unsuccessfully, to match the Ranger's silent movement. With each slither of his feet in the snow, each whip of a branch as he passed, Halt's teeth went more and more on edge. He had just determined that he would have to leave the Skandian behind once they got within striking distance of the Temujai camp when he glimpsed something off to their left in the trees. Quickly, he held up his hand for Erak to stop. The big Skandian, not understanding the imperative nature of the gesture, kept moving till he was alongside Halt.

"What is it?" he asked. He kept his voice low, but to Halt it seemed like a bellow that echoed among the trees.

He placed his own mouth next to the Skandian's ear and breathed, in a barely audible voice, "Listening post. In the trees."

It was a familiar Temujai technique: whenever a force camped for the night, they threw out a screen of concealed, two-man listening posts to give early warning of any attempt at a surprise attack. He and Erak had just passed such a post, so that it now lay to their left and slightly behind them. For a moment, Halt toyed with the idea of continuing down the hill, then he discarded it. The screen was usually deployed in depth. Just because they had passed one post didn't mean there weren't others ahead of them. He decided it might be best to cut their losses and extract themselves as quietly as possible, trusting the gathering darkness to conceal them. It would mean abandoning the idea of getting a closer look at the Temujai force, but it couldn't be helped. Besides, with Erak along, it was unlikely they would get much closer without being seen—or, more likely, heard. He leaned close to the other man and spoke softly once more.

"Follow me. Go slowly. And watch where you put your feet."

The snow under the trees was strewn with dead branches and pinecones. Several times as they'd made their way downhill, he had winced as Erak had trod, heavy-footed, on fallen branches, breaking them with seemingly earsplitting cracks.

Silently, Halt flitted between the trees, moving like a wraith, sliding into cover after he'd gone some fifty paces. He looked back and waved the Skandian on, watched for a moment with mounting apprehension as the big man moved, swaying awkwardly as he placed his feet with exaggerated care. Finally, unable to watch him any longer, Halt looked anxiously to the left, to see if there was any sign that the men in the listening post had seen or heard them.

And heard a ringingly loud crack, followed by a muffled curse, from the hill below him. Erak was poised in midstride, a rotten branch snapped in half on the snow in front of him.

"Freeze," muttered Halt to himself, in the desperate hope that the big man would have the sense to stay motionless. Instead, Erak made the vital blunder that untrained stalkers nearly always made. He dashed for cover, hoping to substitute speed for stealth, and the sudden movement gave him away to the Temujai in the listening post.

There was a shout from above them and a flight of arrows slammed into the tree behind which the Skandian had taken cover. Halt peered around his tree. He could see two shapes in the gloom. One was moving away, sounding a horn as he went. The other was poised, an arrow on the string of his bow, eyes riveted on Erak's hiding place.

Waiting for the Skandian to move. Waiting to let the deadly shaft fly at him.

Somehow, Halt had to give Erak a chance to get clear. He called softly, "I'll step out and distract him. As soon as I do, you make for the next tree."

The Skandian nodded. He crouched a little, preparing to make a run for it. Halt called again.

"Just to the next tree. No farther," he said. "That's all you'll have time for before he's back on you. Believe me."

Again, the Skandian nodded. He'd seen the speed and accuracy with which the Temujai sentry got the first shot away. He wondered how he would get any farther than the next tree. Halt's ploy of distracting the sentry would only work once. He hoped that the Ranger had something else in mind. Fading away now, he could hear the braying notes of the horn sounding the alarm as the other sentry raced downhill, calling for reinforcements. Whatever Halt did, he thought, he'd better do it soon.

Erak saw the dim form of the Ranger as he stepped into the clear from behind the tree. Erak waited a heartbeat, then ran, his legs pumping in the snow, finally diving full length and sliding behind the thick pine trunk as an arrow hissed by, just over his head. His heart was racing, even though he had covered no more than ten meters in his wild, scrambling rush up the hill. He glanced across at Halt and saw the Ranger, back in cover and some five meters farther away. He had his own longbow ready now, an arrow nocked to the string. His face was knotted in a frown of concentration. He felt the Skandian's eyes on him and called across the intervening space.

"Take a look. Carefully—don't give him enough of a target to shoot at. See if he's in the same position."

Erak nodded and edged one eye around the bole of the tree. The Temujai warrior was still where he had been standing, his bow ready and half drawn. As matters stood, he held the upper hand, standing ready to shoot if either of them moved. Halt, on the other hand, would have to step into the clear, sight the man, aim and then shoot. By the time he had accomplished the first two actions, he would be dead.

"He hasn't moved," Erak called to the Ranger.

"Tell me if he does," Halt called softly in return. Lying belly-down in the snow, with just a fraction of his face protruding around the tree, Erak nodded.

Behind his tree, Halt leaned back against the rough bark and closed his eyes, breathing deeply. This was going to have to be an instinctive shot. He pictured again the dark figure of the Tem'uj, silhouetted against the lighter background of the snow. He remembered the position, setting it in his brain, letting his mind take over the control of his hands, willing the aiming and release to become an instinctive sequence. He forced his breathing to settle into a calm, slow, unhurried rhythm. The secret of speed was not to hurry, he told himself. In his mind's eye, he watched the flight of the arrow as he would fire it. He pictured it over and over again until it seemed to be a part of him—a natural extension of his own being.

Then, in an almost trancelike state, he moved.

Smoothly. Rhythmically. Stepping out into the clear, turning in a fluid motion so that his left shoulder was toward the target, the right hand pulling back on the string, left hand pushing the bow away until it was at full draw. Aiming and shooting at a memory. Not even seeing the dark figure in the trees until the arrow was already loosed, already splitting the air on its way to the target.

And, when he finally did see the bowman in his conscious vision, knowing that the shot was good.

The heavy shaft went home. The Tem'uj fell backward in the snow, his own shot half a second too late, sailing high and harmless into the tops of the pines.

Erak scrambled to his feet, regarding the small, gray-cloaked figure with something close to awe.

He realized that there was already a second arrow nocked to the longbow's string. He hadn't even seen the Ranger do that.

"By the gods," he muttered, dropping a heavy hand on the smaller man's shoulder. "I'm glad you're on my side."

Halt shook his head briefly, refocusing his attention. He glared angrily at the big Skandian.

"I thought I told you to watch where you put your feet," he said accusingly. Erak shrugged.

"I did," he replied ruefully. "But while I was busy watching the ground, I hit that branch with my head. Broke it clean in two."

Halt raised his eyebrows. "I assume you're not talking about your head," he muttered. Erak frowned at the suggestion.

"Of course not," he replied.

"More's the pity," Halt told him, then gestured up the hill. "Now let's get out of here."

15

When they reached the crest of the hill, Halt paused to look back. Erak stopped beside him, but he grabbed the bigger man's arm and shoved him roughly toward the two tethered horses.

"Keep going!" he yelled.

In the valley below them, he could hear alarm horns sounding and, faintly, the sound of shouting. Closer to hand, on the slope of the hill below, he could see movement among the trees as those Temujai who had been concealed in listening posts around the hillside now broke cover and headed uphill in pursuit of the two intruders.

"Damned hornets' nest," he muttered to himself. He estimated that there must be at least half a dozen riders on the hill below him, heading upward. A larger party was obviously forming in the camp itself, with a view to heading around the base of the hill and catching him and Erak between two pursuing forces.

Alone, and mounted on Abelard, he was confident that he could outrun them easily. But burdened by the Skandian, he wasn't so sure. He'd seen the man's skill as a rider—which was virtually nonexistent. Erak seemed to stay in the saddle by virtue of an enormous amount of willpower and precious little else. Halt knew that he would have to come up with some kind of delaying tactic, to slow the pursuit down and give him and Erak time to make it back to the larger Skandian force.

Strangely, although they had been nominal enemies up until now, the thought of abandoning the Skandian to the pursuing Temujai riders never occurred to him.

He looked back to where they had tethered Erak's horse—Abelard, of course, needed no tethering. He saw with some slight satisfaction that the wolfship skipper had managed to clamber into the saddle and was sitting clumsily astride his small, shaggy mount. Halt waved a hand now in an unmistakable gesture to him.

"Get going!" he yelled. "Go! Go! Go!"

Erak needed no second bidding. He wheeled the horse to face downhill, swaying dangerously out to one side as he did so and managing to retain his seat only by grabbing at the mane and gripping with his powerful legs around the horse's barrel of a body. Then, half in and half out of the saddle, he drove the former Temujai mount down the slope, skidding and sliding in the soft wet snow, swerving dangerously among the trees. At one stage, Erak neglected to duck as the horse drove under the snow-laden lower branches of a huge pine. There was an explosion of snow and both horse and rider emerged coated in thick white powder.

Halt swung smoothly into Abelard's saddle and the little horse spun neatly, moving at a dead gallop almost before he could draw breath. Halt sat easily as Abelard slid, checked, skidded and regained his footing, gaining on the other horse and rider with every stride.

He'll be lucky to survive another fifty meters, Halt thought as Erak's mount, half out of control, swerved and skidded and slipped among the trees. It seemed only a matter of time before both horse and rider collided full tilt with one of the large pine trunks.

He urged Abelard to a greater effort and the horse responded instantly. They drew level with the plunging horse and rider and Halt, leaning down to one side, was able to grab the trailing reins. Erak had long since abandoned them and was clinging for dear life to the saddle bow.

Now, at least, Halt could exercise some small control over the headlong plunging of the other horse. Abelard, sure-footed and agile, led them through the trees and Halt left the choice to him entirely. The lead rein jerked and tugged at his arm but he clung to it desperately, forcing the other horse to follow in Abelard's tracks. Abelard, as he had been trained to do, chose the most direct and, at the same time, the clearest path down the mountain. They were two-thirds of the way down now and Halt was beginning to feel more positive about their chances of escape when he heard shouting and the sound of those damned horns from the hill crest behind them. He glanced quickly back but the thickly growing trees obscured his view. Nonetheless, he knew that the sudden burst of sound heralded the appearance of the pursuing Temujai at the top of the mountain.

And he knew that it was only a matter of time before they would overhaul him, just as he had overhauled the bulky Skandian on the small horse.

A thin branch whipped across his face, bringing tears to his eyes and punishing him for taking his attention from the direction he was heading. He shook his head to get rid of the accompanying shower of snow that the branch had brought with it, then, seeing the way ahead was clear, he turned briefly again to call encouragement to Erak.

"Keep hanging on!" he yelled and the Skandian promptly did exactly the opposite, releasing his grip with one hand so that he could wave an acknowledgment.

"Don't worry about me!" he yelled. "I'm doing fine!"

Halt shook his head. Frankly, he'd seen sacks of potatoes that could sit a horse better than Erak. He wondered how the Skandian ever managed to keep his feet on the heaving deck of a wolfship. The trees were thinning around them now, he noticed. Then he heard the braying note of one of the Temujai horns out to their left and realized that the first of the parties coming around the base of the mountain from the encampment must be close to heading them off. It would be a near-run thing, he thought grimly. His slight increase in knee pressure sent Abelard bounding even faster. From behind he heard a startled yell from Erak as he nearly lost his seat again. Another quick glance told him that the Skandian was still mounted, and they broke out onto the level ground between the hills.

He had been right. It *was* a close-run race. The leading riders of the Temujai party swept into sight on the flat ground between the hills. They were barely two hundred meters away. Halt dragged Erak's horse around brutally, touched Abelard with his heels and set the two horses galloping back along the track they had followed earlier in the day. On clearer ground now, he could look behind him more easily. He made out at least a dozen riders chasing them. For a moment, the grizzled Ranger had a distinct sense of déjà vu, his mind racing back across the years to the time when he had been driving a herd of stolen horses with another party of Temujai howling for his blood close behind him. He grinned mirthlessly. Of course the horses had been stolen. He simply couldn't bear to disappoint Horace any further when he had told him of his previous encounter with the eastern horsemen. He'd felt at the time that the boy had been disillusioned enough for one day.

Now he eased Abelard fractionally, allowing the other horse

to come level with them, and tossed the reins to the Skandian jarl, who bumped and lurched in the saddle beside him. Surprisingly, Erak caught them. There was nothing wrong with his reflexes, at any rate, Halt thought.

"Keep going!" he yelled at the Skandian.

"What ... you ... got ... in ... mind?" Erak replied jerkily, the words lurching out of him as he was tossed and bumped in the saddle.

"Going to slow them down," Halt replied briefly. "Don't stop to watch. Just keep going as hard as you can!"

Erak gritted his teeth as he came down heavily on the saddle. "This is as hard ... as ... I can!" he replied. But Halt was already shaking his head. The Ranger had unslung his longbow from across his shoulders and was brandishing it in his right hand. Erak saw what was coming, a moment too late to do anything about it.

"No!" he began. "Don't you—!"

But then the bow whipped down across his horse's rump with a resounding crack and the beast leapt forward, stung.

The profanity that Erak was preparing for Halt was lost in his drawn-out howl as he grabbed at the saddle bow once more to keep his seat. For a second or two he was furious. Then he realized that he was still in the saddle, that he could keep his seat even at this accelerated pace. So, when the horse began to slow down to a more comfortable speed, he slapped his big hand across its backside several times, driving it on.

Halt watched in satisfaction as his companion went on ahead, urging the horse on to greater efforts. In a few seconds, Erak swept around a curve in the trail that was formed between two of the hills and was out of sight.

Then, in response to a well-learned knee signal, Abelard reared and pirouetted on his hind legs, spinning in a half circle so that he came to a stop at right angles to the direction they had been following.

In an instant, the horse had gone from a dead run to a full stop. Now he stood rock steady as his master stood in the stirrups, an arrow nocked to the string of his massive longbow.

He knew that the longbow outranged the smaller, flat-shooting re-curve bows of the Temujai. He allowed them to close in a little farther, gauging the pace at which they were eating up the distance between him and them, estimating when he would need to release so as to have the arrow arrive at a given point just as the lead rider did. He did this without thinking, allowing the ingrained instincts and habits of years of endless practice to take over for him. Almost without realizing it, he released and the arrow sped away, sailing in a shallow arc toward the pursuers.

They were one hundred and fifty meters from him when the arrow struck the lead rider from his saddle. He slid sideways to the ground, trying to maintain his hold on the reins and bringing his horse down with him as he did. The rider directly behind him, taken totally by surprise, had no chance to avoid his leader's fallen horse. He and his horse came crashing down as well, adding to the tangle of legs and arms and bodies that rolled in a welter of thrown snow.

The riders behind them were thrown into utter confusion, with riders sawing savagely at the reins to drag their horses away from the tangle ahead of them. Horses plunged and reared, getting in each other's way, sliding stiff-legged to a halt in the snow, heading in all directions to avoid the crash. As they milled in confusion, Halt was already galloping away, rounding the bend and heading after Erak.

Slowly, the Temujai regained order. The leader's horse had re-gained its feet and limped in a circle, blowing and snorting wildly. Its rider lay in the snow in the center of a widening circle of red. Now the others could see the cause of all the trouble: the heavy, black-shafted arrow that had arced down to take him. Accustomed to using the bow themselves with deadly skill, they were unfamiliar with the feeling of being on the receiving end—and at such an extreme range. Perhaps, they realized, a headlong pursuit of the two fleeing riders wasn't such a good idea. The Temujai weren't cowards. But they weren't fools either. They had just seen clear evidence of their quarry's uncanny accuracy. They sorted themselves out and set off in pursuit again—but not quite so eagerly this time, and not quite so quickly.

Behind them, the second rider, who had collided with the fallen leader, was left in a vain attempt to catch the leader's horse. His own had broken its neck in the fall. He didn't seem in too much of a hurry to resume the chase.

16

HALT STOPPED TWICE MORE TO SLOW DOWN THE RIDERS BEHIND them. Both times, he dismounted, allowing Abelard to trot around the next bend in the trail so that he was out of sight. Then Halt waited, standing in the deep shadows thrown by the pine trees, almost invisible in the gray and green mottled cloak.

When the Temujai riders appeared around a bend in the trail behind him, Halt launched two arrows at maximum range, on a high parabolic flight. Each time, the horsemen weren't even aware that they were being fired on until two of their number threw up their hands and tumbled from their saddles into the snow.

Halt chose his ambush positions carefully. He selected places where there was a clear sight of the trail behind him, but he didn't choose every such section. After the third attack, every time the Temujai approached a bend in the trail, they slowed their pursuit, fearing they would be riding into another volley of black-shafted arrows arcing down out of the sky at them.

On the last two occasions they didn't even see Halt before he moved to remount Abelard. They soon began to rationalize, arguing that there was no real need to capture the two men who had been spying on their camp. There was, after all, little that two men could do to harm them and if they alerted the Skandian forces, well, the Temujai had come here prepared to fight anyway.

This was the result Halt had been hoping for. After stopping twice, he urged Abelard into a steady gallop, soon overtaking Erak as he lurched and swayed on the saddle of his now cantering horse. Erak heard the muffled pounding of hooves behind him and swung awkwardly in the saddle, half expecting to see a group of Temujai coming up behind. He relaxed as he recognized the gray-cloaked figure of the Ranger. His horse, without anyone to continue urging it on, slackened its pace as Abelard pounded up alongside. Halt checked him for a few strides, matching the Temujai mount's pace.

"Where have . . . you been?" Erak asked, in that same jerky manner.

Halt gestured to the trail behind him. "Buying us some time," he replied. "Can't you keep that nag of yours running faster than that?"

Erak looked insulted. He'd thought he was doing rather well.

"I'll have you know I'm an excellent rider," he said stiffly. Halt glanced over his shoulder. There was no sign of any pursuit, but there was no knowing how long the Temujai would take to realize that he wasn't waiting for them at every corner. If they continued at this gentle, ambling pace, the riders behind them would make up the lost distance in no time.

"You may believe you're an excellent rider," he called, "but there are a score or so of Temujai back there who actually are. Now get moving!"

Erak saw the longbow rise, and begin to fall on his horse's rump once more. This time, he didn't waste breath or time yelling at Halt not to do it. He grabbed a handful of mane and hung on for dear life as the horse bolted away underneath him. Bouncing and jouncing in exquisite pain, he consoled himself with the thought that, when this was over, he would separate the Ranger from his head.

They swept on, Halt urging the Temujai horse on to greater efforts whenever he began to flag. The landmarks around them began to take on a familiar appearance, then they had galloped into the head of Serpent Pass, coming up to the deserted border post. There, camped outside the log walls of the small fort, Erak's twenty Skandian warriors and Evanlyn and the two apprentices were waiting for them. The Skandians came to their feet quickly, reaching for their weapons, as the two horses entered the pass at a dead run.

Halt brought Abelard skidding to a stop beside his three companions. Erak tried to emulate the action, but his horse pounded on for another twenty meters or so and he had to swing it awkwardly around, swaying and slipping in the saddle as it turned, and inevitably falling in a heap in the snow as the horse finally decided to stop.

Two or three of the Skandians, unwisely, let go short bellows of laughter as Erak picked himself up. The jarl's eyes swept over them, cold as glacier ice, marking them down for later reference. The laughter died as quickly as it had sprung up.

Halt threw his leg over the pommel and slid to the ground. He stroked Abelard's neck in gratitude. The little horse was barely breathing hard. He was bred to run all day if necessary. The Ranger saw the inquisitive looks of those around him.

"Did you find the main party?" Will finally asked.

Halt nodded grimly. "We found them all right."

"Thousands of them," Erak added, and the Skandians reacted with surprise at the news. Erak silenced them with a gesture.

"There are maybe five or six thousand of them out there,

probably heading this way right now." Once again, there were murmurs of surprise and consternation as he mentioned the numbers. One of the Skandians stepped forward.

"What do they want, Erak?" he asked. "What are they doing here?"

But it was the Ranger who answered the question: "They want what they always want," he said grimly. "They want your land. And they're here to take it from you."

His audience looked from one to the other. Then Erak decided it was time he took command of the situation.

"Well, they'll find we're a tough nut to crack," he declared. He swept his battle-ax in a small arc to indicate the fort behind them. "We'll hold the fort here and delay them while one of us takes word back to Hallasholm," he said. "There may be five thousand of them, but they can only come at us in small numbers through the pass. We should be able to hold them for four or five days at least."

There was a growl of assent from the Skandians, and several of them swept their axes through the air in experimental patterns. The jarl was growing in confidence now that he had a definite plan of action. And it was the sort of plan that appealed to the Skandian mind: simple, uncomplicated, easy to put into effect and with a degree of mayhem involved. He looked at Halt, who was watching him in silence, leaning on the man-high longbow.

"We'll trouble you for the use of the horse again," he said. "I'll send one of my men back to Hallasholm on it to raise the alarm. The rest of us will stay here and fight." Again, there was a savage growl from the Skandians in response. The jarl continued: "As for you, you can stay and fight with us or go on your way. It's of no consequence to me."

Halt shook his head, a look of bitter disappointment on his face.

"It's too late for us to go now," he said simply. He turned to his three young companions and shrugged apologetically. "The Temujai main force lies right across our path back to Teutlandt. We've no choice but to stay here."

Will exchanged glances with Evanlyn and Horace. He felt a sinking in the pit of his stomach. They had been so close to escaping, so close to going home.

"It's my fault," Halt continued, addressing his words to the two former captives. "I should have got you out straightaway instead of going to see what the Temujai were up to. I thought, at worst, it would be a reconnaissance in force. I had no idea it was an invasion."

"It's all right, Halt," Will told him. He hated to see his mentor apologizing or blaming himself. In Will's eyes, Halt could do no wrong. Horace hurried to agree with him.

"We'll stay here and hold them back with the Skandians," he said, and one of the sea wolf warriors close by him slapped him heartily on the back.

"That's the spirit, boy!" he said, and several others chorused their approval of Horace's intentions. But Halt shook his head.

"Nobody should stay here. There's no point."

That brought howls of anger and derision from the Skandians. Erak silenced them and stepped forward, staring down at the slight figure in the gray cloak.

"Yes, there's a point," he said, in an ominously quiet tone. "We'll hold them here until Ragnak can muster the main force to relieve us. There are twenty of us. That should be more than enough to hold the little beggars off for a while. It won't be like when they slaughtered the garrison here. There were only a dozen men here then. We'll hold them off, or we'll die in the attempt. It's of no consequence to us as long as we delay them for three or four days."

"You won't last three or four hours," Halt said flatly, and an ugly silence fell over the small group. The Skandians were too shocked by the enormity of his insult to reply. Erak was the first to recover.

"If you believe that," he said grimly, "then you have never seen Skandians fight, my friend." The last two words carried an enormous weight of sarcasm and dismissal. Now the other Skandians found their voices and an angry chorus grew up. The Ranger waited for the shouting to die down. He was uncowed by the Skandians' anger at his words. Finally they fell silent.

"You know that I have," he said, not taking his eyes from Erak's.

The Skandian leader frowned. He knew Halt's reputation, as a fighting man and a tactician. The man was a Ranger, after all, and Erak knew enough about the mysterious Ranger Corps to know that they weren't prone to issuing pointless insults or making ill-considered remarks.

"The question is," Halt continued, "have you seen the Temujai fight?"

He allowed the question to hang in the cold air between them. There was a moment of silence from the Skandians. None of them had, of course. Seeing that he had their attention, Halt continued.

"Because I have. And I'll tell you what I'd do if I were the Temujai general."

He swept his arm up to encompass the steep sides of the pass where they towered above the little fort. Pines grew there, clinging to the almost vertical sides of the pass, managing to find some foothold in the rocks and the snow.

"I'd send a party of men up onto the walls of the pass there above us. Say, two hundred or so. And from there, I'd have them direct a killing fire on anyone foolhardy enough to show his face in the open inside the fort."

The eyes of the group followed the direction of his pointing arm. One of the Skandians snorted scornfully.

"They'd never get up there. Those walls are impassable!"

Halt turned to face him, looking him straight in the eye, willing the man to understand and believe what he was saying by the sheer force of his conviction.

"Not impassable. Very difficult. But they will do it. Believe me, I've seen these men and what they can achieve. It may cost them fifty or so lives in the attempt, but they'll count the cost cheap."

Erak studied the cliffs above the fort, squinting to see more clearly in the rapidly fading light of the late afternoon. Maybe, he thought, the Ranger was right. He figured he might be able to scramble around up there, with ropes and tackle and a small group of hand-picked sailors—the ones who tended the big square sails on the wolfships, who could slip up and down the mast as easy as walking. But the Temujai were cavalry, he thought. He voiced the objection.

"They'll never get their horses up there."

"They won't *need* their horses up there," Halt countered. "They'll simply sit up there and direct a plunging fire on you. The fort may command the pass, but the heights there command the fort."

Erak was silent for a long moment. He looked again up at the walls of the pass. If the trees could find footholds there, he reasoned, so could men—determined men. And he was ready to believe that these Temujai were determined.

"Face it," Halt continued, "this fort was never meant as a real defensive position. It's a checkpoint for people crossing the border, that's all. It's simply not designed or placed to hold an invading army at bay."

Erak studied the Ranger. The more he thought about it, the more sense Halt was making. He could picture the dangers of being caught inside the fort with a hundred or so archers perched on the cliffs above him—and no way to reply to their attack.

"I think you may be right," he said slowly. He was honest enough to admit that Halt's experience of these eastern riders was far greater than his own. Reluctantly, he made the final decision—to pass control over to Halt.

"What do you suggest we do?" he asked. His men looked at him in surprise and he glared them to silence. Halt nodded once, acknowledging the difficulty of the decision the jarl had just reached.

"You were right about one thing," he said. "Ragnak has to be warned. There's no point in our wasting any more time here. It'll take the Temujai at least half a day to get the whole army on the move. Longer for them to come through this narrow pass. Let's use the time we have. We'll ride—and run—like hell back to Hallasholm."

17

FULL NIGHT FELL SHORTLY AFTER THEY HAD SET OUT ON THEIR way back to Hallasholm. But they continued to move, their way lit by a brilliant three-quarter moon that sailed above them in the clear sky.

Halt, Evanlyn and the two apprentices rode, while the Skandians maintained a steady jog, led by the jarl. Halt had suggested that Erak ride the captured Temujai horse again, but he had declined the offer, with a certain amount of alacrity. It seemed now that he had his feet firmly back on the ground, he was determined to keep them that way. His thighs and calves ached from the hours he had spent in the saddle that day, and his backside seemed to be one massive bruise. He was glad of the chance to walk the cramps out of his muscles.

Even allowing for the fact that the Skandians were traveling afoot, Halt was content with the pace they were maintaining. The sea wolves were in superb condition. They could keep up their steady jog all night, with only brief rest periods every hour.

Horace urged Kicker up beside Halt.

"Shouldn't we walk as well?" he suggested. Halt raised an eyebrow at him.

"Why?" he asked. The big youth shrugged, not quite sure how to articulate his thought.

"As a gesture of comradeship," he said finally. "It will give them a feeling of camaraderie."

Camaraderie, Halt knew, was something that was stressed in the early years of Battleschool training. It was part of that inconvenient knightly code. Sometimes he wished that Sir Rodney, the head of Castle Redmont's Battleschool, would give his charges a short course in practicality as well.

"Well, it will give *me* a feeling of sore legs," he replied at last. "There's no point to it, Horace. The Skandians don't care whether we walk or ride. And when there's no point to something, the best idea is not to do it."

Horace nodded several times. Truth be told, he was relieved that Halt had rejected his suggestion. He was far more at home in the saddle than tramping through the snow. And, now that he thought about it, the Skandians didn't seem to resent the fact that the four Araluens were riding while they walked.

During one of the brief rest stops, Halt caught Will's eye and made an almost imperceptible gesture for the boy to follow him. They walked a short distance from the rest of the party, who were sprawled at ease in the snow. A few of the Skandians watched them with mild interest, but most ignored them.

When he judged that there was no one within earshot, Halt drew Will closer to him, his hand on the boy's shoulder.

"This fellow Erak," he said. "What do you make of him?"

Will frowned. He thought back over how Erak had treated them since he had captured them at the bridge in Celtica. In the first place, he had shielded them from Morgarath, refusing to hand them over to the rebel warlord. Then, on the trip across the Stormwhite Sea, and during their stay on Skorghijl, he had shown a certain rough kindness, and even a regard, toward him and Evanlyn. Finally, of course, he had been instrumental in their escape from Hallasholm, providing clothes, food and a pony, and giving them directions to the hunting cabin in the mountains.

There was only one possible answer.

"I like him," he replied. Halt nodded.

"Yes," he said. "So do I. But do you trust him? That's a different matter to liking."

This time, Will opened his mouth immediately to reply, then paused, wondering if his response might not be too impulsive. Then he realized that trust was always impulsive, and went ahead.

"Yes," he said. "I do."

Halt rubbed his chin with his forefinger and thumb. "I must say, I agree with you."

"Well, he did help us to escape, you know, Halt," Will pointed out, and the Ranger nodded his recognition of that point.

"I know," he said. "That's what I was thinking about."

He was conscious of the boy's curious glance, but he said no more. As the members of the small party resumed their progress toward the coast, Halt struggled with the problem of how to protect Will and Evanlyn when they returned to Hallasholm. They might be regarded as allies for the moment, merely from force of circumstance. But once they were back in the Skandians' stronghold, things could go badly for the two escaped slaves. Things could become even worse for Evanlyn should her real identity become known to the Skandian Oberjarl.

Yet, try as he might, the gray-haired Ranger could think of no possible alternative to their present course. The way south was barred by thousands of Temujai warriors and there was no chance that he could make it through their lines with the three young people. He and Will might manage it. But it was a big might. And he knew enough about the Temujai to know that with Horace and Evanlyn along, they would never avoid detection.

So, for the time being, at least, they had no choice but to head toward Hallasholm. In the back of his mind there was a partly formed idea that they might be able to steal a boat. Or even prevail upon Erak to transport them down the coast to the south, leapfrogging the line of advance of the Temujai army. Somehow, sometime, he would have to reach some kind of an accommodation with the Skandian jarl, he knew.

The opportunity came at the next rest stop. And it came from the jarl himself. As the Skandians allowed themselves to sprawl on the ground under the pines, Erak, seemingly casually, approached the spot where Halt was pouring water from his canteen into a collapsible canvas bucket for Abelard. The horse drank noisily as the wolfship commander stood by and watched. Fully aware of his presence, Halt continued with what he was doing.

Then, when the horse stopped drinking, he said, without looking up: "Something on your mind?"

The jarl shifted awkwardly from one foot to another.

"We need to talk," he said finally, and Halt shrugged.

"We seem to be doing that." He kept his voice neutral. He could sense that the Skandian leader wanted something from him and he felt this might be his opportunity to gain some kind of bargaining advantage.

Erak glanced around, making sure that none of his men was in earshot. He knew they wouldn't like the idea he was about to propose. But, all the same, he knew that the idea was a good one. And a necessary one.

"It was you, wasn't it, at the battle of the Thorntree?" he said at last. Halt turned to face him.

"I was there," he said. "And so were a couple of hundred others."

The Skandian made an impatient gesture. "Yes, yes," he said. "But you were the leader—the tactician—weren't you?"

Halt shrugged diffidently.

"That's right, I suppose," he said carefully. The battle at Thorntree forest had been a defeat for the Skandians. He wondered now if Erak might be looking for some kind of revenge over the man who had led the Araluen forces. It didn't seem in character with what he knew of the Skandian, but you never could tell.

Erak, however, was nodding thoughtfully to himself. He hunkered down in the snow, picking up a pine twig and making random marks on the ground with it.

"And you know these Temujai, don't you?" he said. "You know how they fight—how they organize their army?"

It was Halt's turn to nod. "I told you. I lived among them for a while."

"So . . ." Erak paused and Halt knew that he was reaching the crucial part of their conversation. "You'd know their strengths, and their weaknesses?"

The Ranger barked a short, humorless laugh. "There aren't many of those," he said, but Erak persisted, stabbing the twig deeper into the snow as he talked.

"But you'd know how to fight them? How to beat them?"

Now Halt began to have a glimmer of where this conversation was leading. And, with that, he felt a slight surge of hope. He might just be about to be handed the bargaining tool that he would need to protect Will and Evanlyn.

"We fight as individuals," the jarl said softly, seeming to talk almost to himself. "We aren't organized. We have no tactics. No master plan."

"You Skandians have won your share of battles," Halt pointed out mildly. Erak looked up at him and Halt could see how much the sea wolf disliked what he was about to say.

"In a straight confrontation. One on one. Or even against odds of two to one. A straightforward conflict with no complications. Just a simple trial of arms. That sort of thing we can handle. But this . . . this is different."

"The Temujai are probably the most efficient fighting force in the world," Halt told him. "With the possible exception of the Arridi in the southern deserts."

There was silence between them. Halt willed the Skandian to take that one last step that lay in front of him. He saw the intake of breath, then Erak said:

"You could show us how to beat them."

It was out in the open now—exactly what Halt had begun to hope for. Carefully, like a man playing a trout that was yet to be hooked, he answered, making sure no hint of the eagerness he felt showed in his voice.

"Even if I could, I doubt I'd be given that opportunity," he said, trying to sound as dismissive as possible. Erak's head jerked up, a little flare of anger in his eyes.

"I could give it to you," he said. Halt met the other man's gaze, refusing to be intimidated by the anger there.

"You're not the Oberjarl," he said flatly. Erak shook his head, acknowledging the statement.

"That's right," he said. "But I am a senior war leader. I carry a certain amount of weight in our War Council."

Halt appeared unconvinced. "Enough to convince the others to accept an outlander as leader?"

Erak shook his head decisively.

"Not as a leader," he said. "Skandians would never follow your direct orders. Nor any other foreigner's. But as a counselor—a tactician. There are others on the council who know we need tactics. Who will understand that we need to fight as a cohesive unit, not as a thousand individuals. Borsa, for one, will agree with me."

Halt raised an eyebrow. "Borsa?" He knew some of the Skandian leaders' names. This one was unfamiliar.

"The hilfmann—Ragnak's chamberlain," Erak told him. "He's no warrior himself, but Ragnak respects his opinions, and his brain."

"Let me get this straight," Halt said slowly. "You're asking me to come aboard as a tactical adviser and help you find a way to beat the Temujai. And you think you can convince Ragnak to go along with the idea—and not simply kill me on the spot."

Erak looked a question at him. Halt continued.

"I know he has no love for Araluens. His son died at Thorntree, after all."

"You'd be under my protection," Erak said finally. "Ragnak would have to respect that, or fight me. And I don't think he'll be quite ready to do that. Whether I can convince the council or not—and I believe I will be able to—you'll be safe while you're in Hallasholm."

And there, all at once, was the opportunity Halt had been waiting for.

"What about my companions?" he asked. "Will and the girl are escaped slaves."

Erak waved the matter aside, dismissively. "That's a small matter compared to the fact that we're about to be invaded," he replied. "Your friends will be safe as well. You have my word."

"No matter what?" Halt insisted. He wanted the Skandian to

commit totally. He knew that no jarl would ever go back on a sworn vow of protection.

"No matter what," Erak replied, and held out his hand to the Ranger. They clasped hands firmly, sealing the bargain.

"Now," said Halt, "all I have to do is work out a way of beating these horse-riding devils."

Erak grinned at him. "That should be child's play," he said. "The hard part will be convincing Ragnak about it."

18

As it turned out, that task was a lot easier than either Erak or Halt would have thought possible. Ragnak was many things, but he was no fool. When the small party returned to Hallasholm, bringing news that an army of close to six thousand Temujai horsemen was in the process of invading his country, he did the same mental arithmetic that Erak had done. He knew as well as Erak that he could muster a force of no more than fifteen hundred warriors—possibly less, considering that some of the outlying settlements close to the border had probably been overrun and defeated already.

Like most Skandians, Ragnak wasn't afraid of dying in battle. But he also didn't believe that one should seek such an end without first trying all other alternatives. If there were a way of defeating the invaders, he would examine it. Consequently, when Erak told him of Halt's knowledge of the Temujai, and his agreement to lend his services, and when Borsa and several other council members welcomed the idea, he accepted their arguments with no more than token resistance. As for the matter of the recaptured slaves, he dismissed the matter entirely. In normal times, he might seek to punish runaways, as a way of discouraging further escapes. But these weren't normal times, and with an invading army on his doorstep, the matter of two recaptured slaves was of slight interest to him at best.

He did, however, demand to see Halt in his private quarters, with no one else present.

He knew enough about Rangers to respect their abilities and their courage as a group. But he wanted the chance to assess this man as an individual. Ragnak's ability to form such evaluations of men had been one of his principal qualities as leader of the Skandians. Evidence of his skill was the fact that he habitually chose Erak to handle the more difficult tasks that went with ruling a nation of independent-minded, argumentative warriors.

Halt was shown to the low-ceilinged, timber-lined room where Ragnak spent his private hours—and these days, the Oberjarl noted ruefully, there were precious few of those. The room was like all the senior Skandians' quarters—warmed by a pine log fire, with bearskins furnishing the pinewood-carved furniture, decorated with the polyglot results of years of plundering coastal villages and other ships.

The centerpiece of the room was an immense crystal chandelier, taken from an abbey on the coast of the Constant Sea years ago. With no high ceiling to hang it from, Ragnak had chosen to leave it resting on a rough pine table. It dominated the room and was more than a little awkward in the confined space. Furthermore, in its tabletop position it was totally incapable of performing its designed intention. There was no way that the fifty small oil lamps could be lit and kept burning safely.

But Ragnak loved the piece. To him, it represented art at its highest. It was an object of rare beauty, incongruous as it might be in this setting, and so he left it there.

He looked up from a scroll he was reading as Halt knocked at the door and entered, as he had been told to do. Ragnak frowned.

He equated prowess in battle with physical strength and size. The man before him looked wiry enough, but his head would barely come past the Oberjarl's shoulder if both were standing. There were no two ways about it. He was a small man.

"So, you're Halt," he said, not sounding too interested in the fact. He saw the little man's right eyebrow rise momentarily.

Then the man repeated, in exactly the same tone: "So, you're Ragnak."

Ragnak's heavy brows came closer together in an expression of anger. But inwardly, he felt a quick flicker of respect for the man in front of him. He liked Halt's instant reply, liked the way the Ranger was showing no sign of being cowed.

"People address me as 'Oberjarl,'" he said in an ominous tone.

Halt gave just the slightest suggestion of a shrug.

"Very well, Oberjarl," he replied. "I'll do the same."

Halt studied the Oberjarl with a keen eye. He was huge, but that was fairly normal for Skandians. He didn't have the classic, sculptured musculature that a person such as Horace would achieve in the next few years, with broad shoulders and narrow hips. Rather, like all Skandians, he was bulky throughout his entire body, built like a bear.

The arms and legs were massively muscled and the face was bearded, with the long beard lovingly separated into two sweeping masses. The hair had been red originally, but now the onset of age was turning it the color of ashes in a cold fireplace.

There was a faded scar on one cheek, stretching from just under the left eye down to the point of the man's chin. Halt guessed it to be an old injury. Again, there was little to remark on in this. The Skandians chose their leaders from the ranks of warriors, not administrators.

Most of all, Halt noted the eyes. He recognized the dislike that he saw there. He had been expecting to see that. But the eyes were deep-set and he could read an intelligence and cunning there as well. For that, he was grateful.

If Ragnak had been a stupid man, Halt's position might well have become untenable here. He knew of the Oberjarl's ingrained dislike for Rangers, and knew the reasons behind it. But an intelligent leader would be aware of Halt's usefulness to him, and might be prepared to set aside his personal dislike for the greater good of his people.

"I have no love of your kind, Ranger," the Oberjarl said. His mind was obviously running on lines similar to Halt's.

"You have little reason to," Halt agreed. "But you might well find a use for me."

"So I'm told," the Skandian leader replied, once again finding himself admiring the Ranger's forthrightness.

When he'd first heard of his son's death at Thorntree, Ragnak had been overcome with grief and rage—at Araluens, Rangers and, in particular, at King Duncan.

But that had been an immediate and spontaneous reaction to his grief. A realist, he knew that his son had risked death by joining the ill-fated adventure with Morgarath's forces and, indeed, death in battle was commonplace among the Skandians, who lived to raid and pillage. As a result, over the intervening months, Ragnak's anger, if not his grief, had faded. His son had died honorably, with a weapon in his hands. That was all any Skandian could ask. That wasn't to say that he felt any affection for Rangers, but he could respect their abilities and their courage, and their worth as opponents.

Or even, possibly, as allies.

Ragnak's vow against King Duncan and his family was another matter altogether. Chances are, had he waited, his hatred might well have abated and a more reasonable attitude might have prevailed.

But, acting on impulse, he had sworn a vow to the Vallas, the triple deity who ruled Skandian religion, and that vow was inviolable.

Ragnak might be able to accept Halt as an ally. He might be able to recognize that those same qualities that made the Ranger a dangerous opponent could also render him a useful confederate in the upcoming battle against the Temujai invaders. That would be his personal choice. But his Vallasvow against Duncan was irrevocable.

"So," Ragnak said abruptly. "Can you help us?"

Halt answered without any hesitation. "I'm willing to do whatever I can," he said. "What that might be, I have no idea as yet."

"No idea!" Ragnak repeated scornfully. "I was told that Rangers are always full of ideas."

Halt shook his head. "I need to assess your strengths and weaknesses first. And then I'll need maps of the surrounding countryside," he said. "We'll have to find a spot that will offset their superiority of numbers as far as possible. Then I'm going to ride out for another look at the Temujai. Last time I saw them, I had my hands full keeping your senior jarl alive. Then, after I've done all that, I might be able to answer your question."

Ragnak chewed on one end of his mustache, taking in what the Ranger had said. He was impressed, in spite of himself. His ability to plan for a battle usually amounted to the words "Everyone ready? Follow me!" before he led the way in a frontal assault.

Perhaps, he thought, this Ranger might be useful after all.

"Be aware of one thing, however, Oberjarl," Halt continued. Ragnak looked up at him, surprised at the tone of uncompromising command in his voice.

"I'm going to be asking you questions about your establishment, your fighting men, your numbers. They're questions that might give me an advantage in any future disagreement between our two countries."

"I see . . . ," said Ragnak slowly. He didn't like the direction the conversation was taking.

"You'll be tempted to lie to me. To exaggerate your numbers and your abilities. Don't do it."

Once more, the Oberjarl was taken aback at the peremptory tone of command. But Halt's gaze was unwavering.

"If I am to help you, you'll need to be honest with me. And so will your jarls."

Ragnak considered the statement for a moment or two, then nodded ponderously.

"Agreed," he said. "Mind you," he added, "that ax cuts two ways. You'll also be showing us how you think and plan for a battle."

And once more, that trace of a smile hovered around Halt's mouth as he acknowledged the Oberjarl's point.

"That's true," he said. "I guess if we want to win, we both have to be willing to lose a little."

The two men studied each other once more. Each decided that he liked what he saw in the other's eyes. Abruptly, Ragnak gestured to one of the massive pinewood armchairs.

"Sit down!" he said, indicating a flagon of Gallican wine on the table between them, almost lost in the glittering crystal fittings of the chandelier.

"Have a drink and tell me this. Why do you think these Temujai have chosen to make themselves a nuisance in Skandia? Surely the way would have been easier for them to move south, through Teutlandt and Gallica."

Halt poured himself a glass of the brilliant red wine and drank deeply. He raised an eyebrow in appreciation. Ragnak certainly knew the right wines to steal, he thought.

"I've been wondering that myself," he said at last. He wished the chair he was sitting on was made for someone smaller than the normal massive Skandian build. His feet barely brushed the floor as he sat there and he felt like a small boy in his father's study. "Even if they win here, they must know that you'll be a tough nut to crack. Certainly tougher than the Teutlanders."

Ragnak snorted in derision at the mention of the unorganized, squabbling race to the immediate south. Riddled by factions and internecine distrust, the Teutlanders were at the mercy of any would-be conquerors. In fact, if Skandian ambitions had lain in that direction, Ragnak would have felt confident that he could have subjugated the country with his small army of warriors.

"And the Gallicans are nearly as bad," Halt continued. "They'd be almost incapable of agreeing on one overall leader to take command. So I wondered what it was that made the Temujai swing north and risk a bloody nose here in Skandia."

"And?" the Oberjarl prompted. Halt took another swallow of wine and pursed his lips thoughtfully.

"I asked myself what you had that would make the risk worthwhile," he said. "And there was only one thing I could think of."

He paused. It was a theatrical thing to do, he knew, but he couldn't resist it. As he felt sure would happen, the Oberjarl leaned forward.

"What was it? What are they after?"

"Ships," replied Halt. "The Temujai want control of the seas. And that means their ambitions don't stop here. They're planning to invade Araluen as well."

19

EVANLYN WAS WATCHING WILL PRACTICING HIS SHOOTING. It was something that Halt had insisted on, once they had reached the relative safety of Hallasholm. Will's speed and accuracy had fallen far below the levels that Halt found acceptable and he wasted no time making his apprentice aware of the fact.

"Remember the golden rule?" he'd said after he'd watched Will shoot a dozen arrows at different targets set up in a semicircle in front of him, at ranges varying from fifty meters out to two hundred. Most of Will's arrows flew wide of the more distant targets, and it took him far too long to fire the set of twelve shots.

Will had looked up at his mentor, knowing how badly he'd shot. Halt was frowning and shaking his head slightly. It made matters worse that Horace and Evanlyn had chosen that moment to come and watch.

"Practice?" he'd replied glumly, and Halt had nodded.

"Practice," he affirmed. As they'd walked out to collect the arrows he'd fired, Halt had dropped a consoling arm around the boy's shoulders.

"Don't feel too bad about it," he told him. "Your technique is still good. But you can't expect to spend the winter making snow-men in the mountains and retain your edge."

"Making snowmen?" Will replied indignantly. "I'll have you know things were pretty rough up in the mountains . . ." He stopped as he realized that Halt had been pulling his leg. He had to admit that the Ranger was right, however. The only way to attain the al-most instinctive accuracy and speed with the bow that were the hall-marks of a Ranger was to practice, constantly and assiduously.

Over the following days, he took himself to the practice area and gave himself over to the task of perfecting his skills once more. As his old skill returned, along with his strength and fitness, a small crowd would follow and watch. Even though Will couldn't boast the skill levels of a full-fledged Ranger, his ability was far above that of normal archers and he was regarded by Skandians and some of the slaves with a deal of respect.

Evanlyn and Horace, however, seemed to find plenty of other things to fill their days—riding and hiking in the nearby woods, or sometimes taking a small skiff out on the bay. Of course, they had asked Will to join them, but each time, he had replied that he had to attend to his practice.

There were times when he could have gone. But even on these occasions, his feelings injured, he begged off, claiming the need for extra work sessions.

The practice sessions were intensified when Erak produced the double knife scabbard that Will had been wearing when he and Evanlyn had been captured by the Skandians. Erak, a true hoarder, had kept the weapons and now saw fit to return them to their right-ful owner. A word from Halt let Will know that he would soon be tested for his knife-throwing skills as well. Experience had taught Will by now that the long months without practice would have

eroded his abilities in this area too. So he set about restoring them.
The township of Hallasholm soon rang to the repetitive thud of
his throwing knife and saxe knife striking point first into a target of
soft pinewood.

As each day passed, his accuracy and speed improved with both
the bow and the knives. He was beginning to recapture that smooth,
flowing action that Halt had drilled into him over so many hours in
the forest outside Castle Redmont.

Now he switched easily from target to target, his arm raising or
lowering the bow to adjust for the variations in distance, his eyes
wide open, seeing a total sighting picture that included the bow,
the arrow and the eventual target. He was pleased that Evanlyn had
chosen today to come and watch his practice session. He felt a savage exultation as arrow after arrow thudded into the targets, striking
either in the center or close enough to make no difference.

"So," he said casually as he released two arrows at two widely
varying targets in quick succession. "Where's Horace today?"

The arrows thudded, one after another, into their respective
targets and he nodded to himself, turning ninety degrees to loose
another at one of the targets set closer in.

Another hit. Another thud.

The girl shrugged. "I think you made him feel guilty," she replied. "He thought he'd better get some practice in. He's working
out with some of the Skandians from Erak's crew."

"I see," replied Will, then paused to put an arrow into one of
the farthest targets, watching it arc smoothly through the air before
burying its point in the center ring.

"And why didn't you go along to watch him?" He felt a little
pleased that Evanlyn had chosen, finally, to see how proficient he
was becoming and hadn't bothered to watch her constant compan-

ion of the past few days. Her next words dashed that small glow of pleasure, however.

"I did," she replied. "But after you've seen two people whack at each other for several minutes, you develop a sense of déjà vu. I thought I'd come and see if you'd improved since the other day."

"Oh, really?" Will replied, a little stiffly. "Well, I hope you don't feel you've wasted your time."

Evanlyn looked up at him. He was facing away from her, firing a sequence of shots at three targets—one at fifty meters, one at seventy-five and one at a hundred. She could hear the stiff tone in his voice and wondered what was bothering him. She decided not to answer the question. Instead, she commented on the three-shot sequence, as all three arrows found their marks.

"How do you do that?" she asked. Will stopped and turned toward her. There was a genuine note of inquiry in her voice.

"Do what?"

She gestured toward the three targets.

"How do you know how far to lift the bow for each distance?" she asked. For a moment the question left him nonplussed. Finally, he shrugged.

"I just . . . feel it," he replied uncertainly. Then, frowning, he tried to elaborate. "It's a matter of practice. When you do it over and over again, it becomes sort of . . . instinctive, I suppose."

"So, if I took the bow, could you tell me how high to hold it for that middle target, for instance?" she asked, and he cocked his head to one side, thinking the question through.

"Well . . . it's not just that. I suppose I could, but . . . there are other factors."

She leaned forward, her face querying, and he continued.

"Like your release . . . it has to be smooth. You can't snatch at it or the arrow goes off line. And your draw weight would probably vary."

"Draw weight?"

He indicated the tension on the bowstring as he pulled it back to full draw. "The longer your draw, the more weight you put behind the arrow. If you didn't draw exactly the same distance as I did, the result would vary."

She thought about the answer. It seemed logical. She pursed her lips pensively and nodded once or twice.

"I see," she said. There was a slight tone of disappointment in her voice.

"Is there some kind of problem?" Will asked, and she sighed deeply.

"I was kind of hoping that maybe you could show me how to shoot so that I could actually do something when the Temujai turn up here," she replied, a little downcast.

Will laughed. "Well, maybe I could—if we had a year to spare."

"I don't want to be an expert," she said. "I thought maybe you could just show me one or two basic things so I could . . . you know . . ." She tailed off uncertainly.

Will shook his head apologetically, regretting the fact that he'd laughed at her.

"I'm afraid the real secret is a whole lot of practice," he said. "Even if I showed you the basics, it's not something you can just learn in a week or two."

She shrugged again.

"I suppose not." She realized that her request had been unrealistic. She felt foolish now and seized the opportunity to change the subject. "Is that when Halt thinks they'll get here—a week or two?"

Will fired the last arrow in the set and laid his bow down.

"He said they could be here then. But he thinks they'll take a little longer. After all, they know the Skandians aren't going anywhere." He gestured to her to accompany him as he collected his arrows and they started across the practice field together.

"Did you hear his theory?" she asked him. "About attacking here because they want the Skandians' ships?"

Will nodded. "It makes sense when you think about it. They can overrun Teutlandt and Gallica almost as they choose. But they'd be leaving a dangerous enemy behind them. And the Skandians could raid them anywhere along the coast, hitting them where and when they choose."

"I can see that," Evanlyn replied, tugging one of the arrows from the fifty-meter target. "But don't you think his theory about invading Araluen is a little far-fetched?"

"Not at all," Will replied. "Hold them closer to the head as you pull them out," he said, indicating the next arrow as she reached for it. "Otherwise you'll break the shaft, or warp it. There's no reason why the Temujai should stop at the Gallican coast. But if they tried to transport their army by ship without taking care of the Skandians first, they could be in big trouble."

Evanlyn was silent for a few seconds. "I suppose so," she said eventually.

"It's only a theory, after all," Will replied. "Maybe they're just making sure their flanks are secure before they move into Teutlandt. But Halt says you should always plan for the worst-case scenario. Then you can't be disappointed."

"I guess he's right about that," she replied. "Where is he, anyway? I haven't seen him around for a few days."

Will nodded his head toward the southeast. "He and Erak have gone to scout the Temujai advance," he said. "I think he's looking for a way to slow them down."

He collected the last of his arrows and stowed them in his quiver. Then he stretched and flexed his arms and fingers.

"Well, I guess I'll shoot another set," he said. "Are you staying to watch?"

Evanlyn considered for a moment, then shook her head. "I might go see how Horace is doing," she said. "I'll try to spread the encouragement around." She smiled at him, waggled her fingers in farewell and strode off across the field, back toward the palisade. Will watched her slim, upright figure as she walked away.

"You do that," he muttered to himself. Once more, he felt a flutter of jealousy as he thought of her watching Horace. Then he shook the feeling off, as a duck shakes water away. Head down, he began to mooch back to the firing line.

"Women," he muttered to himself. "They're nothing but trouble."

A shadow fell across the ground beside him and he glanced up, thinking for a moment that Evanlyn might have changed her mind. After all, the prospect of watching two muscle-bound hulks whacking each other with practice weapons was a little boring, he thought. But it wasn't Evanlyn, it was Tyrelle—blond, pretty, fifteen years old and the niece of Svengal, Erak's first mate. She smiled shyly at him. Her eyes were amazingly blue, he realized.

"Can I carry your arrows back for you, Ranger?" she asked, and he shrugged magnanimously, unclipping the quiver and handing it to her.

"Why not?" he said, and her smile widened.

After all, he thought, it would have been churlish to refuse.

20

THE PINE HAD FALLEN SEVERAL YEARS BACK, FINALLY DEFEATED by the weight of snow in its branches, the insidious rot at the heart of its massive trunk and one too many seasons of gale force winter winds. Even in death, however, its neighbors had tried to support it, keeping it from the ignominy of the ground, holding it in the grip of their tangled branches so that it lay at an angle of thirty degrees to the horizontal, seemingly supported between heaven and earth by its closely packed fellows.

Halt leaned now on the rough bark that still coated the dead trunk and peered down into the valley below, where the Temujai column moved slowly past.

"They're taking their time," Erak said, beside him. The Ranger turned to look at him, one eyebrow raised quizzically.

"They're in no hurry," he replied. "It's going to take them some time to get their wagons and supply train through the passes. Their horses don't like confined spaces. They're used to the open plains of the steppes."

The cavalry army continued its slow advance. There seemed little order to their march, Halt thought, frowning. There were no outriders, no patrols screening the flanks of the mob of men, horses

and wagons as they made their way toward Hallasholm, ninety kilometers to the north.

Halt, Erak and a small party of Skandians had come southeast,
moving over the mountains along steep, narrow paths where the
Temujai cavalry found it more difficult to move, to scout the invaders' progress. Now, as Halt watched them, a thought struck him.

"Mind you, we could make sure they move a little slower," he
said softly. Erak shrugged impatiently at the idea.

"Why bother?" he asked bluntly. "The sooner we come to grips
with them, the sooner we settle this."

"The longer they take, the more time we have to prepare," Halt
told him. "Besides, it bothers me to see them just ambling along, taking no precautions, riding in no order. It's too damned arrogant."

"I thought you said they were smart?" the Skandian queried, and
it was Halt's turn to shrug.

"Maybe it's because they expect you to simply come at them
head-on when they finally reach Hallasholm," he suggested. The
Skandian war leader considered the thought, looking a little of-
fended by it.

"Don't they give us any credit for strategy?"

Halt tried to hide a grin. "How *would* you plan to fight them?"

There was a pause, then Erak replied reluctantly, "I suppose
I'd simply wait till they reached our position, then . . . attack them
head-on." He looked carefully at the shorter man, but Halt was
being very obvious about not saying anything further. Finally, Erak
added, in an injured tone: "But there's no need for them to simply
assume that."

"Exactly," Halt replied. "So perhaps we should give them something to think about. Something to put them a little off balance—
and maybe put a little doubt in their minds."

"Is that good strategy?" Erak asked. The Ranger grinned at him.

"It's good therapy for us," he replied. "And besides, an enemy with a worm of doubt working away at his mind is less likely to make bold and unexpected moves. The more we can dissuade them from doing the unexpected, the better it will be for us."

Erak thought about the point. It seemed logical. "So what do you want to do?" he asked.

Halt looked around at the twenty warriors who had accompanied them.

"This Olgak," he said, indicating the young leader of the troop. "Is he capable of following orders, or is he a typical Skandian berserker?"

Erak pursed his lips. "All Skandians are berserkers, given the right conditions," he replied. "But Olgak will follow orders if I give them."

Halt nodded his understanding. "Let's talk to him then," he said.

Erak beckoned the broad-shouldered younger man to join them. Olgak, seeing the signal, moved forward, his ax swinging easily in his right hand, his large circular shield on his left arm. He looked expectantly at Erak, but the jarl gestured toward Halt.

"Listen to what the Ranger has to say," he ordered, and the young man's eyes turned to Halt. The Ranger studied him for a few moments. His clear blue eyes were guileless and straightforward. But he saw a light of intelligence there. Halt nodded to himself, then gestured to the Temujai army below them.

"See that rabble down there?" he asked, and when the younger man nodded, he continued, "They're riding with no formation, with no covering scouts, and with their supply wagons and support personnel mixed up with their warriors. They don't usually travel that way. Do you know why they're doing it now?"

Olgak hesitated, then shook his head, frowning slightly. Not only didn't he know, but he didn't know why it should be important for anyone to know such a thing.

"They're doing it because they feel safe," Halt continued. "Because they believe you Skandians are simply going to wait for them and meet them head-on."

Olgak nodded now. They had reached a point that he understood. "We are . . . aren't we?"

Halt exchanged a glance with Erak. The jarl shrugged. Skandians took a simple view of things.

"Well, yes, you are," Halt admitted. "Eventually. But for now, it might be nice to make them a little less comfortable, mightn't it?" He paused, then added, with a slight edge in his voice, "Or do you enjoy seeing them swan through your country as if they're on holiday?"

Olgak pursed his lips, looking down at the invaders. Now that the Ranger had mentioned it, they did appear to be having an altogether too easy time of things, he thought.

"No," he replied. "I can't say I enjoy seeing that. So what are we going to do about it?"

"Erak and I are going back to Hallasholm," Halt told him, feeling the Skandian leader stiffen beside him as he said it. Obviously the jarl had been looking forward to a little skirmish and he wasn't thrilled to hear he was going to miss it. "But you and your men are going to raid their lines tonight and burn those wagons."

He pointed with the end of his longbow to half a dozen supply wagons, trundling carelessly along at the edge of the army. Olgak grinned and nodded his approval of the idea.

"Sounds good to me," he said. Halt reached out and laid a firm grip on his muscular forearm, compelling the younger man to meet his steady gaze.

"But listen to me, Olgak," he said intensely. "You are going to hit and run. Don't get tangled up in an extended fight, understand?"

The young Skandian was less pleased with that command. Halt shook his arm fiercely for emphasis.

"Understand?" he repeated. "We do not want you and these twenty men to go down in a blaze of glory when you burn those wagons. And do you know why?"

Olgak shook his head—a small, reluctant movement. Halt continued.

"Because tomorrow night, I want you to move along the column and burn more wagons—and kill a few more Temujai while you're at it."

The idea was beginning to appeal to the younger man now.

"And if you're all killed on the first attempt, no matter how glorious it may seem at the time, by tomorrow the Temujai will simply continue on as they are, won't they?" the Ranger asked him. Olgak nodded his understanding.

"Then each night, I want you to hit a different part of the column. Burn their supplies. Set their horses loose. Kill their sentries. Get in and out fast and don't let them trap you into a standing battle. Stay alive and keep harassing them. Got the picture?"

Olgak nodded again, now more convinced of the good sense behind the plan. "They'll never know where we're going to hit them next," he said enthusiastically.

"Exactly," Halt said. "Which means they'll have to set guards along the entire column. They'll have to post extra sentries at night. And all of that will slow them down."

"It's like coastal raiding, isn't it?" the young Skandian said, thinking how the wolfships would appear from over the horizon without warning on an enemy coast and attack unprepared settlements. "Do you only want us to do it at night?" he added.

Halt thought for a minute.

"For the first couple of days, yes. Then pick a spot where you can withdraw quickly into the trees and uphill—somewhere their horses won't follow easily—and hit them in daylight. Maybe toward the end of the day—or the beginning."

"Keep them guessing?" Olgak said, and Halt patted his arm approvingly.

"You've got the idea," he said, smiling at the younger man. "And remember the golden rule: hit them where they aren't."

Olgak pondered that. "Hit them where they aren't?" he asked finally, sounding uncertain.

"Attack in those places where their troops are spread thinnest. Make them come to you. Then fade away before they really make contact. Remember that part. It's the most important of all. Survive."

He could see the younger man understood. Olgak repeated the word to himself. "Survive," he said. "I understand."

Halt turned and looked at Erak, raising an eyebrow. "Is there any reason why you should make it an order to Olgak that he's not to get tied down in a fight, Jarl?" he asked. Erak turned the question to the younger man.

"Well, Olgak, is there?" he said, and the troop leader shook his head.

"I understand what you have in mind, Ranger," he said. "Trust me. It's a good idea."

"Good man," Halt said quietly, then he turned to face the question he knew was coming from Erak.

"And what will we be doing while Olgak and his men are having all the fun?" the Jarl asked.

"We're going back to Hallasholm to start preparing a reception for our friends down there," Halt told him. "And while we're at it, we might send another half dozen parties out to harass the column the way Olgak will be doing. Everything we can do to slow them down will help us."

Erak shuffled his feet in the snow. He looked, Halt thought, remarkably like a child who has been told he must hand over his favorite toy.

"You could do that," he said finally. "Maybe I should stay and give Olgak and his men a hand." But Halt shook his head, the ghost of a smile touching the corners of his mouth.

"I need you back with me," he said simply. "I need your authority behind me if I'm going to be able to get things organized."

Erak opened his mouth to reply, but Olgak interrupted.

"The Ranger's right, Jarl," he said. "You'll be more valuable at Hallasholm. And besides, you're getting a little long in the tooth for this sort of work, aren't you?"

Erak's eyes widened with anger and he started to say something. Then he noticed that Olgak was grinning broadly and realized that the younger man was joking. He shook his head warningly, glancing at his own broadax.

"One of these days, I might just show you how long in the tooth I am," he said meaningfully. Olgak's grin widened. Halt regarded the two of them for a moment, then, slinging his longbow over his right shoulder, he turned and led the way back to where Abelard was tethered, along with the pony that Erak had reluctantly ridden when they came on this scouting expedition. He gathered Abelard's reins in one hand and turned back to the troop leader.

"I'm sure you'll do a good job, Olgak," he said. Then, glancing sidelong at the still indignant jarl, he added quietly: "You're obviously a very brave young man."

21

GENERAL HAZ'KAM, COMMANDER OF THE TEMUJAI INVASION force, looked up from his meal as his deputy entered the tent. Even though Nit'zak was by no means a tall man, he had to stoop as he came through the low opening. The general gestured to the cushions that were scatted on the felt rug floor and Nit'zak lowered himself to sit on one of them, uttering a sigh of relief. He had been in the saddle the past five hours, checking up and down the length of the Temujai column.

Haz'kam shoved the fragrant bowl of meat stew that he had been eating across to the other man and indicated for him to help himself. Nit'zak nodded his thanks, took a smaller bowl from the rug between them and scooped several handfuls into it, wincing slightly as his hand made contact with the hot food. He selected a large chunk and scooped it into his mouth, chewing heartily and nodding his appreciation.

"Good," he said finally. Haz'kam's concubine—the general never brought any of his three wives on campaign with him—was an excellent cook. The general considered that ability of far greater importance during a campaign than any physical beauty. He nod-

ded now, belched softly and pushed his own eating bowl away. The
woman moved quickly forward to remove it, then returned to her
position against the curved felt wall of the tent.

"So," the general asked. "What did you find?"

Nit'zak screwed his face into an expression of distaste—not at
the next morsel of food, but at the subject matter he was about to
report.

"They hit us again this evening," he replied. "This time in two
places. Once at the tail of the column. They stampeded a small herd
of horses there. It'll take half the day tomorrow to recover them.
Then another group came in from the coastal side and burned half
a dozen supply wagons."

Haz'kam looked up in surprise. "From the coast?" he asked, and
his deputy nodded confirmation. Up until now, the nuisance raids
mounted by the Skandians had been launched from the thickly
wooded hills inland from the narrow coastal flatlands. The raiders
would dash out, strike an undefended part of the column, then retreat into the cover of the forests and the hills where pursuit would
be too risky. This new eventuality complicated things.

"They seem to have several of their ships at sea," the deputy told
him. "They stay out of sight during the day, then steal in after dark
and land troops to hit us. Then they retreat to sea once more."

Haz'kam probed with his tongue at a piece of meat wedged between two back teeth. "Where, of course, we can't follow them," he
said.

Nit'zak nodded. "It means now that we'll have to cover both
sides of the column," he said.

Haz'kam muttered a low curse. "It's slowing us down," he said.

Each morning, hours were wasted as the massive column formed
up in disciplined ranks for the day's march. And, of course, once the

march began, the pace was limited by the slowest sections of the column—which were the supply carts and the baggage train. It had been much faster simply moving as one vast mass.

Nit'zak agreed. "So is the problem of having to screen the camp each night."

Haz'kam took a deep swig of the fermented barley drink that the Temujai favored, then handed the leather drinking skin to Nit'zak.

"It's not what I expected," he said. "They're far more organized than our intelligence had led us to believe."

Nit'zak drank deeply and gratefully. He shrugged. In his experience, intelligence was usually inaccurate at best and dead wrong at worst.

"I know," he said. "Everything we'd heard about these people led me to believe that they would simply attack us in a frontal assault, without any overall strategy. I'd half expected that we'd be finished with them by now."

Haz'kam pondered. "Perhaps they're still gathering their main force. I suppose we have no option but to continue as we are. I imagine they'll finally make a stand when we reach their capital. Although now we'll take longer to do that."

Nit'zak hesitated for a moment with the next suggestion. Then he said: "Of course, General, we could simply continue as we were, and accept the losses their raids are causing. They're quite sustainable, you know."

It was a typically callous Temujai suggestion. If the loss of lives or supplies could be balanced out by greater speed, it might well be worthwhile opting for that course. Haz'kam shook his head. But not through any sense of care for the people under his command.

"If we don't respond, we have no way of knowing that they won't hit us with a major raid," he pointed out. "They could have hundreds of men in those mountains and if they chose to change from pinprick attacks to a major assault, we'd be in big trouble. We're a long way from home, you know."

Nit'zak nodded his acquiescence. That idea hadn't occurred to him. Still, he demurred slightly.

"That isn't the sort of thing we've been led to believe they're capable of," he pointed out, and Haz'kam's eyes met his and locked onto them.

"Neither is this," he said softly, and when the younger man's eyes dropped from his, he added, "Have the men keep forming into their sixties for each day's march. And I suppose now we'd better put sentries out on the seaward side at night too."

Nit'zak muttered his assent. He hesitated a few seconds, wondering if this were one of those times when his commander wanted to continue to talk and pass the drinking skin back and forth for a few hours. But Haz'kam waved him away with a small hand gesture. Nit'zak thought that the general looked tired. For a moment, he thought about the years they had spent on campaign together and realized that Haz'kam was no longer a young man. Neither was he, he thought, as the ache in his knees testified. He bowed his head in a perfunctory salute, rose to his feet with another barely suppressed groan and went, crouching, out through the felt hanging that covered the tent doorway.

In the distance, he heard men shouting. Looking in the direction from which the noise came, he saw a bright flare of flame against the night sky. He cursed softly. The damned Skandians were raiding again, he thought.

A troop of horsemen clattered by him, heading for the site of the attack. He watched them go, tempted for a moment to join them, but resisting the temptation as he realized that by the time they reached the point of the attack, the enemy would be long gone.

22

THE SKANDIAN WAR COUNCIL WAS MEETING IN THE GREAT Hall. Will sat to one side, listening as Halt addressed the Skandian leader and his principal advisers. Borsa, Erak and two other senior jarls, Lorak and Ulfak, flanked the Oberjarl as they clustered around the table where Halt had spread an immense map of Skandia. The Ranger tapped a spot on the map with the point of his saxe knife.

"As of last night," he said, "the Temujai were here. Maybe sixty kilometers away from Hallasholm. The delaying raids are having exactly the sort of effect we wanted. The advance has gone from thirty kilometers a day to less than twelve."

"Shouldn't cavalry move faster than that?" asked Ulfak. Halt perched one leg on the bench beside the table and shook his head.

"They'll move fast enough when they're fighting," he told them. "But right now, they're conserving their horses' strength, letting them feed and move easily. Besides, now that we've reinforced Olgak's men with another half dozen raiding groups, it's taking them half the day to simply form up, then set up camp again in the evening."

He glanced up at Erak as he added: "Your idea of sending a few wolfships to raid their seaward flank was a good one."

The jarl nodded. "It seemed logical," he replied. "It's what we're good at, after all."

Ragnak thumped one massive fist on the pine planks that formed the table.

"Raids and skirmishes, nuisance attacks! They achieve nothing! It's time we hit them with our main force and settle this once and for all," he declared, and three of his council growled agreement.

"There'll be plenty of time for that," Halt cautioned. "The most important thing is to engage them in a place that suits us—one that we choose ourselves."

Again, the Oberjarl snarled. He knew he'd agreed to listen to Halt's advice. But these damned invaders had been flaunting themselves in his country now for several weeks. It was an affront to him and to every Skandian and he wanted to wipe the affront out, or die in the attempt. "What's the difference where we fight them?" he said. "A fight is a fight. We win or we lose. But if we do lose, we'll take plenty of them with us!"

Halt removed his foot from the bench and stood straight, ramming the saxe knife back into its scabbard.

"Oh, don't worry," he said icily. "There's every chance that we'll lose. But let's make sure we take as many of them with us as possible, shall we?" The Skandians, used to bluster and boasting, were taken aback by his cold assessment of their chances for survival—as he had intended them to be.

"They're cavalry," he continued. "They outnumber us at least four to one. They can outmaneuver us, outrun us. And they'll look for the widest possible front to engage us on. That way, all the advantages are with them. They'll flank us, surround us and draw us out if they can." He saw that he had their attention. They weren't happy about the situation, but at least they were prepared to listen.

"How will they do that?" Erak asked. He and Halt had discussed this briefing the day before. Halt wanted certain questions to be asked, and Erak was to ask them if none of the others seemed prepared to do so. The Ranger glanced quickly at Erak, but directed his answer to all of the group.

"It's a standard tactic of theirs," he said. "They'll attack on a wide front, probing, hitting and retiring. Then they'll appear to become fully engaged at one or two given points. They'll stop their hit-and-run tactics and fight a pitched battle—just the sort of thing that will suit your men," he added, glancing at Ragnak. The Oberjarl nodded.

"Then," Halt continued, "they will begin to lose. Their attack will lose its cohesion and they will try to withdraw."

"Good!" said Borsa, and the two other jarls grunted agreement. Ragnak, however, sensed that there was more to come. He didn't comment for the moment, but gestured for Halt to continue. The Ranger obliged.

"They'll give ground. Slowly at first, then faster and faster as panic seems to set in. Somehow they'll never move so fast that your men lose contact with them. Gradually, more and more of your warriors will be drawn out of our line, away from the shield wall, away from our defenses. As they pursue the enemy, the Temujai will become more and more desperate. At least, they'll seem to. Then, at the right moment, they'll turn."

"Turn?" said the Oberjarl. "How do you mean?"

"They'll stop retreating when your men are strung out and in the open—the strongest and fastest well ahead of their comrades. Suddenly, they'll find themselves cut off, surrounded by the Temujai cavalry. And remember, every one of their cavalrymen is an expert archer. They won't bother coming to close quarters. They can pick your men off at their leisure. And the more they kill the leaders, the more enraged those behind will become. They'll stream out to save their friends—or avenge them. They'll be surrounded in turn. And wiped out."

He paused. The five Skandians all looked at him, struck silent. They could imagine the scenario he described. They knew the temper of their men and could see how easily such a stratagem could succeed against them.

"This is how they fight?" Ragnak asked finally.

"I've seen it, Oberjarl. Time and time again, I've seen it. They aren't concerned with glory in battle. Only efficient killing. They'll challenge our warriors to single combat, then ambush them with ten or twenty warriors at a time. If they can't shoot to kill immediately, they'll shoot to disable. Even your strongest warriors can't continue with ten to fifteen arrow wounds in the legs. Then, when they're helpless, the Temujai will kill them."

He swept his gaze around the table. Satisfied that they could all see the danger that faced them, he sat down, straddling the bench. Finally, it was Borsa, the hilfmann, who broke the long silence that had fallen in the room.

"So ... where do you want to engage them?" he asked. Halt spread his hands wide in a questioning gesture.

"Why engage them at all?" he asked. "We have time to withdraw before they arrive. We could move into the hills and the forest and keep hitting them as they come farther and farther along the coastal plain here."

"Run away, you mean?" Ragnak asked, his tone angry.

Halt nodded several times. "Yes. Run away. But continue to hit them at twenty or thirty or fifty points along their column. Kill them. Burn their supplies. Harass them. Make their life one long, insufferable misery until they realize that this invasion was a bad idea. Then harass them back to the border until they're gone."

He paused. He knew there was little chance of winning this one. But he had to try. It was the best course open to them. His heart sank as Ragnak shook his head. Even Erak's lips were compressed into a thin, disapproving line.

"Abandon Hallasholm to them?" asked Ragnak.

Halt shrugged. "If necessary. You can always rebuild."

But now all the Skandians were shaking their heads and he knew what was behind it.

"Abandon everything in Hallasholm to them?" Ragnak persisted. This time Halt made no answer. He waited for the inevitable.

"Our booty—the results of hundreds of years of raiding—leave that to them?" Ragnak asked.

And that, Halt knew, was the crux of the matter. No Skandian would ever abandon the loot he had stored up over the years—the gold, the armor, the tapestries, the chandeliers, the thousand and one items that they hoarded and kept and gloated over in their storehouses. He caught Will's eye and shrugged slightly. He'd tried. Halt moved to the map once more and indicated the flatlands outside Hallasholm with his knife point.

"Alternatively," he said, "we stop them here, where the coastal plain contracts to its narrowest point."

The Skandians craned to look again. They nodded cautious approval, now that Halt had withdrawn the suggestion that they should abandon Hallasholm and its contents to the invaders.

"This way, they can't attack on a wide front. They'll be cramped. And we can conceal men in the trees here—and even in the outbuildings along the shore."

Lorak, older of the two jarls, frowned at the suggestion. "Won't that weaken our shield wall?"

Halt shook his head. "Not noticeably. We'll have more than

enough men to form a solid defensive position here where the land is narrowest. Then, when the Temujai try their trick of falling back and bringing our men along with them, we'll appear to go along with it."

Erak moved forward to inspect the narrow neck of land that Halt was indicating.

"You mean we'll do as they want?" he asked. Halt pushed out his bottom lip and cocked his head to one side.

"We'll appear to," he admitted. "But once they stop withdrawing to counterattack, we'll bring our ambush forces out of hiding and hit them from behind. If we time it correctly, we could make life very unpleasant for them."

The Skandians stood, staring down at the map. Borsa, Lorak and Ulfak had blank looks as they tried to visualize the movement. Erak and Ragnak, Halt was glad to see, were slowly nodding as they understood the idea.

"Our best chance," he continued, "is to force them into the sort of engagement that suits your men best—close quarters, hand to hand, every man for himself. If we can catch them that way, your axmen will take a heavy toll on them. The Temujai rely on speed and movement for protection. They're only lightly armed and armored. If we had even a small force of archers, it could make an enormous difference," he added. "But I suppose we can't have everything." Halt knew that the bow wasn't a Skandian weapon. It was no use wishing for things that couldn't be. But in his mind's eye, he could see the devastation that an organized party of bowmen could cause. He shrugged, pushing the thought aside.

Erak looked up at the gray-cloaked Ranger. He's small, he thought, but by the gods, he's a warrior to reckon with.

"We have to depend on our men keeping their heads," he

said. "Then we have to time it just right when we spring our trap—otherwise the men coming from the forest and the out-buildings will be exposed themselves. It's a risk."

Halt shrugged. "It's war," he replied. "The trick is to know which risks to take."

"And how do you know that?" Borsa asked him, sensing that the small, bearded foreigner had gained the trust and the acceptance of the Oberjarl and his War Council. Halt smiled wolfishly at him.

"You wait till it's over and see who's won," he said. "Then you know those were the right risks to take."

23

"HALT," WILL SAID THOUGHTFULLY AS HE WALKED AWAY FROM the council with Halt and Erak. "What did you mean when you said that about archers?"

Halt looked sideways at his apprentice and sighed. "It could make a big difference to the outcome," he said. "The Temujai are archers themselves. But they rarely have to face an enemy with any particular skill with the bow."

Will nodded. The longbow was traditionally an Araluen weapon. Perhaps because of the island kingdom's isolation from the countries on the eastern landmass, it had remained peculiar to Araluen. Other nationalities might use bows for hunting or even sport. But only in the armies of the Araluens would you find the massed groups of archers that could provide a devastating rain of arrows on an attacking force.

"They understand the value of the bow as a strategic weapon," he said. "But they've never had to cope with facing it themselves. I got some inkling of that when Erak and I were running from them near the border. Once I'd put a few arrows close to them, they were decidedly reluctant to come dashing around any blind corners."

The jarl laughed quietly at the memory. "That's true enough," he agreed. "Once you'd emptied a few saddles, they slowed down remarkably."

"You know, I've been thinking . . . ," said the boy, and hesitated. Halt grinned quietly to himself.

"Always a dangerous pastime," he said gently.

But Will continued: "Maybe we should try to put together a force of archers. Even a hundred or so could make a difference, couldn't they?"

Halt shook his head. "We haven't the time, Will," he replied. "They'll be on us within two weeks. You can't train archers in that short a time. After all, the Skandians have no skill with the bow to begin with. You'd have to teach them the very basics—nocking, drawing, releasing. That takes weeks, as you know."

"There are plenty of slaves here," Will persisted. "Some of them would know the basics. Then all we'd have to do is control their range."

Halt looked at his apprentice again. The boy was deadly serious, he could see. A small frown creased Will's forehead as he thought through the problem.

"And how would you do that?" the Ranger asked. The frown deepened for a few seconds as Will gathered his thoughts.

"It was something Evanlyn asked me that suggested it," he said. "She was watching me shoot and she was asking how I knew how much elevation to give to a particular shot and I told her it was just experience. Then I thought maybe I *could* show her and I was thinking, if you created—say—four basic positions. . ."

He stopped walking and raised his left arm as if it were holding a bow, then moved it through four positions—beginning horizontally and ultimately raising it to a maximum forty-five degree angle. "One, two, three, four, like that," he continued. "You could drill a group of archers to assume those positions while someone else judged the range and told them which one to go to. They wouldn't need to be very good shots as long as the person controlling them could judge range," he finished.

"And deflection," Halt said thoughtfully. "If you knew that at the second position your shafts would travel, say, two hundred meters, you could time your release so that the approaching enemy would reach that spot just as the arrow storm did."

"Well, yes," Will admitted. "I hadn't taken it that far. I was just thinking of setting the range and having everyone release at the same time. They needn't aim for individual targets. They could just fire away into the mass."

"You'd need to anticipate," Halt said.

"Yes. But essentially, it would be the same as if I were firing one arrow myself. It's just that, as I released, I could call a hundred others to do the same."

Halt rubbed his beard. He glanced at the Skandian. "What do you think, Erak?"

The jarl merely shrugged his massive shoulders. "I haven't understood a word you've been saying," he admitted cheerfully. "Range, defraction . . ."

"Deflection," Will corrected him, and Erak shrugged.

"Whatever. It's all a puzzle to me. But if the boy thinks it might be possible, well, I'd tend to think he might be right."

Will grinned at the big war leader. Erak liked to keep things simple. If he didn't understand a subject, he didn't waste energy wondering about it.

"I tend to think the same way," Halt said quietly, and Will looked at him in surprise. He'd been waiting for his mentor to point out the fundamental flaw in his logic. Now he saw that Halt was considering his proposal seriously. Then he noticed the look of exasperation that grew on Halt's face as he found the flaw.

"Bows," the Ranger said, disappointment in his voice. "Where would we find a hundred bows in time to let people train with them? There probably aren't twenty in all of Skandia."

Will's heart sank. Of course. There was the problem. It took weeks to shape and craft a single longbow, trimming the bowstave just so, providing just the right amount of graduated flex along both arms. It was a craftsman's job and there was no way they would have time to make the hundred bows they would need. Disconsolately, he kicked at a rock in his path, then wished he hadn't. He'd forgotten that he was wearing soft-toed boots.

"I could let you have a hundred," Erak said in the depressed silence that followed Halt's statement. Both the others turned to look at him.

"Where would you find a hundred longbows?" Halt asked him. Erak shrugged.

"I captured a two-masted cob off the Araluen coast three seasons ago," he told them. He didn't have to explain that when a Skandian said *season* he meant the raiding season. "She had a hold full of bows. I kept them in my storeroom until I could find a use for them. I was going to use them as fence palings," he continued. "But they seemed a little too flexible for the job."

"Bows tend to be that way," Halt said slowly, and when Erak looked at him, uncomprehending, he added: "More flexible than fence palings. It's one of the qualities we look for in a bow."

"Well, I suppose you'd know," Erak said casually. "Anyway, I've still got them. There must be thousands of arrow shafts as well. I thought they'd come in handy one day."

Halt reached up and laid a hand on the massive shoulder. "And how right you were," he said. "Thank the gods for the Skandian habit of hoarding everything."

"Well, of course we hoard," Erak explained. "We risk our lives to take the stuff in the first place. There's no sense in throwing it away. Anyway, do you want to see if you could use them?"

"Lead on, Jarl Erak," Halt said, shaking his head in wonder and lifting an eyebrow at Will.

Erak set out toward the large, barnlike storehouse by the docks where he kept the bulk of his plunder.

"Excellent," he said happily, rubbing his hands together. "If you decide to use them, I'll be able to charge Ragnak."

"But this is war," Will protested. "Surely you can't charge Ragnak for doing something that will help defend Hallasholm?"

Erak turned his delighted smile on the young Ranger. "To a Skandian, my boy, all war is business."

24

Evanlyn had been waiting for Halt and Will to leave Ragnak's War Council. As the two gray-cloaked figures, in company with the burly Jarl Erak, emerged from the Great Hall and walked across the open ground that fronted it, she started forward to intercept them. Then she stopped, uncertain how to proceed. She had been hoping that Will might come out by himself. She didn't want to approach him in front of Erak and Halt.

Evanlyn was bored and miserable. Worse, she was feeling useless. There was nothing specific she could do to contribute to the defense of Hallasholm, nothing to keep her mind occupied. Will had obviously become part of the inner circle of the Skandian leadership, and even when he wasn't in meetings with Halt and Erak, he was off practicing with his bow. It sometimes seemed that he used his practice sessions to avoid her. She felt a little flare of anger as she recalled his reaction when she asked him to teach her to shoot. He'd laughed at her!

Horace was no better. Initially, he'd been happy to keep her company. But then, seeing Will constantly practicing, he'd felt guilty and began spending time on the practice field himself, honing his own skills with a small group of Skandian warriors.

It was all Will's fault, she thought.

Now, as she watched him talking with his old teacher, and saw the two of them stop as Will made a point, she realized with a sense of sadness that there was a part of Will's life from which she would always be excluded. Young as he was, he was already a part of the mysterious, close-knit Ranger clan. And Rangers, she had been told since she was a small child, kept themselves to themselves. Even her father the King had been frustrated from time to time by the closemouthed nature of the Ranger Corps. As the realization hit home, she turned sadly away, leaving the two Rangers, master and apprentice, to their discussion with the Skandian jarl.

Morosely, she kicked at a stone on the ground in front of her. If only there were something for her to do!

She stood uncertainly, undecided about where to go next. She turned abruptly to see if Will and Halt were still where she'd last seen them. They had moved on, but her sudden turn brought her into unexpected eye contact with a familiar, though unwelcome, figure.

Slagor, the thin-lipped, shifty-eyed wolfship captain whom she had first seen on the rocky, windswept island of Skorghijl, had just emerged from one of the smaller buildings that flanked Ragnak's Great Hall. He stood now, staring after her. There was something in his look that made her uncomfortable. Something knowing, something that boded ill for her. Then, as he realized she had seen him, he turned away, walking quickly into the dark-shadowed alleyway between the two buildings. She frowned to herself. There had been something suspicious about the Skandian's manner, she thought. Half because she wanted to know more, and half because she was bored, with nothing constructive to do, she set out after him.

There had been something in the way he looked at her that told her it might be better if he didn't know she was following him. She moved to the end of the alley and peered cautiously around, just catching sight of him as he turned right at the rear of the building. She paralleled his path, moving cautiously to the next alley, pausing, then peering around again. Once more, she caught a quick glimpse of Slagor and she guessed from his general direction that he was heading for the quays, where the wolfships docked. Realizing that her own actions might appear highly suspicious, she glanced quickly around to see if anyone might be watching her. Apparently not, she decided. Still, she crossed back to the far side of the street before following in the pursuit of the wolfship skirl.

As she slid unobtrusively from building to building, she saw him several more times, confirming her first impression that he was heading for the docks. That was logical. Presumably his ship was among the fleet moored there. Probably Slagor had some ship's business to attend to, she thought. The suspicious manner that she had noticed was probably nothing more than his normal shifty-eyed demeanor.

Then she cast the doubts aside. There had been something else: something knowing. Something calculating.

Evanlyn was, naturally, constantly aware of her precarious position here in Hallasholm. Ragnak might have no interest in punishing a recaptured slave. But if her real identity were to become known, his reaction was a foregone conclusion. He had vowed to kill any member of the Araluen royal family. Now it seemed important to her to find out what had been behind Slagor's look. She quickened her pace and hurried down one of the narrow connecting alleys, emerging in the broad waterfront thoroughfare that Slagor had taken.

He was twenty meters ahead of her as she peered cautiously around the end of the building. His back was turned and she realized that he had no idea that she had been following him. To the left, the masts of the moored wolfships formed a forest of bare poles, bobbing and swaying with the movement of the water. On the right of the street were a series of waterfront taverns. It was toward one of these that Slagor was hurrying now, she realized.

Some instinct made her ease into a doorway as the skirl reached the tavern entrance. It was as well she did, for he turned and looked back the way he had come, apparently checking to see if anyone had followed him. She frowned to herself as she shrank into the shadows of the doorway. Why should Slagor be nervous, here in the middle of Hallasholm? Certainly he was one of the less popular wolfship captains, but it was unlikely that anyone would actually do him harm. There was obviously something going on, she thought, and she determined to get to the bottom of it. Close by, moored to one of the timber quays, she saw Slagor's ship, *Wolf Fang*. She recognized it by the distinctive carved figurehead. No two wolfships had the same figurehead and she remembered this one all too well from the day when *Wolf Fang* had come limping into the anchorage at Skorghijl. With it had come the news of Ragnak's Vallasvow against her father and herself, so she had good reason to remember the grotesquely carved icon.

For a moment, she hesitated in the doorway. Then, the door behind her opened and two Skandian women emerged, shopping baskets in hand. They stared at the stranger on their doorstep and she hurriedly apologized and moved away. Behind her, she heard the angry comments of the women as they headed for the market square. She was too obvious here, she realized. Any moment, Slagor might emerge from the tavern and see her. She glanced uncertainly at the ship, then came to a decision and, moving at a half run, she made her way down the waterfront to the quay where *Wolf Fang* was moored. It was reasonable to assume that Slagor might come here eventually, and then she might get an inkling of what he was up to.

There was an anchor watch aboard, of course. But it was just one man and he was at the stern, leaning on the bulwark and staring at the harbor and the sea beyond. Crouching below the level of the high prow, she approached the ship and vaulted lightly over the railing, her soft-shod feet making virtually no sound as she landed on the planks of the deck. She dropped immediately into the rowing well, set below the main deck, where the rowing crew would normally sit to wield their heavy, white oak oars. The area was deserted at the moment, and she was concealed from the sight of the solitary guard at the stern. But it was only a temporary hiding place and she looked now for a better one.

Right at the prow of the ship was a small triangular space, screened by a canvas flap. It was large enough to accommodate her if she crouched, and she moved quickly into it now, letting the canvas screen fall back into place behind her. She found herself sitting on coils of stiff, coarse rope, and something hard jabbed into her side. Shifting to a better position, she realized that it had been the fluke of the anchor, and the coils of heavy rope were the anchor cable. With the ship moored alongside the quay, they weren't in use. This would be as good a hiding place as any, she thought. Then she wondered if she might not be wasting her time here. Odds were that Slagor had simply come this way to visit the tavern and that after he'd drunk his fill of the harsh spirits the Skandians favored, he'd probably head on back to his lodge.

She shrugged morosely. She had nothing better to do with her time. She might as well give it an hour or so and see if anything transpired. What that *anything* might be, she really had no idea. She'd followed Slagor on an impulse. Now, following the same impulse, she was crouched here, waiting to see what she might overhear if and when he came aboard.

It was warm in the confines of the forepeak and, once she'd

moved a few of the coils, the rope made a relatively comfortable resting place. She wriggled herself into a better position and rested her chin on her elbows, peering through a small gap in the canvas to see if anything was happening outside. She felt the footsteps of the sentry as he crossed to the landward side of the ship, giving up his scrutiny of the harbor, and heard him call to someone on the shore. There was an answering voice but the words were too muffled for her to make out. Probably just a casual greeting to a passing friend, she reasoned. She yawned. The warmth was making her drowsy. She hadn't slept well the night before, thinking about Will and how their friendship seemed to be eroding with every passing day. She tried to dislike Halt, blaming him for the sudden estrangement between them. But she couldn't. She liked the small, roughly bearded Ranger. There was a dry sense of humor about him that appealed to her. And after all, he had rescued her from the Temujai reconnaissance party. She sighed. It wasn't Halt's fault. Nor Will's. It was just the way things were, she guessed. Rangers were different to other people. Even princesses.

Especially princesses.

She woke suddenly, thinking she was falling. She hadn't realized that she'd drifted off to sleep, lying here on the coils of rope. But she knew what had woken her. The deck beneath her had dropped suddenly as *Wolf Fang* heaved herself into a short head sea. Now she could hear the creak and thump of the oars in their rowlocks and she realized, with a terrible sinking feeling, that *Wolf Fang* had put to sea and she was trapped on board.

25

Between them, Halt and Will had found a hundred slaves who claimed to have some level of skill with the bow. Finding them had been one matter. Convincing them that they should volunteer to help defend Hallasholm was something else.

As a burly Teutlander forester, who seemed to have assumed the role of spokesman for them, told the two Rangers, "Why should we help the Skandians? They've done nothing except enslave us, beat us and give us too little food to eat."

Halt eyed the man's ample girth speculatively. If some of the slaves were underfed, this one could hardly claim to be one of them, he thought. Still, he decided to let that matter pass.

"You might find it more agreeable to be a slave of the Skandians than to fall into the hands of the Temujai," he told them bluntly.

Another of the assembled men spoke up. This one was a southern Gallican and his outlandish accent made his words almost indecipherable. Will finally pieced the sounds together in sufficient order to know that the man had asked: "What do the Temujai do with their slaves?"

Halt turned a steely gaze on the Gall. "They don't keep slaves," he said evenly, and a buzz of expectation ran through the assembled men. The big Teutlander stepped forward again, grinning.

"Then why would you expect us to fight against them?" he asked. "If they beat the Skandians, they'll set us free."

There was a loud mumble of consent among the others behind him. Halt held up a hand and waited patiently. Eventually, the hubbub died away and the slaves looked at him expectantly, wondering what further inducement he could offer them—what he would consider to be more attractive to them than the prospect of freedom.

"I said," he intoned clearly, so that everyone could hear him, "they don't keep slaves. I didn't say they set them free." He paused, then added, with a slight shrug of his shoulders, "Although the religious ones among you may consider death to be the ultimate freedom."

This time, the commotion among the slaves was even louder. Finally, the self-appointed spokesman stepped forward again and asked, with a little less assertion, "What do you mean, Araluen? Death?"

Halt made a careless gesture. "The usual, I suppose: the sudden cessation of life. The end of it all. Departure for a happier place. Or oblivion, depending upon your personal beliefs."

Again a buzz ran through the crowd. The Teutlander studied Halt closely, trying to see some indication that the Ranger was bluffing.

"But . . ." He hesitated, not sure whether to ask the next question, not sure that he wanted to know the answer. Then, urged by his companions, he went on: "Why should these Temujai want to kill us? We've done nothing to them."

"The truth of the matter is," Halt told them all, "you *mean* nothing to them either. The Temujai consider themselves a superior race. They'd kill you out of hand because you can do nothing for them—but left behind their backs, you could constitute a threat."

A nervous silence settled over the crowd now. Halt let them digest what he had said, then he spoke again.

"Believe me, I've seen what these people are like." He looked into the faces of the crowd. "I can see there are some Araluens among you. I'll give you my word as a Ranger that I'm not bluffing. Your best chance of survival is to fight with the Skandians against these Temujai. I'll leave you for half an hour to consider what I've said. You Araluens might tell the others what a Ranger's word means," he added. Then, beckoning for Will to follow, he turned on his heel and walked some distance away, out of earshot.

"We're going to have to offer them more," he said when the others couldn't hear him. "Reluctant recruits will be almost useless to us. A man's got to have something worth fighting for if he's going to do his best. And that's what we're going to need from this bunch—their best effort."

"So what are you going to do?" Will asked, almost jogging to keep pace with his teacher's urgent stride.

"We're going to see Ragnak," Halt told him. "He's going to have to promise to free every slave who fights for Hallasholm."

Will shook his head doubtfully. "He won't like that," he said. Halt turned and looked at him, a faint grin touching the corner of his mouth.

"He'll hate it," he agreed.

"Freedom?" Ragnak exploded. "Give them their freedom? A hundred slaves?"

Halt shrugged disdainfully. "Probably closer to three hundred," he replied. "A lot of them will have women and children they'll want to take with them."

The Oberjarl gave an enormous snort of incredulous laughter. "Are you mad?" he asked the Ranger. "If I give three hundred slaves their freedom, we'll have virtually no slaves left. What will I do then?"

"If you don't, you may find you have no country left," Halt replied. "As to what you would do next, you could try paying them. Make them servants instead of slaves."

"Pay them? To do the work they're doing now?" Ragnak spluttered indignantly.

"Why not? The gods know you can afford it well enough. And you might find they do a better job if they've got something more than a beating to look forward to at the end of the day."

"To hell with them!" Ragnak said. "And to hell with you, Ranger. I agreed to listen to you, but this is ridiculous. You'll turn me into a beggar if I let you have your way. First you want me to abandon Hallasholm to this rabble of horsemen. Now you want me to send all my slaves off back to where they came from. To hell with you, I say."

He glared at the Ranger for a few seconds, then, with a contemptuous wave of his hand, he turned away, refusing even to make eye contact. Halt waited a few seconds, then spoke to Erak, who was standing by his Oberjarl, an uncomfortable look on his face.

"I'm telling you, we need these men," he said forcefully. "Even with them, we can still lose. But with them fighting willingly for us, we'll have a chance." He jerked a thumb in the direction of the Oberjarl. "Tell him," he said finally, then turned on his heel and left the council room, Will hurrying behind him as he went.

As they left the hall, Halt said, almost to himself, but loud enough for Will to hear, "I wonder if it occurs to them that if the slaves agree unwillingly to fight for them, and if, by some mad mischance, we do win, there's nothing to stop the slaves from turning their weapons on the Skandians." That thought had occurred to

Will. He nodded agreement. "That's why," Halt continued, "we've got to give them something worth fighting for."

They waited at the training field for over an hour. The slaves had come to a decision, agreeing to fight against the Temujai. However, a few shifty eyes among the group told Halt and Will that, once the battle was over, the newly armed men were not going to return meekly into slavery.

There was a buzz of expectation as Erak arrived. He walked up to Halt and Will, who were standing a little apart from the archers.

"Ragnak agrees," he said quietly. "If they fight, he'll free them."

Halt nodded his head gratefully. He knew where the real impetus for Ragnak's decision had come from.

"Thank you," he said simply to Erak. The Skandian shrugged and Halt turned to Will. "They'll be your men. They need to get used to taking orders from you. You tell them."

Will hesitated, surprised. He had assumed that Halt would do the talking. Then, at an encouraging nod from his master, he stepped forward, raising his voice.

"Men!" he called, and the low murmur of conversation among the group died instantly. He waited a second or two to make sure he had their full attention, then continued.

"Ragnak has decided. If you fight for Skandia, he'll set you free."

There was a moment of stunned silence. Some of these men had been slaves for ten years or more. Now, here was this slightly built youth telling them that the end to their suffering was in sight. Then a mighty roar of triumph and jubilation swept through them, at first wordless and inchoate, but rapidly settling into a rhythmic chant of one word from one hundred throats:

"Free-dom! Free-dom! Free-dom!"

Will let them celebrate for a while longer. Then he climbed onto a tree stump where he could be seen by all of them and waved his arms for silence. Gradually, the chant died away and they crowded closer around him, eager to hear what else he had to tell them.

"That's all very well," he said when they had quieted down. "But first, there's the small matter of beating the Temujai. Let's get to work."

Halt and Erak watched as Will supervised the issuing of arrows to the men. Unconsciously, both men nodded their approval of the boy. Then Erak turned to Halt.

"I nearly forgot, Ragnak had a further message for you. He said if we lose this battle and he loses his slaves as well, he's going to kill you for it," he said cheerfully.

Halt smiled grimly. "If we lose this battle, he may have to get in line to do it. There'll be a few thousand Temujai cavalrymen in front of him."

26

WILL CALLED THE LAST GROUP OF TEN MEN FORWARD TO THE firing line. The preceding group moved to the rear of the waiting ranks and sat down to watch. He was working the men in small groups at this stage. That gave him a manageable group to work with as he tested their ability to follow his orders and shoot at a predetermined elevation.

"Ready!" he called. Each man took an arrow from the bin in front of him and nocked it to the string. They stood ready, their heads turned toward him, waiting for his next order.

"Remember," he said, "don't try to judge the shot yourself. Just go to the position I call, make a full draw and a smooth release when I call it."

The men nodded. Initially, they hadn't liked the idea of having their shooting controlled by someone as young as Will. Then, after Halt had encouraged his apprentice to give a demonstration of high-speed pinpoint shooting, they had reluctantly agreed to the system Will had devised.

Will took a deep breath, then called firmly: "Position three! Draw!"

Ten arms holding bows rose to a position approximately forty degrees from the horizontal. Will quickly glanced down the line to see that each man had remembered the correct position. He'd been drilling the four different elevations into them all day. Satisfied, and before the strain of holding the bows at full draw became too great, he called:

"Shoot!"

Almost as one, there was a rapid slither of released bowstrings and a concerted hiss of arrows arcing through the air.

Will watched the small flight of shafts as they arced upward, then nosed over and plunged down to bury themselves up to half their length in the turf. Again he called to the waiting line of men: "Position three, ready!"

As before, the ten men nocked arrows to the strings, waiting for Will's next call.

"Draw . . . shoot!"

Again there was the slithering slap of released bowstrings hitting the archers' arm guards, and the sound of the wooden shafts scraping past the bows as they were hurled into the air. This time, as the arrows came down, Will changed his command.

"Position two . . . ready!"

The line of left arms holding the bows extended and tilted up to a thirty-degree angle.

"Draw . . . shoot!"

And another ten-shaft volley was on its way. Will nodded to the ten men, who were watching him expectantly.

"All right," he said. "Let's see how you did."

He began to pace across the open field, followed by the ten men who had just shot. There were markers set out down the middle of the field, marking 100, 150 and 200 meter distances. Position three, with the bow arm elevated forty degrees from the horizontal, should have equated to the 150 meter marker. As they approached that marker, Will nodded with satisfaction. There were sixteen arrows slanting up from the turf within a ten-meter tolerance of the mark. Two had gone long, he noticed, and two more had dropped short. He studied the long shots. The shafts were numbered so that he could assess how each member of the shooting line had performed. He saw now that the two overshoots belonged to two different archers.

Moving back to the arrows that had undershot the target, he frowned slightly. The arrows were both marked with the same number. That meant the same archer had dropped his shot short of the mark both times. Will took note of the number, then moved back to view the results of the final volley. The frown deepened as he saw that nine arrows were well grouped, with one falling short by the same margin. He didn't really need to check, but a quick glance showed him that, once again, the same archer had undershot the distance.

He grunted thoughtfully.

"All right!" he called. "Recover your arrows." Then he led the way back to the firing point, the ten men following behind him.

"Who was at number four position?" he asked.

One of the archers stepped forward, hesitantly holding up a hand and looking like a nervous pupil in school. He was a heavyset bearded man of about forty, Will noticed, yet his demeanor showed that he was totally in awe of the young Ranger facing him.

"That was me, your honor," he said. Will beckoned him closer.

"Bring your bow and two or three arrows," he said. The man picked up his bow, and selected two arrows from the bin that stood by his firing position. He was nervous at being singled out and promptly dropped the arrows, scrabbling awkwardly to retrieve them.

"Relax," Will told him. "I just want to check your technique."

The man tried to smile in return. He'd seen they were his arrows that had fallen short and he assumed he was about to be punished. That was the way life went for a slave in Hallasholm. If you were told to do something and you didn't do it, you were punished. Now the brown-haired youth who was directing the session was grinning at him and telling him to relax. It was a novel experience.

"Take a stance," Will told him, and the man stood side-on to the firing range, left foot extended, left hand holding the bow at waist height.

"Position three," Will said quietly, and the man assumed the position that had been drilled into him all the previous day, his left arm holding the bow at forty degrees—almost maximum distance. Will studied him. There seemed to be little wrong with the man's stance.

"All right," he said. "Draw, please."

The man was using too much arm muscle and not enough of his back muscles to draw the bow, Will thought. But that was a minor fault and the result of long habit. There would be no way of changing that in the time they had left.

"And . . . shoot."

There it was, Will thought. A fraction of a second before the man released his shot, he relaxed the draw length slightly—letting the arrow ease down a little before actually letting his fingers slip from the string. That meant that at the moment of release, the arrow was at something less than full draw, which in turn meant it was receiving less than the full power of the bow behind its flight. Halt and Will had tested all the bows to make sure they were similar in draw weight and the arrows were all exactly the same length to ensure results were as consistent as possible. The main cause for variation would be little technical errors like this one.

He looked down the range to where the colored flights of the arrow were visible against the brown, sodden grass of the spring thaw. As he had suspected, it was short again.

Will explained the reason for the problem to the man, seeing from the surprised expression that he had no idea that he was relaxing the draw at the crucial moment.

"Work on it," he told him, giving him an encouraging slap on the shoulder. Halt had impressed on him the fact that a little encouragement in matters like these went a great deal further than scathing criticism. Will had been surprised when Halt had put him in charge of the archers' training. Even though he knew he'd be directing the archers during the battle, he'd assumed that Halt would supervise their training. But the Ranger had repeated his earlier sentiment.

"You're the one who'll be directing them once we're fighting. It's as well they get used to following your orders from the start."

Will remembered another piece of advice the Ranger had given him. "Men work better when they know what you have in mind," he told the young apprentice. "So make sure you tell them as much as possible."

He stepped up onto a raised platform that had been placed here for the purpose of addressing the entire group.

"We'll break for today," he said in a raised voice. "Tomorrow we'll shoot as one group. So if I've picked any technical faults in your shooting today, practice getting rid of them before the evening meal. Then get a good night's rest." He started to turn away, then turned back, remembering one thing more. "Good work, all of you," he said. "If you keep this up, we're going to give those Temujai a very nasty surprise."

A growl of pleasure rose from the hundred men. Then they broke off, heading back for the warmth of the halls and lodges. Will realized that it was later than he'd thought. The sun was touching the tops of the hills beyond Hallasholm and the shadows were lengthening. The evening breeze was chilly and he shivered, reaching for the cloak that he'd hung from the platform railing as he'd directed the shooting.

A half dozen boys had been assigned to help and without orders from him they gathered the arrow bins and arrows, putting them under cover in one of the store sheds that fronted the practice field. Will couldn't help noticing the admiring glances they cast his way as they went about their work. He was only a few years older than they were, yet here he was, directing a force of one hundred archers. He smiled to himself. He wouldn't have been human if he hadn't enjoyed their hero worship.

"You look pleased with yourself," said a familiar voice. He turned and realized Horace must have approached while he had been talking to the men. He shrugged, trying to act diffident.

"They're coming along quite well," he said. "It's been a good day's work."

Horace nodded. "So I noticed," he said. Then, in a worried tone, he continued, "Evanlyn hasn't been here with you, has she?"

Will looked up at him, instantly on the defensive. "What if she has been?" he asked, an argumentative tone creeping into his voice. Instantly, he saw the worried look clear from Horace's face and realized he'd misinterpreted the reason for his friend's question.

"Then she has been here?" Horace said. "That's a relief. Where is she now?"

Now it was Will's turn to frown. "Just a moment," he said, putting a hand on Horace's muscular forearm. "Why is it a relief? Is something wrong?"

"Then she hasn't been here?" Horace asked, and his face fell again as Will shook his head.

"No. I thought you were being . . . you know . . ." Will had been about to say *jealous*, but he couldn't quite manage it. The idea that Horace might have something to be jealous about had too much of a sense of boasting about it. He saw instantly that such thoughts were far from Horace's mind. The apprentice warrior had hardly seemed to notice Will's hesitation.

"She's missing," he said, in that same worried tone. He cast his hands out and looked around the empty practice field, as if he somehow expected to see her appear there. "Nobody's seen her since midmorning yesterday. I've looked everywhere for her, but there's no sign."

"Missing?" Will repeated, not quite understanding. "Missing where?"

Horace looked up at him with a sudden flare of asperity. "If we knew that, she wouldn't be missing, would she?"

Will put up his hands in a peacemaking gesture.

"You're right!" he said. "I didn't realize. I've been a little tied up trying to get these archers organized. Surely somebody must have seen her last night. Her room servants, for example?"

Horace shook his head miserably. "I've asked them," he said. "I was out on patrol most of yesterday myself, keeping an eye on the Temujai approach. We didn't get back in to Hallasholm till well after supper time, so I didn't realize she wasn't around. It was only this morning when I went to find her that I found out she hadn't been in her room last night and that nobody had seen her today. That's why I was hoping that maybe you'd . . ." The sentence tailed off and Will shook his head.

"I haven't seen hide nor hair of her," he told his friend. "But it's ridiculous!" he exclaimed after a short silence. "Hallasholm isn't a big enough place for someone to go missing. And there's nowhere else she could have gone. Let's face it, she can't have simply disappeared . . . can she?"

Horace shrugged. "That's what I keep telling myself," he said morosely. "But somehow, it looks as if she has."

27

UNITED NOW IN THEIR CONCERN FOR EVANLYN, THE TWO apprentices headed for Halt's quarters. All of the Araluen party had been assigned rooms in the main hall. As Halt was their leader, he had been given a small suite of three rooms. At the door, Will knocked perfunctorily and heard Halt's gruff reply: "Come."

As they entered, he took in the fact that Erak was in the room with Halt. It was hard to miss the bulky Skandian. He seemed to fill most spaces he occupied. He was sprawled in one of the comfortable, carved wood armchairs that decorated the room—doubtless liberated on some wolfship raid down the coast. Halt was standing by the window, framed against the low-angled light of the late afternoon. He looked quizzically at the doorway as the two boys entered hurriedly.

"Halt," Will began urgently, "Horace says Evanlyn's disappeared. She's—"

"Safe and sound and back in Hallasholm." A familiar voice finished the sentence for him. Both boys turned to the speaker. Standing a little back, in the shadows of the room, she hadn't been evident as they'd entered.

"Evanlyn!" Horace exclaimed. "You're all right!"

The girl smiled. Now that his eyes were accustomed to the darker part of the room, Will could make out that her face and clothes were smeared with grease and dirt. Her eyes met his and she smiled at him, a little wistfully. Then she upended the flask of juice that she had in her hand and drank greedily from it.

"Apparently," she said, setting the flask down. "Although I have a thirst on me that I doubt I'll ever quench. All I've had to drink in the last eighteen hours was a little rainwater that made its way through the canvas covers over the . . ." She hesitated and looked to Erak to supply the word she was after. The jarl obliged.

"Forepeak," he said, and Evanlyn repeated the word.

"Forepeak, exactly, of Slagor's ship," she said. Will and Horace exchanged puzzled glances.

"What in the devil's name were you doing there?" Will asked. Halt answered for her.

"The devil's name is right," he said. "It seems our friend Slagor has sold out to the Temujai—and he's planning to betray Hallasholm to them."

"What?" asked Will, his voice cracking with surprise. He looked at Evanlyn. "How do you know?"

The girl shrugged her slim shoulders. "Because I heard him discussing it with the Temujai leader. They were barely two meters away from me."

"It seems," Halt put in, by way of explanation, "that your old friend Slagor sailed down the coast yesterday to a rendezvous with the Temujai Shan—one Haz'kam. And since our traitor obviously didn't trust his new allies too far, he insisted on all negotiations being carried out on board his ship—just to keep Haz'kam's retainers at a distance."

"Which is how I came to hear it," Evanlyn finished. But now Horace was scratching his head in bewilderment.

"But . . . what were you doing on the ship?" he said.

"I told you," Evanlyn replied. "Eavesdropping on Slagor and the Temujai."

Horace made an impatient gesture. "Yes, yes, so you've said. But why were you there in the first place?"

Evanlyn went to answer, hesitated, then stopped altogether. All eyes in the room were on her now and she realized she didn't really have a logical answer to that question.

"I . . . don't know," she said finally. "I was bored, I guess. And feeling useless. I was looking for something to do. And besides, Slagor looked sort of . . . shifty."

"Slagor always looks sort of shifty," Erak put in, helping himself to fruit from a bowl on the table in front of him. Evanlyn thought about it, then conceded the point.

"Well, that's true, I suppose. But he looked even shiftier than usual," she said. "So I decided someone had better keep an eye on him and see what he was up to."

Truth be told, Evanlyn was quite enjoying herself now. She had gone from feeling useless and unnecessary to being the bearer of important, even vital news to Halt and Erak. She couldn't help preening, just a little. Horace's next reaction was exactly what she'd hoped for.

"But . . . you could have been spotted! What if they'd found you there? They would have killed you," he said, his concern for her evident in the worried tone of his voice.

That thought had occurred to Evanlyn on more than one occasion as she'd crouched in the damp space in the bow of the wolfship. Once she had fully realized the situation she was in, her skin had crawled with the fear of discovery with every second. But now she affected a nonchalant air about the entire episode.

"I suppose so. But let's face it, someone had to do it."

She was delighted to notice that Horace was looking at her with something approaching awe. She glanced quickly at Will, hoping to see the same look of admiration there. His next words dashed that hope.

"All very well," he said dismissively. "But the important thing is that Slagor is planning to betray us. How is he aiming to do it?"

"That's the point, of course," Halt agreed. He indicated a chart of the Skandian coast that he and Erak had spread on the table between them. "Apparently, friend Slagor plans to put to sea quietly the day after tomorrow and make for the same rendezvous point down the coast. Only this time, there'll be one hundred and fifty Temujai warriors waiting. He'll take them aboard and ferry them back here to Hallasholm—"

"He'll never fit a hundred and fifty men into one wolfship!" Will interrupted.

Halt nodded. "Apparently, he has another two ships waiting for him out behind this island, halfway to the rendezvous."

"They left a week ago," Erak put in. "Supposedly, they were going to raid behind the Temujai lines. It seems the skirls are in league with Slagor and they're waiting at this prearranged point." He tapped the map with his dagger, with which he'd been peeling fruit. A few spots of apple juice fell onto the parchment. Halt raised an eyebrow at him and wiped them away as the Jarl continued. "With three ships, they'll carry one hundred and fifty men easily."

"Then what?" Horace asked. Evanlyn, piqued that attention had been diverted from her and that Will had ignored the danger she'd been in, leapt back into the conversation.

"They'll be able to attack our forces from the rear," she explained. "Think of it, one hundred and fifty men, with the element of surprise, suddenly appearing behind our lines!"

"That could be very nasty indeed," Horace said thoughtfully. "So what do we do?"

"We've already taken the first step," Erak told him. "I've sent Svengal with two of my ships out to Fallkork Island here." Again he tapped the juice-stained knife on the map and again Halt raised his eyes at him. "To make sure Slagor's other two ships don't keep any rendezvous."

"Two against two?" Will asked. "Is that enough?"

The jarl cocked his head to one side and smiled at him. "Count yourself lucky that Svengal wasn't here to hear you say that," he replied. "He'd consider his crew alone to be more than a match for two ships full of Slagor's followers. But in fact, Slagor's ships will have only rowing crews. They need all the space they have to cram those Temujai on board with them."

"But what do we do about Slagor?" Will asked, and this time it was Halt who answered.

"That's the problem. If he gets wind that we know what he's up to, he'll simply abandon the plan. We'll be able to prove nothing. It'll be his word against the word of a former slave—and an escaped one at that." He smiled at Evanlyn to show he meant no insult, but was merely stating the facts. She nodded her understanding.

"But if Slagor finds the other two ships at this island, surely that's proof?" Horace interjected. Halt shook his head.

"Proof of what? The crews will hardly admit they were waiting to go fetch the Temujai," he said.

Horace sat back, frowning. This was getting too complicated for him.

"Then what can we do?" Will asked. But at that moment there was a heavy knock at the door. They all looked at each other in surprise. The clandestine nature of their discussion had made them speak in lowered tones and the sudden interruption had made them all start guiltily, as if discovered.

"Anyone expecting visitors?" Halt asked, and as the others shook their heads, he called once more: "Come."

The door opened to admit Hodak, one of Erak's younger followers. He glanced about the room, noting the identities of all present. He looked uncomfortable as he noticed Evanlyn.

"Thought I might find you here," he said to Erak. "Ragnak's calling a special council in the Great Hall. He wants you there, Jarl." He indicated Evanlyn. "And you'd better bring the girl with you."

"Evanlyn? Why should she go?" Halt asked. He saw the girl shrink back from the young Skandian. Maybe she had some premonition of what was to come.

"The council's about her," Hodak said awkwardly. "Slagor has invoked Ragnak's Vallasvow. He says the girl is really Princess Cassandra, daughter of King Duncan."

28

"BRING HER FORWARD!" RAGNAK'S MASSIVE VOICE, USED TO dominating the howling gales of the Stormwhite, boomed painfully in the low-ceilinged Hall. Evanlyn shrank back instinctively, then recovered as Halt touched her arm and met her eyes with a reassuring smile. She straightened her shoulders and drew herself up to full height. Will watched in admiration as she walked down the cleared space in the center of the hall. Halt, Erak and the two apprentices followed close behind her. Horace, Will noticed, was continually easing his sword in its scabbard, lifting it to free the blade, then allowing it to drop back again. Will's own hand strayed to the hilt of his throwing knife. If things went as badly as they all feared, he decided that knife was for Slagor, who was standing beside and slightly behind Ragnak. Once before, on Skorghijl, Will had demonstrated his skill with the knife to Erak's and Slagor's crews, throwing it across the room and skewering a small wooden keg next to Slagor's hand. This time, there would be no keg.

The room watched in utter silence as Evanlyn stopped before Ragnak's raised dais.

She met the Oberjarl's glower with a calm, composed expression on her face. Again, Will found himself almost overwhelmed by her courage and her composure. Slagor signaled to a pair of attendants by a side door.

"Bring in the slave," he called. His voice was soft and silky, totally unlike Ragnak's forceful bellow. He sounded very pleased with the current turn of events, Will thought. The two men, rowers from Slagor's crew, opened the door and dragged in a protesting, weeping figure. She was a middle-aged woman, her hair graying and her face lined before its time with the strain of unending labor, poor food and the threat of constant punishment that was the lot of a slave in Hallasholm. The sailors dragged her forward and cast her down on the floor in front of Evanlyn. She crouched there miserably, her eyes down.

"Look up, slave," Slagor told her in that same quiet voice. Her sobbing continued and she shook her head, her eyes still cast down at the floor. Slagor moved quickly, stepping down from the platform and drawing his saxe knife in one smooth movement. He held the razor-sharp blade below the woman's chin, pressing it into the flesh of her neck with not quite sufficient force to break the skin.

"I said, 'look up,'" he repeated, and applied pressure to the knife to raise her eyes until she was gazing at Evanlyn. As she saw the girl, the woman began sobbing even louder.

"Shut up," Slagor told her. "Shut up that noise and tell the Oberjarl what you told me."

There were angry welts across the woman's face. Obviously, she had been recently beaten. Her ragged shift was torn in several spots as well, and more red marks were visible on her body through the gaps. In some places, blood had soaked through the thin material. Her tear-filled eyes pleaded with Evanlyn.

"I'm sorry, my lady," she said, her voice breaking. "They beat me until I told."

Evanlyn took an involuntary step toward her. But Slagor's knife swung up and around to confront her and stop her from coming closer. Beside him, Will heard Horace's quick intake of breath and saw his hand fall to the sword hilt once more. He placed his own hand over Horace's, stopping him from drawing the sword. The heavily built apprentice looked at him, surprised. Will shook his head slightly. He realized that Horace's movement had been a reflex reaction and he knew that in this tinderbox atmosphere, if his friend ever drew that sword it could mean the end of all of them.

"Not yet." He mouthed the words. If the time came, he was willing to join Horace in an attack on Slagor and Ragnak. But first, he thought, they should see if Halt couldn't talk their way out of this situation.

"Leave the talking to me," the Ranger had told them before they left his apartment. "And don't do anything until I tell you. Clear?"

The two boys had nodded. Then Halt had added: "This puts an altogether different slant on our accusing Slagor, of course."

"But surely you're still going to tell Ragnak?" Will had burst out. Halt shook his head doubtfully.

"The problem is, he's got in first. If we make a counter accusation now, it will look as if we're simply doing it to save Evanlyn. Chances are, Ragnak will ignore it altogether."

"But you can't let him get away with . . . ," Will began, but Halt held up a hand to silence him.

"I'm not letting him get away with anything," he reassured them. "We'll just have to pick the right time to bring the matter up, that's all."

Now Slagor turned back to the woman on the floor. "Tell the Oberjarl," he repeated.

The woman said nothing and Slagor turned to Ragnak in exasperation. "My head slave overheard her talking to some of the others," he explained. "She's Araluen originally and she said she recognized this girl here"—he jerked a thumb in Evanlyn's direction—"as the Princess Cassandra—Duncan's daughter."

Ragnak's eyes narrowed and he turned slightly to inspect Evanlyn. Her chin went up and she stood a little taller under his gaze.

"She does have something of the look of Duncan about her," he said suspiciously.

"No! No! I was mistaken!" the slave burst out suddenly. On her knees, she stretched her hands out to Slagor in supplication. "Now I see her close to, I realize I was wrong, Lord Slagor. I was mistaken!"

"You called her 'my lady,'" Slagor reminded her.

"It was a mistake, that was all. A mistake. Now I see her properly, I can tell it's not her," the woman insisted.

Slagor regarded her with a pained expression on his face. He turned to Ragnak again. "She's lying, Oberjarl," he said. "I'll have my men beat the truth out of her."

He made a signal to the two men again and one of them came forward, uncoiling a short, thick whip as he came. The woman cringed away from him.

"No! Please, my lord, please!" Her voice was shrill with fear as she tried to crawl away. Slagor's man grabbed a handful of her hair to stop her and she cried out again, in pain as well as fear. He raised the vicious-looking whip over his head, ready to bring it down.

"Leave her alone!" Evanlyn cried, and her voice froze the sailor where he stood. He looked uncertainly to Slagor for direction, but the wolfship captain was watching Evanlyn, waiting for her to say more.

"All right," she said quietly, "There's no need to torture her further. I'm Cassandra."

The silence in the room was almost a physical force. Then an excited buzz broke out among the assembled crowd. Will distinctly heard the word *Vallasvow* from several different sources.

"Silence!" roared Ragnak, and instantly the noise ceased. He rose and moved forward to confront Evanlyn, glaring down at her. "You are Duncan's daughter?"

She hesitated, then replied.

"I am King Duncan's daughter," she said, with a slight emphasis on his title. "Cassandra, Princess of Araluen."

"Then you are my enemy," he said, spitting the words out. "And I've sworn that you should die."

Erak stepped forward. "And I've sworn that she will be safe here, Oberjarl," he said. "I gave my word when I asked the Ranger to help us."

Ragnak looked up angrily. Again there was a buzz of conversation through the room. Erak was a popular jarl among the Skandians and Ragnak hadn't reckoned on having to contend with him over this matter. With an invading army only days away from his stronghold, he knew he couldn't afford a split with his senior war leader.

"I am Oberjarl," he said. "My vow is of greater importance."

Erak folded his arms across his chest. "Not to me it isn't," he said, and there was a chorus of agreement from the crowd.

"Erak cannot defy you like this! You are Oberjarl!" Slagor suddenly interjected. "Have him imprisoned! He is defying your vow to the Vallas!"

"Shut up, Slagor," Erak told him in an ominously calm voice. Then he readdressed himself to Ragnak. "I didn't ask you to take your death vow, Ragnak," he said. "But if you want to carry it out, I'm afraid you'll have to go through me to do it."

Now Ragnak stepped down from his podium and walked closer to where Erak stood. They were of equal height, both massively built. He faced his old companion, the anger burning in his eyes.

"Erak, did you know? Did you know who she was when you brought her here?"

Erak shook his head.

Slagor snorted in disgust. "Of course he knew!" he cried, then stopped suddenly as the point of Erak's dagger appeared under his nose.

"I'll allow that once," Erak told him. "Say it again and you're a dead man."

Wordlessly, Slagor backed away from the bigger man, putting a safe distance between himself and the point of the knife. Erak sheathed the dagger and turned back to Ragnak. "I didn't know," he said. "Otherwise I would never have brought her here, knowing of your vow. But the fact remains, I vouched for her safety and my word is all-important to me—as is yours to you."

"Damn and blast it, Erak!" Ragnak shouted. "The Temujai are only three or four days' march from here! We can't afford to be fighting amongst ourselves now!"

"It would be a shame if you had to face the Temujai with at least one, and possibly both, of your best leaders dead," Halt put in mildly, and the Oberjarl rounded on him in a fury.

"Shut up, Ranger! I'm of half a mind to believe that this is all your doing! No good ever came of dealing with your kind!"

Halt shrugged, unimpressed by the Skandian's fury. "Be that as it may," he said, "it occurs to me that there might be a solution to your problem—for the time being, at least."

The buzz of conversation through the room was cut short as Ragnak swung his gaze around angrily. He watched Halt with narrowed eyes, expecting some trick or some kind of subterfuge.

"What are you talking about? My vow is binding upon me," he said. Halt nodded agreement.

"I understand that. But is there any time factor involved?" he asked. Now Ragnak looked puzzled as well as suspicious.

"Time factor? How do you mean?"

"If we accept that you plan to do your best to kill Evanlyn, knowing that Erak will try to stop you when you do—not to mention the fact that if he doesn't, I most certainly will—have you vowed that you'll do it at any particular time?" Halt continued.

The puzzled expression on Ragnak's face grew more intense.

"No. I didn't specify any time. I just made the vow," he said finally, and Halt nodded several times.

"Good. So, as far as these Vallas are concerned, they don't care whether you try to fulfill your vow today or if you choose to wait until, say, after we've sent the Temujai packing?"

Understanding was beginning to dawn on the Oberjarl's face. "That's right," he said slowly. "As long as the intent is there, the Vallas will be satisfied."

"No!" A shrill voice cut across them. It was Slagor, the silky, self-satisfied tones gone from his voice now. "Can't you see, Oberjarl, he's trying to trick you? He has something in mind. The girl must die and she must die now! Otherwise your sworn word is worthless!" Slagor's anger and his long-held desire for revenge on Evanlyn for the events that had occurred on Skorghijl had caused him to go too far. Ragnak turned on him now, a flame of anger burning in his eyes.

"Slagor, I would advise you to get rid of this reckless habit of telling your peers that they are liars," he said, and instantly the wolf-ship captain retracted his accusation.

"Of course, Oberjarl. I didn't mean—"

Ragnak cut him off.

"My first concern is for the safety of Skandia. With these Temujai on our doorstep, Erak and I cannot afford to be fighting. If he'll agree to postpone our differences until after we've settled with them, then I will too."

Erak nodded agreement instantly. "It sounds like a good compromise to me."

There was still one thread of suspicion in Ragnak's mind. He turned back to Halt, his heavy brows knitted together in a frown.

"I can't help wondering what's in it for you, Ranger. All you've done is win a postponement."

Halt inclined his head slightly to one side as he considered the matter. "True," he replied. "But a lot can happen in the next few days. You might be killed in the battle. Or Erak. Or me. Or all three of us. Besides that, my immediate priority is the same as yours: to see these Temujai driven back. After all, if they win here, it won't be long before they're invading Araluen as well. I have a sworn duty to try to prevent that." He smiled grimly. "That's another of those vows that we all seem to rush around taking. Damned nuisances, aren't they?"

Ragnak turned and stepped back up on the dais to his massive council chair.

"We're agreed then," he said. "We'll settle the Temujai question first. Then we'll come back to this problem."

Erak and Halt exchanged glances, then both men nodded. Only Slagor seemed to be in disagreement with the compromise. He muttered a curse under his breath. Halt took Evanlyn's arm and began to guide her from the Great Hall, followed by the two apprentices and Erak. They hadn't gone half a dozen paces when Halt turned back to Ragnak.

"Of course, there is one more question that I'd like to hear Slagor answer," he said. As he hoped, at the mention of his name, everyone in the room involuntarily glanced at Slagor. Then, when all eyes were on him, Halt continued.

"Perhaps he could tell us what his ships are doing at Fallkork Island?"

29

EVERYONE SAW SLAGOR'S GUILTY START OF SURPRISE WHEN Halt mentioned the name of the island. Slagor recovered quickly, but the moment had been there and it had been witnessed.

"I'm not here to answer to you, Ranger!" he blustered angrily. "You have no authority in this council!"

Erak stepped forward, rocking on his heels, his face only centimeters from Slagor's. "But I have," he told the other man. "And I'd like to hear your answer."

"What's this about, Erak?" Ragnak interrupted before Slagor could reply. Erak kept his gaze fixed on Slagor.

"Two of Slagor's ships are currently at Fallkork Island," he replied. "In another day, he plans to rendezvous with them and sail down the coast to Sand Creek Bay."

Erak saw the color draining from Slagor's face as he realized that his plans had been discovered. He continued inexorably, his voice rising in volume as Slagor attempted to speak, drowning the other man out. "There, he plans to embark one hundred and fifty Temujai warriors and land them behind our lines to attack us from the rear."

The room erupted as people began to shout all at once. In vain,

Slagor spat abuse at Erak and protested his innocence. His followers in the hall, and there were more than a few, roared their protests, while those who favored Erak roared back, calling for Slagor's head. The bedlam continued for a full minute until Ragnak rose from his seat.

"*Silence!*" he bellowed.

In the ensuing quiet, you could almost hear a pin drop.

"How do you know this?" the Oberjarl asked. He disliked Slagor. Many of the Skandians did. But the concept of such treachery was so absolutely abhorrent to the simple Skandian code of conduct that Ragnak found it impossible to believe it of anyone, even Slagor.

"His plans were overheard, Ragnak," Erak told him.

Instantly Slagor was screaming his innocence. "This is lies! It's a pack of filthy lies! Who heard me? Who claims I'm a traitor? Let them face me now!"

"As a matter of fact, Ragnak," said Halt, raising his voice so that he was heard clearly in every corner of the room, "the informant is here with us."

That piece of news stilled Slagor's protests immediately. Ragnak eyed the Ranger with distaste. Since he had arrived in Hallasholm, the comfortable, established order of things had been continually disturbed.

"Then let's hear from him," the Oberjarl said.

"Not him, Ragnak. Her. The informant is Evanlyn. Perhaps that's why Slagor is so keen to have her discredited and killed."

Uproar once again filled the room and Will realized how cleverly Halt had played this hand. In the confusion of the moment, nobody asked the obvious question: how could Slagor have known that Evanlyn had discovered his plan? For if he didn't know, he would have no reason to try to discredit the girl. But now that Halt had planted the seed, the Skandians would all half believe that Slagor's actions were intended to forestall Evanlyn, rather than the other way around. In that light, her accusation could not be dismissed out of hand. It had to be investigated.

"Proof!" Slagor was shouting now, and some of his followers, realizing their own necks were close to the heads-man's ax, were shouting it too. "Anyone can accuse me! But where's the proof?"

Ragnak silenced the shouting with a gesture. "Well, Ranger," he asked Halt, "can you offer us proof of these accusations?"

Erak hurriedly stepped into the breach, before Halt had to answer. "Svengal is bringing in the two ships from Fallkork," he said. "He should be in port by tomorrow."

But now Slagor saw the way out, saw there was no concrete evidence of the plan. "So two of my ships are waiting at Fallkork?" he cried, his voice shrill once more. "What does that prove? How does that make me a traitor? It doesn't, does it, Erak?"

A few of those in the hall started to echo the thought—and not just his own followers. As Halt had pointed out earlier, the mere presence of the ships at the rendezvous was no proof of Slagor's treachery. Emboldened now, Slagor stepped toward the crowd, addressing them and not the Oberjarl.

"They accuse me of treachery! They slander me! They take the word of an enemy of this country, the sworn enemy of our Oberjarl! Yet they can show no way to prove their vile claims! Is this Skandian justice? Let them find a way to prove it, I say."

A growing chorus of voices agreed with him. Then, as if he were conducting a choir, Slagor signaled for silence and turned back to Halt.

"Can you, Ranger?" he said, spitting the last word out as if it were an insult. "Can you show some kind of proof?"

Halt hesitated, knowing they'd lost the momentum and the sentiment of the crowd. Knowing they'd lost. Then Will pushed forward to stand beside his mentor and friend.

"There is a way," he said.

It took a lot to silence a noisy crowd of Skandians, but Will's statement managed to do the trick. The voices died away as if cut by a knife and all eyes turned to the small figure, standing now between Halt and Erak. As Will might have guessed, it was Ragnak himself who broke the silence.

"How?" he said simply.

"Well, Slagor's ships at this island, taken on their own, may be no proof of his intention to sell out to the Temujai," Will said carefully, thinking through his words before he spoke them aloud, knowing that all their safety hung by a hairsbreadth on the way he expressed his idea. He saw Ragnak draw breath to speak and hurried on before the Oberjarl could interrupt him. "But ... if Erak took *Wolfwind* to this Sand Creek Bay, and if they happened to find, say, a hundred and fifty Temujai warriors waiting there to embark, it's a fair indication that someone is planning to betray you, isn't it?"

There was a murmur of agreement among the assembled crowd. Ragnak frowned as he thought through the idea. Beside Will, Erak muttered: "Good thinking, boy."

"That's true," Ragnak said finally. "It shows there's treachery been planned. But who's to say Slagor's involved?"

Will chewed his lip as he thought over that one. But now Halt spoke up.

"Oberjarl, there's a simple way to find out. Let Erak take not one ship, but three. After all, that's the number the Temujai are expecting to see. Then he can speak with the leader of any Temujai who might happen to be there and tell them that Slagor has been detained and has sent him in his place. If the Temujai leader responds with words along the lines of 'Who the devil is Slagor?,' then our friend here is as innocent as he claims to be." He paused and saw that Ragnak was nodding as he considered the idea. Then he added, more deliberately, "On the other hand . . . if the name Slagor seems familiar to the enemy, then there is all the proof you need."

"This is ridiculous!" Slagor burst out. "I swear to you, Oberjarl, that I am no traitor to Skandia! This is a plot cooked up by these Araluens." He gestured contemptuously at Halt and Will. "And somehow they seem to have tricked Erak into believing it."

"If you're innocent," Ragnak said heavily, "then you have nothing to fear from all this, do you?" He was gazing steadily at Slagor now, noting the sheen of perspiration on the other man's forehead, noting the shrill tone that pervaded all his statements now. Slagor was scared, he thought. The more he saw that, the more he was prepared to believe that the man was a traitor.

"I don't see any reason why—" Slagor began, but Ragnak cut him off with a gesture.

"I do!" he snapped. "Erak, take three ships to Sand Creek Bay immediately and do as the Ranger suggests. Once you've established whether or not Slagor is involved in this plot, get back here and report. As for you . . ." He turned to Slagor, who was beginning to edge toward the side door of the room. "Don't try to go anywhere. I want you where I can see you until Erak returns. Ulfak, see to it!" He addressed this last comment to one of his other senior jarls, who nodded and moved to stand beside Slagor, laying a hand on his arm.

"One thing, Oberjarl," Erak said, and the Skandian leader turned to him again. "Once I've established that Slagor is involved, is it all right if we reduce the Temujai numbers a little? That'll be a few less we have to fight here, at least."

"Good idea," Ragnak said. "But don't take any risks. I need to know the traitor's identity and you can't tell me that if the Temujai kill you."

"Why not go ahead with the plan they're expecting?" Will said, before he could stop himself. The Skandian leader regarded him as if he were mad.

"Are you out of your mind?" he said. "Are you suggesting that Erak actually brings the Temujai back here as prisoners? We'd have to subdue them and guard them and that would take men away from our own battle line."

"Not back here," Will said, turning to appeal to Erak. "But couldn't you find some pretext to make them get off the ships at this Fallkork Island—then just leave them there?"

Again a silence, broken this time by a deep, throaty chuckle from Erak. "Oh, what a prize idea!" he said, grinning fondly at Will. "If we take these ... horsemen ... through the Vulture Narrows, I'm sure we can have them begging to get ashore for a few hours. The seas there are terrible at this time of year—guaranteed to make any inexperienced sailors seasick!"

Ragnak rubbed his chin thoughtfully. "I take it these Temujai are unused to sailing?" he asked Halt.

The Ranger nodded. "Totally, Oberjarl."

Ragnak looked from Halt to his young apprentice. "This boy of yours shows a certain talent for the sort of devious thinking we expect from you Rangers."

Halt dropped one hand lightly on Will's shoulder, and said, with a completely straight face, "We're very proud of him, Oberjarl. We think he'll go far."

Ragnak shook his head wearily. This sort of plot and counterplot was beyond him. He waved one dismissing hand at Erak.

"Get your ships ready and go," he said. "Then dump these Temujai on Fallkork Island and get back here." The matter was done as far as he was concerned, but Slagor had one last, desperate objection.

"Oberjarl! These are the people who accuse me! They're all in it together! You can't send them to verify their own charges!"

Ragnak hesitated. "Fair point." He turned to his hilfmann. "Borsa, you go with them as an independent witness." Then, returning his gaze to Slagor, he concluded, "As for you, you'd better hope there are no Temujai at Sand Creek Bay."

30

ERAK LOOKED AT THE FIGURE STANDING BESIDE HIM IN THE stern of the wolfship and, for the hundredth time, was unable to prevent a broad grin from breaking out across his face.

Halt noticed the look, and the grin, and said in a sour tone, "It must lose its fascination after a while, surely?"

The jarl shook his head, his grin broadening. "Not for me," he replied cheerfully. "Every time, it's just as fresh as the first."

"I'm so glad that Skandians have such a lively sense of humor," the Ranger said, scowling. It didn't serve his ill temper any better to see that several of the other Skandians were grinning as well. In truth, he was a comical figure. He had forsaken his Ranger's cloak and garb and was dressed in Skandian clothing—sheepskin vest, a short fur cloak and woolen breeches, wound around with leather bindings from the knees down. At least they should have been wound from the knees down. In fact, since Halt was considerably smaller in stature than any of the adult Skandians, the leggings were bound from his thighs down, the breeches sagged alarmingly at the crutch and the sheepskin vest hung loosely on him, seemingly with room for another person of his own size inside.

"It's your own fault," Erak replied. "For deciding to try to disguise yourself as one of us."

"I told you," Halt muttered. "The Temujai got a good look at me when they were chasing us near the border—and even without that, they have no reason to love anyone dressed as a Ranger."

"So I've heard," Erak said, still grinning. He bent to the sighting ring before him, checked the position of the floating lodestone and adjusted the sight ring to conform with it. Then he read off the bearing to the next headland.

"A little east to east of south," he said to himself, then, raising his voice, he called to his men: "Look alive now! Sand Creek Bay lies beyond that next headland!"

There was an expectant shuffle on the decks of the wolfship as the Skandians made sure their weapons were close to hand—although not obviously so. At a nod from Erak, the masthead lookout relayed the message to the other two wolfships sailing in close company with them. Very obviously making an effort not to grin, the wolfship skipper nudged Halt in the ribs with a not too gentle elbow.

"You'd better put on your helmet," he told the Ranger, whose countenance darkened even further than before as he reached for the huge horned helmet that every Skandian warrior wore.

This had been the most contentious piece of equipment. Erak had maintained that no Skandian would ever appear in public without a helmet, and that there was no question of Halt's not wearing one. Yet the sizes were immense compared to what Halt considered to be his own perfectly normal head size. Even the very smallest helmet that Erak could find wobbled loosely on Halt, and came down over his ears and eyes. By dint of much padding with cloths, they had finally managed to get the helmet to sit more or less firmly on his head. But it still gaped amazingly all around.

The Skandians looked on with ill-concealed amusement as Halt carefully placed the helmet on his head. Borsa, who had joined the expedition on Ragnak's orders, shook his head and chuckled. The unwarlike hilfmann, who'd never seen a day of battle in his life, knew he looked more the part than Halt did.

"Even if this turns out to be a wild-goose chase," he said cheerfully, "it will have been worth it to see this."

Halt turned away angrily. It was a mistake. With the rapid head movement, his helmet became dislodged and tipped down over his eyes. He cursed quietly to himself, straightened the ridiculous headgear and resigned himself to the smothered laughter of the Skandians.

They had been running before a quartering wind, but now, as Erak prepared to bring *Wolfwind* around the headland and across the wind, there was a flurry of activity on board as the big square sail was gathered in and furled to the cross yard. The long, heavy oars clattered in their tholes as the crew ran them out, and before the ship had time to lose way, they began their smooth, rhythmic stroking. Glancing behind, Halt saw the other ships had followed suit. Once again, the helmet tilted awkwardly on his head and, with a gesture of disgust, he ripped it off and dropped it to the deck. He glared at Erak, daring the big Skandian to make some comment. The jarl merely shrugged his shoulders and smiled.

They were almost around the last promontory now and those without any duties involved in keeping the ship moving and on course craned eagerly to see whether the beach would be empty—or whether there would be a war party of Temujai warriors waiting for them. With tantalizing slowness, the boat crept past the headland, gradually revealing the strip of sandy beach beyond. Halt felt a sinking feeling in the pit of his stomach, as the first sight of the beach showed no sign of any Temujai. But they were only looking at the southern end of the beach, and as they came farther around, there was a soft sigh from those watching and the sinking feeling in Halt's stomach turned to a flame of fierce exultation.

There, drawn up at the center of the beach, were three squadrons of Temujai cavalry.

Their dome-shaped felt tents were pitched in neatly ordered rows. Horses were tethered on a grass sward where the beach ended. There were sixty men to a squadron, Halt knew. He presumed each squadron would be leaving ten men to tend the horses, which, of course, couldn't travel on the wolfships. The discordant blare of a Temujai horn from the beach told them that they had been sighted.

Borsa shook his head sadly at the evidence of Slagor's treachery. "I'd been hoping that this would be an empty quest," he said bitterly. "The thought of any Skandian turning traitor is a bitter one to face."

He moved away from Halt and Erak and the two men exchanged glances. Erak shrugged. His was a more cynical temperament than the hilfmann's, and he had better knowledge of Slagor's character.

"Time to make absolutely sure," he said quietly, and heaved on the steering oar to bring *Wolfwind*'s prow heading straight toward the beach. As arranged, the other two ships hove to, the rowers maintaining a slow, relaxed stroke to hold them in position against wind and tide, some two hundred meters off the beach. They were still within bowshot there, but the huge, circular Skandian shields that were ranged along the bulwarks gave the sailors protection against any Temujai attack.

Those on *Wolfwind* weren't so fortunate. They were heading straight inshore, every stroke of the oars making them more vulnerable to a sudden volley of Temujai arrows.

"Keep your heads down," Erak growled at his rowers. It was

an unnecessary warning. They were hunched down as far as they could be, trying to prevent any part of their persons from showing above the oak bulwarks. Halt noticed that the jarl's right hand strayed from the steering oar from time to time, and brushed almost unconsciously against the haft of the massive battle-ax that leaned close by.

Activity on the beach was growing now, and a party of half a dozen Temujai had moved to the water's edge. Behind them, orders were being shouted and squads were forming as troop leaders prepared their men to embark on the three wolfships.

The deep water continued in quite close to the beach. Of course, the wolfships were designed to beach in water as shallow as one meter, but the Temujai weren't aware of the fact and Halt and Erak had agreed that it made better sense to keep the enemy at a distance. Twenty meters from the water's edge, Erak gave a brief command and the oars on one side of the ship backed while the others went ahead, swinging the narrow craft through ninety degrees, virtually in her own length.

Erak nodded to his second in command, who hurried to the tiller. Then the jarl stepped to the shoreward side of the ship and raised his voice in his familiar storm-quelling bellow.

"Ahoy the beach!" he called, and Halt, standing close by, hastily moved a few paces farther away.

The Tem'uj standing in the center of the small group on the beach cupped his hands and called back.

"I am Or'kam, commander of this force," he called. "Where is Slagor?"

Behind him, Halt heard a quick intake of breath and turned to see Borsa shaking his head sadly, his eyes downcast. Several of the other Skandians also exchanged glances at this incontrovertible confirmation that Slagor had been involved in the plan.

"Keep still!" Halt warned them, and the men hurriedly masked their reactions. Erak was answering now, with the story that he, Borsa and Halt had agreed upon.

"Oberjarl Ragnak was growing suspicious of our movements. It was too dangerous for Slagor to come on this expedition. He will join us at Fallkork Island."

There was a hurried consultation between the Temujai leaders.

"They don't like it," Erak muttered out of the side of his mouth.

"They don't have to like it. They just have to believe it," Halt told him in the same undertone. After several minutes' discussion, Or'kam stepped away from the group and called again.

"We expected Slagor. How can we be sure we can trust you? Did he give any message? Any password?"

On the ship, the men exchanged worried glances. This was the one eventuality they had feared. If Slagor had arranged a password with the Temujai, then their plan was spoiled. Of course, their main aim had already been achieved. They had proved Slagor's complicity in the plot. But now that they were here, the chance of taking 150 men out of the enemy's battle line, without any loss to their own forces, was tempting in the extreme.

"Bluff it out," Halt said quickly. "He already said he was expecting Slagor, so they didn't need a password." Erak nodded. It made sense.

"Look, horseman," Erak bellowed again. "I don't need a password, do I? I'm here to pick you up. And I'm risking my neck to do it! Now if you choose to come aboard, then do so. If not, I'm going raiding and leaving you and Ragnak to your little war. Now you choose!"

Once again there was an urgent consultation on the beach. They could see Or'kam's reluctance in his movements, but equally, they could see him weighing his options, and after a long, searching glance at the wolfship, he obviously decided he had nothing to fear from the skeleton crews of rowers on the three ships.

"Very well!" he called. "Bring your ships in and we'll board."

But now Erak shook his head.

"We'll bring you out on the skiffs," he called. "We can't beach here."

Or'kam made an angry gesture. Obviously he didn't like it when things didn't go precisely according to his wishes.

"What are you talking about?" he yelled. "Slagor beached his ship right here. I saw him do it!"

Erak moved to the bulwark and stood up on it, completely exposed to any possible fire from the beach.

"Careful," Halt muttered, trying not to let his lips move.

"And tell me, horseman," Erak said, his voice heavy with sarcasm, "did Slagor then load fifty men aboard his ship and take her *off* the beach?"

There was a pause as the Temujai leader thought through the reasoning in what Erak had said. Erak saw the hesitation and pressed on.

"If I beach now and load your men aboard, we'll never get her off again. Particularly with the tide falling the way it is."

That seemed to clinch it. Or'kam reluctantly signaled his agreement.

"Very well!" he called. "How many can you take at a time?"

Erak resisted the temptation to heave a sigh of relief.

"Three skiffs, eight men each," he called. "Twenty-four at a time."

Or'kam nodded. "All right, Skandian, send in the skiffs."

31

"POSITION TWO ... SHOOT!" CALLED WILL, AND THE HUNDRED archers' arms rose to the same angle, drew and released, more or less simultaneously. The slithering hiss of the release was magnified a hundred times, and Will and Horace watched in satisfaction as a dark cloud of arrows arced across the intervening space to the target that had suddenly popped up.

Evanlyn was sitting on an old broken cart a few meters behind the line of archers, watching the scene with interest.

They could hear the distinctive soft thudding of arrows striking into the turf around the target, and the harder, clearer smack of those arrows that actually hit it.

"Shields!" bellowed Horace. Beside each archer, a foot soldier stepped forward with a rectangular wooden shield held on his left arm, positioned to cover both himself and the archer as he reloaded. It had been an idea the warrior apprentice had come up with while he'd been watching an earlier practice shoot. Will had readily adopted the improvement. With only one hundred archers, he couldn't afford to lose any to the return fire the Temujai were sure to mount once they saw his men in action.

Will glanced quickly around to make sure his men were ready

for the next shot. Then he turned back to the practice field, searching for the next target to appear.

There! As the team of men behind him hauled on a set of ropes, another flat board swung up out of the grass. But he had nearly missed the movement, waiting to see if the archers were ready. He felt a slight twinge of panic. Things were moving too fast.

"Clear!" he called, wishing his voice wouldn't tend to break when he did this, and the shield bearers stepped clear.

"Half right! Position three . . . shoot!"

Again they heard the slithering hiss. Another cloud of arrows cast its fleeting shadow across the field and riddled the area around the target. Already, another target was rising out of the grass, much closer in this time.

"Shields!" Horace called again and once more the archers were hidden from return fire. As he ordered his men to do this, Horace performed the same action, concealing Will behind one of the large shields.

"Come on, come on," Will muttered, shifting from one foot to the other as he watched the men select new arrows and nock them to the string. The archers sensed his urgency and hurried their reloading. The extra haste made for clumsiness. Three of them dropped the arrows they were about to nock; others fumbled like beginners.

Frustrated, Will realized he'd have to go with the men who were ready. He swung his gaze back to the target. But the men on the ropes were hauling it in, so that it slid toward them on its sled-like runners, matching the speed of an enemy advance. The range had closed too quickly for him to make an instant assessment. In the time that he'd been watching his men, he'd lost his concentration and his sense of the battlefield.

He stepped down angrily from his command position, a low platform built at the end of the line of archers.

"Stand down!" he called. "Everyone take a break."

He realized he'd been sweating freely with the tension and wiped a corner of his cloak across his forehead. Horace set the large shield down and joined him.

"What's the trouble?" he asked.

Will shook his head, defeated. "It's hopeless," he said. "I can't keep track of the targets and the men at the same time. I lose my perspective. You'll have to watch the men and tell me when they're ready."

Horace frowned.

"I could," he agreed. "But on the day, I think I'm going to be a little busy shielding you from any return shots. I really need to keep my eye on the enemy too. Unless you want to be turned into a pincushion."

"Well, someone's going to have to do it!" Will said angrily. "We haven't even begun to practice against the Kaijin and the whole thing's falling apart already!"

Halt had told them about the Kaijin. They were specialist marksmen and each group of sixty Temujai riders would have one with them. The Kaijin were assigned to pick off the leaders in any enemy group. It would be Will's task to counteract them and he'd devised a drill for it, with additional, smaller targets set in the field, ready to rise into view unexpectedly. But if Will was dividing his attention between his own archers and the enemy, his chances of nullifying the enemy marksmen would be low indeed.

On the other hand, his chances of being shot by one of them were considerably higher.

"I could do it," said Evanlyn, and both boys turned toward her. She saw the doubt in their expressions. "I could do it. I could keep an eye on the archers and call when they're ready."

"But that'll put you in the battle line!" Horace objected instantly. "It'll be dangerous!"

Evanlyn shook her head. She noticed Will hadn't objected so far. She could see he was at least considering her idea. She hurried on before he could veto the suggestion.

"The archers aren't actually in the front line. You'll be behind it, and protected by a trench and an earth mound. You could build me a kind of a dugout at the end, beneath your command position. I'd be safe from arrows there. After all, I don't need to see the enemy, just our men."

"But what if the Temujai break through our line?" Horace said. "You'll be right in the middle of it then!"

Evanlyn shrugged. "If the Temujai break through, it won't matter where I am. We'll all be dead. Besides, if everyone else is taking a risk, why shouldn't I?"

Horace was wise enough not to reply *Because you're a girl*. And he had to admit that she had a point. But he wasn't convinced. He turned to Will.

"What do you think, Will?" he said. He expected the apprentice Ranger to agree with him and he was a little surprised when Will didn't answer immediately.

"I think," Will said slowly, "she may be right. Let's try it."

"Ready," Evanlyn said calmly. She was crouched below the platform where Will and Horace stood.

"Clear!" That was Horace. The shield bearers dropped to one knee beside the archers.

"Left left! Position one . . . shoot!"

The volley was ragged and Will knew that was his fault. He'd called the order to shoot a fraction too quickly and some of the men hadn't reached full draw. He mentally kicked himself. He heard Horace calling for the shields again and saw the arrow strikes on the target—as well as those that missed and fell short.

But now another danger reared its head. As the next large target swung up and began moving toward them, another, smaller one swung out from the target they had just engaged. This was a man-sized figure and it was Will's responsibility. He drew and loosed and saw his arrow slam into the target, just as Evanlyn called "ready" once more. He turned his attention quickly to the main target as Horace ordered the shield bearers down.

"Left! Position three . . ." He waited, then added a correction. "Down a half . . ."

He forced himself to wait the full term, then called: "Shoot!"

This time, the volley flew truly, with the majority of arrows slamming into the target or close around it. If it had been a charging group of horsemen, the volley would have taken a severe toll.

"Shields!" bellowed Horace, and the pattern began to repeat itself. But now Will waved a weary hand.

"Stand down," he said, and Horace repeated the order in a louder voice. The archers and shield bearers, who had been working at this drill for the past two hours with only a few short breaks, dropped gratefully to the grass to rest. Horace grinned at Will.

"Not bad," he said. "I make it twenty out of twenty-five of those targets peppered pretty solidly. And you hit every one of the Kaijin."

The smaller targets attached to each large board represented the Kaijin. Freed from the need to check on both his own men and the enemy, Will had coped easily with them.

"True," Will said in response to Horace's comment. "But they weren't shooting back."

Secretly, he was pleased with his performance. He had shot well, in spite of the distractions involved in estimating range and trajectory for the larger group.

He grinned at Horace and Evanlyn. It was good to feel some of the old camaraderie back.

"Nice work, everyone," he said, then, raising his voice: "Let's take a break for half an hour."

There was a murmur of satisfaction from the archers and they moved to the side of the practice area, where barrels of drinking water were available. Behind Will, a familiar voice spoke.

"Take a break for the rest of the day. You've done enough for the moment."

The three young Araluens turned at the sound of Halt's voice. Instantly, Will felt reinvigorated, bursting with curiosity about events at Sand Creek Bay.

"Halt!" he cried eagerly. "What happened? Were the Temujai there? Did you manage to fool them?"

But Halt held up a hand to stop the flow of questions he knew he was about to face. He was troubled by what he had just seen as he approached.

"Why have you got Evanlyn involved in this, Will?" he asked. He saw the hesitation in the young man's eyes, then saw his jaw set in a determined line.

"Because I need her, Halt. I need someone to keep track of the men, to let me know when they're ready. Without that, the system won't work."

"Couldn't someone else do that?"

"I can't think of anyone else I can trust. I want someone who won't panic. Someone who'll keep her head."

Halt scratched his beard thoughtfully. "How do you know Evanlyn won't panic?"

The answer came immediately.

"Because she didn't in Celtica—at the bridge."

Halt looked at the three young faces before him. All set. All determined. He knew Will was right. He would need someone he could trust.

"All right then," he said, then added, as the three beamed at him, "But don't look so happy about it. I'm the one who'll have to explain to her father if she's shot."

"Now what about the Temujai?" Will asked. "Did you find them at Sand Creek Bay?"

At the mention of Slagor's plot, the smile on Evanlyn's face faded, replaced by a look of anxiety.

"They were there," Halt said quickly, dispelling her worst fears. "And they made it clear that they were expecting to see Slagor." He nodded at the girl as she let go a pent-up breath in relief. "It puts a different complexion on things as far as you're concerned, Princess," he said.

"Ragnak still has his vow," she said dully.

Halt nodded. "True. But at least he's agreed not to act on it until after we've driven off the Temujai." Evanlyn made an uncertain little gesture with her hands.

"It's just postponing things," she said.

"Problems postponed have a habit of solving themselves, more often than not," Halt told her, putting an arm around her slim shoulders. Evanlyn smiled at him. But it wasn't much of a smile.

"If you say so," she replied. "But Halt, don't address me as 'Princess' if you would. No point in reminding Ragnak about me at every opportunity."

The Ranger nodded. "I stand corrected," he said. Then he added, in a lower tone that only Evanlyn heard, "By the way, there's no need to mention it to him, but don't be too surprised if Erak's wolfship is standing by to get you out of here the minute we've seen these damned Temujai off."

She looked up at him then, hope in her eyes. He met her gaze and nodded meaningfully. She looked from him to the burly Skandian Jarl, who was now approaching over the field, then she leaned forward to kiss Halt lightly on the cheek.

"Thanks, Halt," she said softly. "At least now I know there is an alternative."

The Ranger shrugged and grinned at her. "That's what I'm here for," he said, pleased to see the light of hope back in her eyes. She smiled at him again and slipped away, heading back to her quarters. All at once, overwhelmed by her sense of relief that Halt had contrived a possible way out of her predicament, she felt the need to be alone for a while.

Some of the Skandians who had been working the targets were calling to Erak now as he came closer, wanting to know how events had turned out at Sand Creek Bay. As the jarl confirmed Slagor's treachery, there were angry mutterings and dark looks cast toward the lodge, where Slagor was being held under guard.

"What about the Temujai, Erak?" Will asked. "How did you convince them to go ashore on Fallkork Island?"

Erak's laughter rang around the practice field. "We would have had to fight to stop them!" he told the assembled audience. "They were scrambling over each other to get back on solid land."

The Skandians in the crowd standing around him echoed his laughter as he continued: "I managed to find a spot where we had the wind from astern, a steep head sea on our starboard quarter and the tide race through the narrows at the same time. A few hours of that and our fierce horse soldiers were like little lambs—sick little lambs."

"They weren't the only ones," Halt replied with some feeling. "I've been through some rough seas in my time, but I've never felt anything like the plunging and leaping you had us doing."

Once again Erak bellowed with laughter. "Your master here went nearly the same shade of green as his cloak," he told Will. Halt raised one eyebrow.

"At least I finally found a use for that damned helmet," he said, and the smile disappeared from Erak's face.

"Yes. I'm not sure what I'm going to tell Gordoff about that," he said. "He made me promise I'd look after that helmet. It's his favorite—a real family heirloom."

"Well, it certainly has a lived-in feel to it now," Halt told him, and Will noticed there was a hint of malicious pleasure in his eye. The Ranger nodded at the group of archers who were standing by.

"You seem to have this group working pretty well," he said.

Will felt absurdly pleased at his mentor's praise.

"Oh," he said, trying to sound casual. "We're not doing too badly."

"Better than that from what I saw," Halt told him. Then he repeated his earlier suggestion. "I meant what I said, Will. Give them the rest of the day off. Yourself too. You've earned a break. And unless I miss my guess, we're going to need all the rest we can get in the next few days."

32

It was a muted sound—surf on a beach a long way away, or maybe the rolling of distant thunder, Will thought. Except no thunder had ever sounded like this. This sound never seemed to start and never seemed to end. It just continued, over and over, repeating itself constantly.

And, gradually, growing louder. It was the sound of thousands of horses cantering slowly toward them.

Will flexed the string on his bow a couple of times, testing the feel and the tension. His eyes were fixed on the point where they all knew the Temujai army would appear—a kilometer away, where the narrow coastal strip between the hills and the sea jutted out in a promontory, temporarily blocking their view of the approaching army. His mouth was dry, he realized, as he tried, unsuccessfully, to swallow.

He reached down for the water skin that was hanging by his quiver and missed the first sight of the Temujai horsemen as they swept around the bend.

The men around him let out an involuntary cry. The horsemen rode stirrup to stirrup, in one long extended line, each horse cantering easily, matching the pace of the horse beside it.

"There must be thousands of them!" one of the archers said, and Will could hear the fear in his voice. It was echoed in another dozen places along the line. From the ranks of Skandian warriors beyond them, there was not a sound.

Now, above the dull rumble of the hooves, they could hear the jingle of harness as well, a lighter counterpoint to the rumbling hoof-beats. The horsemen came on, moving closer to the waiting ranks of silent Skandians. Then, at the single blaring note of a bugle, they reined in and came to a halt.

The silence, after the rumbling beat of their approach, was almost palpable.

Then a massive roar rose from the throats of the Skandian war-riors who stood by their defenses. A roar of defiance and challenge, accompanied by the ear-shattering clash of axes and broadswords on shields. Gradually, the sound died away. The Temujai sat their horses silently, staring at their enemies.

"Keep still!" Will called to his archers. Now that he saw the Temujai front rank, his force seemed ridiculously small. There must have been six or seven hundred warriors riding side by side in that first rank. And behind them were another five or six times that num-ber. At the center of the army, where the commander sat his horse, a sequence of colored signal flags waved. Others answered from posi-tions in the line of horsemen. There was another horn blast—a dif-ferent note this time—and the front rank began to walk their horses forward. The jingling of harness was apparent once more—then a massive metallic slithering sound filled the air and the weak sun gleamed on hundreds of saber blades as they were drawn.

"They're going to fight close in," Horace said softly beside him.

Will nodded. "Remember what Halt told us? Their first move will be a feint—an attack and then a false withdrawal to draw the Skandians out from behind their breastworks. They won't commit to their real attack until they have the Skandians strung out in pursuit."

The eighteen hundred Skandians were drawn up in three ranks on a narrow strip of flatland between the sea and the heavily timbered hills. They waited behind carefully constructed earthen breastworks. The sloping ramparts facing the Temujai were thick with sharpened stakes of various lengths, designed to impale the enemy's horses.

Halt had located their main defensive position at the spot where the strip was narrowest, with their flanks protected by the steep, wooded mountains on the left and the sea on the right. Hallasholm itself was barely two hundred meters behind their line. Will's force of archers were on an earthwork berm on the right, some meters behind the main defensive line. At the moment, earth-covered wicker ramparts kept the archers hidden as they crouched behind them.

Halt, Erak and Ragnak were in the command position, more or less in the center of the Skandian line, on a small knoll.

Now, more signal flags were seen and the advancing cavalry broke into a trot, beginning to wheel slightly toward the Skandian left flank.

There was a stir among the archers crouched behind the breastworks. Several of them reached for the arrow bins in front of them, instinctively feeling the need to arm themselves.

"Stay down!" Will called, wishing, as ever, that his voice wouldn't crack. Halt didn't want him revealing the presence of the archers until the Skandians had made several of their usual probing attacks.

"Wait till they're committed to a full attack, then we'll surprise them," he had told his apprentice.

The line of archers turned now to look at their young commander. Will forced himself to smile at them, then, feigning a casualness he certainly didn't feel, leaned his bow against the breastworks in front of him, signifying that there would be no action required of the archers for some time yet.

Some of the other men copied the action.

"Nice work," Horace said quietly beside him. "How can you stay so calm?"

"It helps if you're terrified," Will replied, speaking out of the corner of his mouth. He was surprised at the warrior apprentice's question. Horace himself seemed to be the epitome of calm, totally unworried and seemingly unconcerned. His next statement dispelled that idea.

"I know what you mean," he said. "I nearly dropped my sword when they rode around the bend there."

The Temujai charge was gathering pace now, breaking into a fast canter, then a gallop. As they neared the Skandian line, a major part of the force swung away, seemingly deterred by the fortifications and the sharpened stakes. They wheeled their horses to run parallel to the Skandian line for a few seconds, then began to curve back toward their own army. The Skandians yelled abuse and scorn at them. A shower of spears, rocks and other missiles erupted from the Skandian line. Most of them fell short of the galloping horsemen.

A smaller group, maybe less than a hundred, continued to close on the left wing of the Skandian line. Leaning forward in their stirrups, shouting their war cries, they forced their shaggy mounts up the earth breastworks, ignoring the screams of those horses who were struck by the stakes. About two-thirds of their numbers made it to the Skandian line and they leaned down from their saddles, striking left and right with their long, curved sabers.

The Skandian defenders joined the battle eagerly. Huge axes rose and fell and more horses came down, with tortured screams.

Will tried to shut his ears to the sound of horses in agony. The small, shaggy Temujai mounts were nearly identical to Tug and Abelard and it was all too easy to imagine his own horse bleeding and terrified, just as the Temujai horses were. Obviously, the Temujai thought of their horses as a means to an end, and had little affection for them.

The seething battle occupied one corner of the Skandian line. For some minutes, there seemed to be no clear picture of what was happening. Then, gradually, with cries of panic, the Temujai began to give ground, backing down the sloped earthworks, wheeling their horses and moving away, and letting the Skandians come after them with increasing eagerness.

Yet, to the more distant observers, it was obvious that the retreating enemy wasn't moving as fast as they might. Even those still mounted made no real effort to gallop clear. Rather, they withdrew gradually, maintaining contact with the foremost of their pursuers, drawing them farther and farther from the defensive positions they occupied and into the open ground.

"Look!" said Horace suddenly, pointing with his sword. In response to more flag signals, and unseen by the defenders on the left flank, several hundred riders from the original Temujai charge had now completed a full circle and were wheeling back to the aid of their embattled companions.

"Just as Halt said they would," Horace muttered, and Will nodded wordlessly.

In the command post near the center of the Skandian line, Erak was saying much the same thing.

"Here they come, Halt, just as you said," he muttered. Ragnak, standing beside him, peered anxiously over the breastworks at his exposed men. Nearly a hundred Skandians had streamed out of the defenses now and were engaged with the Temujai.

"You called it correctly, Ranger," he agreed. From this remote position, he could see the trap about to be sprung. Had he taken his normal place, at the thick of the fighting, he would have been totally unaware of the tactic.

"Can Kormak be trusted to keep his head out there, and not let his men get out of control?" Halt asked the Oberjarl. Ragnak scowled at the question.

"I'll kill him if he doesn't," he said simply. The Ranger raised one eyebrow.

"You won't have to," he said. Then, turning, he gestured to one of Ragnak's signalers, who stood nearby with a huge ram's horn in his hand. "Get ready," he said, and the man raised the horn to his lips, pursing his mouth to form the right shape to create the mournful but penetrating note.

It was a game of cat and mouse. The smaller group of Temujai were pretending to retreat, all the while managing to stay engaged with the leading elements of the pursuing Skandians. For their part, they were simulating a wild and undisciplined pursuit, and getting farther and farther from their own lines. And all the while, the first Temujai force were circling back to fall on the exposed Skandians.

There was only one more element in the game, which was unknown to the Temujai leaders. Before dawn, Halt had directed a hundred Skandian axmen to take up positions in the fringe of the wooded slope bordering the valley. Concealed in hastily dug shallow trenches and behind fallen logs, they waited now for the signal that would tell them to make a surprise attack on the Temujai who were planning to surprise their comrades.

"Signal one," Halt said quietly, and the ram's horn sounded a single, extended note that echoed across the valley.

Instantly, the pursuing Skandians, strung out in a long line behind the retreating Temujai riders, broke contact with the enemy and ran to form a defensive circle, their round shields forming an impenetrable wall. They were none too soon, as the second wave of Temujai horsemen was nearly upon them. As the eastern riders swept in, they were surprised to find an enemy already in a defensive formation and obviously awaiting them. The charge broke against the shield wall and another seething, struggling skirmish formed, with the hundred Skandians defending desperately against at least five times their number of horsemen.

Haz'kam, commanding general of the Temujai invasion force, frowned from his command position as he watched the well-rehearsed, coordinated movement of the Skandians as they formed their shield wall.

"I don't like the look of this," he muttered to his second in command. "This is not how these savages are supposed to react." And then the ram's horn rang out again, this time sounding three short, staccato notes that seemed to punch the air. A signal of some kind, he realized. But for what? And to whom?

The answer wasn't long in coming. There was a roar from the main Skandian ranks as a group of foot soldiers broke from the cover of the trees and ran to fall upon the encircling riders from the rear. The Skandian battle-axes took a terrible toll of the surprised Temujai, who found themselves suddenly and unexpectedly caught between the hammer of the new attacking force and the anvil of the shield wall. Surprised and confused, and with the momentum of their charge long since spent, the horsemen were easy marks for the savage northerners. In a matter of a few seconds, Haz'kam estimated that he had lost at least a quarter of his engaged force. It was time to cut his losses, he knew. He turned to his bugler.

"Retreat," he said quickly. "Disengage and retreat."

The silver notes of the bugle spilled over the battlefield, cutting through the consciousness of the highly disciplined Temujai cavalry. This time, as they withdrew, they made no pretense of staying in contact with the Skandians. Their rapid disengagement showed how false their previous feigned retreat had been. In a matter of a few minutes, the riders were streaming back toward their own lines.

For a moment, it looked as if discipline and reason had forsaken the Skandians. Ragnak realized that, in the heat of the moment, they were on the verge of pursuing the retreating Temujai back to their own lines—and to certain death for the Skandians. He quickly jumped up on the breastworks and bellowed, in his loudest storm-quelling voice: "Kormak! Back here! Now!"

There was no need for the ram's horn to reinforce the order. The Oberjarl's voice carried clearly to the Skandians and, as one, they ran for the shelter of the fortifications. Realizing what was happening, some of the Temujai sheathed their sabers and turned back to send a volley of arrows sailing after the Skandians.

But it was too little and too late. Apart from a few minor flesh wounds, there were no injuries.

Will and Horace exchanged glances. So far, things had gone pretty well as Halt had predicted. But they didn't think the Temujai would be trying that particular trick again.

"Next time," said Will, "it'll be our turn."

33

GENERAL HAZ'KAM TROTTED HIS HORSE ALONG THE FRONT rank of his army, watching as the first skirmish party made their way back to his lines. He had lost perhaps two hundred men, killed and wounded in that first encounter, he estimated. And perhaps half that number of horses. With an army of six thousand combat troops, of course, the numbers in themselves weren't terribly significant.

What was significant, however, was the behavior of the Skandians. That first attack had been designed to reduce *their* numbers by several hundred, not his own. In fact, there had even been the slight hope that the majority of the Skandians might have been drawn out from behind their defensive positions, into the exposed ground where they would have been easy meat for his mounted archers.

He reined in as he came level with a group of his officers. Among them, he recognized Colonel Bin'zak, his head of intelligence. The colonel was looking decidedly uncomfortable, he saw. As well he might be.

Haz'kam caught his eye now and jerked his head toward the Skandian defenses.

"That was not what I was led to expect," he said. His voice was deceptively mild. The colonel urged his own horse forward a few paces and saluted as he came level with his commander.

"I don't know what happened, Shan Haz'kam," he replied. "Somehow, they seemed to see through the trap. It's not the way I expected them to react. It's . . ." He searched for the right words, finally saying weakly, "It totally un-Skandian behavior."

Haz'kam nodded several times. He held in his anger with an effort. It was undignified for a Temujai commander to show emotion on the field of battle.

"Does it occur to you, perhaps," he said eventually, when he was sure he could keep control of his voice, "that the Skandians may have someone with them who knows our way of fighting?"

Bin'zak frowned as he turned this thought over. In truth, it hadn't occurred to him. But now that the Shan mentioned it, it seemed the logical conclusion. Except for one factor.

"It would be unlike the Skandians to give field command to a foreigner," he said thoughtfully. Haz'kam smiled at him. But it was a smile without the faintest touch of humor in it.

"It was unlike them to break off their pursuit, form a shield wall and then hit us with a surprise attack from the woods too," he pointed out. The colonel said nothing to that. The truth of the statement was self-evident.

"There have been reports," the Shan continued, "that a foreigner has been seen with the Skandians . . . one of those cursed Atabi."

Atabi, literally meaning "the green ones," was the Temujai term for Rangers. In the years since Halt had made his successful horse raid, the Temujai leaders had attempted to gather as much knowledge as they could about the mysterious force of men who wore green and gray cloaks and seemed to meld into the forest. In the past few years, in preparation for this campaign, spies had even reached as far as Araluen itself, asking questions and seeking answers. They had learned little. The Rangers guarded their secrets jealously and the ordinary Araluens were reluctant to discuss the Ranger Corps with foreigners. There was a strong undercurrent of belief among Araluens that Rangers dabbled in magic and the black arts. Nobody was too keen to discuss such matters.

Now, at this mention of an Atabi among the enemy, Colonel Bin'zak shrugged.

"They were rumors only, Shan," he protested. "None of my men could confirm the fact."

The general's gaze locked on his. "I think we've just had it confirmed," he said, holding the colonel's eyes until the officer looked down and away.

"Yes, Shan," he said bitterly. He knew his career was finished. Haz'kam now raised his voice, addressing the other officers gathered around and dismissing the matter of the disgraced intelligence colonel.

"It might also explain why our own planned surprise attack from the ocean failed to materialize," he said, and there were a few assenting grunts. The plot with Slagor had also been hatched by Bin'zak. Now, it seemed, the 150 men who had embarked on the Skandian ships four days ago had simply vanished into thin air.

The general came to a decision. "No more subterfuge. We've wasted enough time here. We've been delayed by three weeks already. Standard attack from now on: rolling arrow storm until we create a weakness, then we drive through their line."

His commanders nodded their assent. He looked around at them, seeing their determination, their grim confidence. The Temujai were about to do what they did best, using their mobility and the devastating force of their mounted archers to probe and weaken the enemy line. Then, when the moment was right, they would drive in with their sabers and lances and finish the job. There was no shouting of battle cries, no histrionics from these men.

This was a normal day at work for them.

"Give your orders," Haz'kam told them. "Watch for my commands."

He wheeled his horse, ready to ride back to the knoll where he had set up his command position. Already, signal flags were beginning to order the standard assault. A voice from behind made him pause.

"General!" It was Bin'zak. He had forsaken the social honorific of "Shan," Haz'kam noticed, and addressed him by his military title. The general faced his intelligence colonel now, waiting for his next words.

"Permission to ride with one of the Ulans, sir," Bin'zak said, his head held high. *Ulan* was the Temujai word for the formation of sixty riders that was the basic unit of the Temujai force. Haz'kam considered the request. Normally, field grade officers were kept out of the close contact part of battles. They had no need to prove their courage or dedication. The general finally nodded permission.

"Granted," he said, and spurred his horse back to the command position.

"Now what?" said Ragnak irritably as he watched the Temujai cavalry forming into groups.

Halt watched too, his eyes narrowed. "Now, I think, it's the end of the opening gambits. Now they're going to hit us in earnest." He pointed with his bow, sweeping it along the line of mounted horsemen facing them. "They'll fight in their Ulans, sixty men in each unit, hitting us all along the line and wheeling away before we can respond. The idea is to pick off as many of our men as possible with arrows before launching a concentrated attack at a selected spot."

"Which is where?" Erak asked. This tactical talk was making him increasingly cross. All he wanted was a dozen or so Temujai within reach of his ax. Now it appeared he would have to continue waiting for that eventuality.

Halt turned to the signaler with the horn.

"Give the 'ready' call for the archers," he said, and as the man blew a series of long short, long short notes, he replied to Erak's question: "Wherever their general decides they've created a weakness in our line."

"So what do we do while we're waiting for him to make up his mind?" Ragnak asked irritably. Halt grinned to himself. Patience certainly wasn't high on the Skandian list of virtues, he thought.

"We surprise them with our own archers," he said. "And we try to kill as many of them as we can before they become used to the fact that someone's shooting back at them."

All of Will's hundred archers heard the horn signal and there was an instant stirring among them. He held up a hand to calm them.

"Stay down!" he called. He took his time and was pleased that his voice didn't crack. Maybe that was the answer for the future, he thought. He climbed up on the raised step that had been built into his command position. Horace, his shield ready, stood beside him. The wicker breastworks still concealed the archers but, when the time came, they would be pushed aside and the shield bearers would have the responsibility of protecting them from the answering storm of arrows that the Temujai would send their way.

Below Horace and Will's more exposed position, protected by earthworks and a wicker overhang, Evanlyn crouched in her position, with a clear sight of the line of archers.

The assembled troops of horsemen began to move now, cantering slowly at first, then at increasing speed. Will could see that this time, each man was armed with a bow.

They thundered toward the Skandian line—not in one extended line as they had before, but in a dozen separate groups. Then, a hundred meters from the Skandians, each group wheeled so they were heading in a dozen different directions and sending volley after volley of arrows arcing up and over the Skandian lines.

Will drummed his fingers nervously on the breastworks before him. He wanted to see the Temujai pattern before he committed his men. The first surprise would have the maximum potential to disrupt the enemy and he wanted to make sure he didn't waste it.

Now there was a continuous rattle as the raised Skandian shields caught the majority of the arrows that the Temujai were pouring in. But not all. Men were falling along the Skandian lines and being dragged back out of the battle line by those behind them, who then stepped in to replace them. Now the second and third ranks of Skandians held their shields high, to protect them against plunging fire, while the front rank presented their shields to the more direct frontal fire.

It was an effective ploy. But it left the men blinded to the approach of the Temujai. Now, as Will watched, one group of sixty quickly slung their bows, drew sabers and darted into the Skandian line in a slashing attack, killing a dozen men before the Skandians even realized they were there. As the Skandians re-formed and moved to counterattack, the Temujai withdrew rapidly and another Ulan, waiting for this exact opportunity, poured a deadly hail of arrows into the disrupted shield wall.

"We'd better do something," Horace muttered. Will held his hand up for silence. The seemingly random movements of the Temujai Ulans actually had a complex pattern to them, and now that he had seen it, he could predict their movements.

The horsemen were wheeling again, galloping away from the Skandian line and back to re-form. Behind them, more than fifty Skandians lay dead, victims of either the arrows or the slashing Temujai sabers. Half a dozen Temujai bodies lay around the breastworks where the Ulans had made their lightning attack.

The Temujai riders were back in their own lines now. They would rest their horses, letting them recover their wind, while another ten Ulans took up the attack. It would be the same pattern, forcing the Skandians to cover up behind their shields, then attacking with sabers when they were blinded and, finally, pouring in volley after volley of arrows as their own men withdrew, leaving a gap in the shield wall. It was simple. It was effective. And there was a deadly inevitability about it.

Now the Ulans began their wheeling, galloping dance once again. Will fixed his attention on a troop at the middle of the line, knowing that it would curve and turn and eventually come at them on a diagonal. He muttered to Horace.

"Get those breastworks down."

He heard the muscular apprentice bellow: "Shields! Uncover!" The shield bearers rushed to shove the wicker walls down, leaving the archers behind a waist-high earth berm and with a clear field.

"Ready!" called Evanlyn, indicating that each man in the line of archers had an arrow nocked to the string. Then it was up to Will.

"Half left!" he called, and the archers all turned to the same direction.

"Position two!"

A hundred arms raised to the same angle as Will watched the approaching group of riders, seeing in his mind's eye the galloping Temujai and the flight of arrows converging to meet at the same point in time and space.

"Down a half . . . draw!"

The elevation corrected and one hundred arrows came back to full draw. He paused, counted to three to make sure he wasn't too soon, then yelled:

"Shoot!"

The slithering, hissing sound told him that the arrows were on their way. Already, the archers were reaching for their next shafts.

Horace, about to call for the shield bearers, waited. They were under no direct attack at the moment and there was no need to disrupt the sequence of shooting and reloading at this stage.

Then the first volley struck home.

Maybe it was luck. Maybe it was the result of the weeks of practice, hour after hour, but Will had directed that first volley almost perfectly. One hundred shafts arced down to meet the galloping Ulan and at least twenty of them found targets.

Men and horses screamed in pain as they crashed to the ground. And instantly, the disciplined, structured formation of the Ulan was shattered. Those who were unhurt by the arrows were confronted by their comrades and their horses tumbling and rolling headlong. And as each stricken man fell, he took another with him, or caused his neighbor to swerve violently, reining his horse in, sawing on the reins until the tight formation was a milling mass of plunging horses and men.

"Ready!" called Evanlyn. From her position, she couldn't see the result. Quickly, Will realized he had the chance now to deal a devastating blow to the enemy.

"Same target. Position two. Draw . . ." He heard the scrape of arrows against bows as the men drew back their right hands until the feathered ends of the shafts were just touching their cheeks.

"Shoot!"

Another volley hissed away at the tangle of men and horses. Already, Will was yelling for his men to reload. In their haste, some of them fumbled, dropping the arrows as they tried to nock them. Wisely, Evanlyn decided not to wait until they had recovered.

"Ready!" she called.

"Same target. Position two. Draw . . ."

They had the range and the direction now and the Temujai troop was stalled, caught in the one spot, losing their most valuable protection—their mobility.

"Shoot!" yelled Will, not caring that his voice cracked with excitement, and a third volley was on its way.

"Shields!" bellowed Horace, shoving his own shield forward to cover himself and his friend. He had seen that some of the other Ulans had finally noticed what was happening and were riding to return fire. A few seconds later, he felt the drumming of arrows against the shield, heard the rattle as they struck other shields along the line of archers.

There was no way that the Temujai could send a squad with sabers in toward the archers. Halt had placed Will and his men to one side and behind the Skandian main line of defense. To reach them, the Temujai would have to fight their way through the Skandian axmen.

The troop that Will had engaged had taken three carefully aimed volleys—nearly three hundred arrows—in quick succession. Barely ten men of the original Ulan remained alive. The bodies of the others littered the ground. Their riderless horses were galloping away, neighing in panic.

Now, as the other riders wheeled away toward their own lines, Will saw a further opportunity. Another two Ulans were riding in close proximity and still well within range.

"Shields down," he said to Horace, and the warrior passed the message along.

"Target: right front. And a half . . . Position three . . . draw . . ."
Again, he made himself wait, to be sure. "Shoot!"

The arrows, dark against the clean blue of the sky, arced after
the withdrawing cavalry.

"Shields!" Horace called as the arrows struck home and another
dozen or so Temujai tumbled from their saddles. Behind the shelter
of the big, rectangular shield, he and Will exchanged grins.

"I think that went rather well," said the apprentice Ranger.

"I think it went rather well indeed!" the apprentice warrior
agreed with him.

"Ready!" called Evanlyn once more, her gaze fixed on the archers
as they fitted arrows to their bowstrings. The call reminded Will, a
little belatedly, that she had no way of knowing how successful their
first action had been.

"Stand down!" Will called. There was no point keeping the
men tensed up while the Temujai were re-forming. He gestured to
Evanlyn.

"Come on up and see the results," he told her.

34

It took several minutes for the Temujai commander to realize that something had gone badly wrong—for the second time. There was a gap in his line as the riders returned, he realized. Then, as he cast his glance over the battlefield, he saw the tangled bodies of men and horses and frowned. He had been watching the overall action and had missed the four rapid volleys that had destroyed the Ulan.

He pointed with his lance at them. "What's happened there?" he demanded of his aides. But none of them had seen the destruction as it took place. His question was greeted with blank stares.

A single horseman was pounding toward them, calling his name.

"General Haz'kam! General!"

The man was swaying in the saddle and the front of his leather vest was slick with blood from several wounds. Blood stained the flanks of his horse as well, and the Temujai command staff were startled to see that the horse had been hit by at least three arrows.

Horse and rider skidded to a stop in front of the command position. For the horse, it was the final effort. Weakened by loss of blood, it sank slowly to its knees, then rolled over on its side, its injured rider only managing to escape being pinned at the last moment. Haz'kam frowned as he peered at the wounded man, then recognized Bin'zak, his former chief of intelligence. True to his word, the colonel had taken his place in the front line of one of the Ulans. It had been his incredible misfortune that he'd chosen the one destroyed by Will's archers.

"General," croaked the dying man. "They have archers . . ."

He staggered a few paces toward them and now they could see the broken-off stubs of arrows in two of his wounds. On the ground beside him, the horse heaved a gigantic, shuddering sigh and died.

"Archers . . ." he repeated, his voice barely audible, and he sank to his knees.

Haz'kam tore his gaze away from the stricken colonel and scanned the enemy ranks. There was no sign of archers there. The Skandians stretched in three ranks across the narrowest part of the valley, behind their earthworks. On the seaward side, and a little behind the main force, another group stood—also behind earthworks and holding large rectangular shields. But he could see no sign of archers.

There was one sure way to find them, he thought. He gestured toward his next ten Ulans.

"Attack," he said briefly, and the bugler sounded the call. Once more, the valley filled with the jingle of harness and the thunder of hooves as they drove forward.

In front of him, the colonel slumped forward, facedown in the sodden grass. Haz'kam made the Temujai gesture of salute, raising his left hand to his lips, then extending it out to the side in an elaborate, flowing movement. His staff did likewise. Bin'zak had redeemed himself, he thought. In the end, he had brought his general a vital piece of intelligence, even if it had cost him his own life.

✦   ✦   ✦

Will watched the approaching cavalry as, once again, they began their wheeling, circling dance. Horace stirred beside him, but some sense warned the young Ranger not to expose his men yet.

"Wait," he said quietly. He had half expected that a concerted attack would be launched toward their position, in an attempt to wipe them out. But this attack was like the previous one, launched along the entire front. That could mean only one thing: the Temujai leaders hadn't pinpointed the archers' position.

Arrows began falling on the Skandian lines and once more, the three ranks covered up with their shields. As before, a troop of Temujai broke off their maneuvering and drew sabers to launch a lightning attack on the unsighted Skandians. This time, however, Will was looking beyond them, to identify the support group who would open fire on the Skandians as their comrades withdrew. He saw them: a Ulan that had drawn to a halt some fifty meters from the Skandian front rank.

"Load!" Will yelled down his line. Then, in an aside to Horace: "Keep the shields up." He had felt the larger youth draw breath to call his next order. But Will wanted to keep his men hidden as long as possible.

"Ready!" Evanlyn called as the last arrow nocked onto the string.

"Face left half left again!" he called, and the archers, luckily, understood his meaning. As one, they all turned to face the direction he had picked. He had varied their drill by calling direction first but they seemed to understand what he wanted.

"Position three!" he yelled. The arms came up to maximum elevation, the hundred of them moving as one.

"Shields down," he muttered to Horace and heard him repeat the order.

"Draw!"

Beneath his breath, he told himself, "Count to three as each arm brings back its arrow to the full draw."

Then, aloud: "Shoot!" and instantly, he screamed: "Shields! Up shields!" As Horace took up the cry, the shields swung back into position to conceal the archers from return fire—and, hopefully, from observation.

Again the wait, then the volley of arrows slammed down into the Temujai Ulan, just as they were on the point of firing into the gap their comrades had forced in the shield wall. Once more, men and horses went down in screaming, tangled heaps. Grouped together as they were, and not moving, the Ulan made a perfect target for the massed arrows.

At least twenty of them were down, including their commander. Now their sergeants were yelling at the survivors to get moving. To get out of this killing ground.

Haz'kam never saw the volley that struck his men. But he did see, in his peripheral vision, the concerted movement of the hundred shields as they swung back and forth like so many gates opening and closing. A few seconds later, he saw one of his foremost Ulans collapse and disintegrate.

And then the shields moved again and he saw the archers. At least a hundred of them, he estimated, working smoothly and in unison as they launched another volley at the retreating Ulan that had attacked the Skandian line. The shields swung closed to cover the archers as more Temujai riders went down.

Again, the shields swung aside in unison, and this time he saw the solid flight of arrows, black against the sky, as they arced up and struck into another of his galloping Ulans. He turned and caught the eye of his third son, a captain on his staff. He pointed with his lance to the line of shields on the slight rise behind the Skandian ranks.

"There are their archers!" he said. "Take an Ulan and investigate. I want information."

The captain nodded, saluted and clapped spurs to the barrel-shaped body of his horse.

He was shouting commands to the leader of the nearest troop of sixty as he galloped down the front line of the Temujai army.

In their raised position behind the Skandian lines, Will and Horace were working smoothly together, pouring volley after volley into the wheeling riders. Inevitably now, they were beginning to take casualties as individual Temujai saw them and returned fire. But the shield drill worked smoothly and their improvised method of exposing the men to return fire for only a few seconds at a time was paying dividends.

What was more, the Skandians were beginning to see the effect of the disciplined, concentrated fire on their enemies. As each volley hissed down, as arrows found their marks and Temujai saddles emptied, the waiting axmen roared their approval.

For the first time, Will had seen the Kaijin sharpshooters attached to each Ulan as they attempted to take him and Horace under fire. He had just dueled with two of them and watched in satisfaction as the second slumped sideways out of his saddle. Horace nudged his arm and pointed.

"Look," he said, and Will, following the line he indicated, saw a Ulan galloping from the Temujai lines and heading straight for them. There was no wheeling and turning for these riders. They were coming straight on at a dead run. And it was obvious where they were heading.

"We've been spotted," he said. Then, calling to his men: "Face front half right. Load!"

Hands reached for arrows, nocked them firmly to strings.

"Ready!" That was Evanlyn once more. He grinned as he thought of how Halt had questioned the need for her to be here. Suddenly, he was glad the grizzled Ranger had lost that argument. He shook the thought aside, estimating the speed of the oncoming riders. Already, they were shooting, and arrows were rattling on the shields along the line. But all the advantages lay with Will and his men. Shooting from a stable, unmoving, elevated position, and from behind cover, they held the upper hand in any exchange.

"Position two!" he called. "Draw!"

"Shields down!" Horace yelled, giving Will just the right pause.

"Shoot!" shouted Will.

"Shields up!" roared Horace, covering his friend as he did so.

The archers were exposed to return fire for no more than a few seconds. Even so, under the constant barrage of arrows from the Temujai, they took a few casualties. Then their volley hit the on-rushing Ulan and wiped out the front rank of twelve, sending men and horses tumbling yet again. The riders in the following ranks tried to avoid their fallen comrades, but in vain. More horses came down; more riders tumbled out of their saddles. Some managed to leap their horses over the tangle of bodies and they were the ones who rode clear. As the others tried to reorganize, another volley, ten seconds behind the first, fell on them.

Haz'kam's son, with one arrow through his right thigh and another in the soft flesh between neck and shoulder, lay across the body of his horse. He watched as the shields opened and shut and the arrows poured out in a constant, disciplined stream. He saw the two heads moving in the fortified position at the end of the archer's line.

That was what his father needed to know. He watched as another two volleys hissed into the sky. Thankfully, these were directed at another Ulan as it galloped past. He could actually hear the commands as the two men in the command position called them. One of the voices sounded absurdly young.

It was growing dark early, he reflected, and promptly realized that it could be no later than midmorning. He craned painfully to look at the sky. But it was a brilliant blue and, with a sudden thrill of fear, he realized he was dying. He was dying, with urgent information that he must pass on to his father. Groaning in pain, he dragged himself to his feet and began to stumble back toward the Temujai lines, picking his way through the tangle of fallen bodies.

A riderless horse cantered past him and he tried to catch it but was too weak. Then he heard a thunder of hooves behind him and a strong hand gripped the back of his sheepskin jacket and hauled him up and over a saddlebow, where he gasped and moaned with the pain in his neck and leg.

He angled around to see his savior. It was a sergeant from one of the other Ulans.

"Take me . . . to General Haz'kam . . . urgent message," he managed to croak, and the sergeant, recognizing the staff insignia on his shoulders, nodded and wheeled his horse toward the command post.

Three minutes later, the mortally wounded captain told his father all that he had seen.

Four minutes later, he was dead.

35

From the central command position, Halt and Erak watched as the smooth drill of the archers caused havoc among the Temujai ranks. Now that the attacking force was aware of them, Will's men had no chance to repeat the devastating casualties of those first three volleys that had all but wiped out a complete Ulan. But the regular, massed fire of one hundred archers, and Will's accurate direction, was breaking up attack after attack.

In addition, the Temujai now realized that their own favorite tactic had been effectively countered. If they sent one group into close combat while another stood off to provide covering fire during the withdrawal, they knew that the second group would instantly come under fire from the archers on the Skandian right flank. It was a new experience for the Temujai. Never before had they encountered such disciplined and accurate return fire.

But they were no cowards, and some of the commanders were now substituting raw courage and ferocity for tactical ploys. They began to storm toward the Skandian line, abandoning their bows and drawing sabers, trying to break through in close-in fighting, determined to bury the Skandians under sheer numbers if necessary.

They were brave and skillful fighters, and against most adver-

saries they might have faced, their ploy would probably have suc-
ceeded. But the Skandians reveled in hand-to-hand fighting. To the
Temujai it was a matter of skill. To the northerners, it was a way
of life.

"This is more like it!" Erak bellowed cheerfully as he moved forward to intercept three Temujai scrambling over the earthen bulwark. Halt felt himself shoved to one side as Ragnak rushed to join
his comrade, his own battle-ax causing terrible havoc among the
small, stocky warriors who were swarming over their position.

Halt stood back a little, content to let the Skandians take on
the brunt of the hand-to-hand fighting. His gaze roamed outside
the area of immediate engagement until he saw what he was looking
for: one of the Temujai marksmen, recognizable by the red insignia
on his left shoulder, was searching the milling crowd of men for the
Skandian leaders. His eyes lit on Ragnak as the Oberjarl called more
of his men into the breach the Temujai had forced. The Temujai's
recurve bow came up, the arrow already sliding back to full draw.

But he was two seconds behind Halt's identical movement, and
the Ranger's huge longbow spat its black-painted shaft before the
Temujai had reached full draw. The rider never knew what hit him
as he tumbled backward over the withers of his horse.

Suddenly, the savage little battle was over and the surviving
Temujai were scrambling back down the earth slope, capturing any
horses they could and hauling themselves into the saddles.

Ragnak and Erak exchanged grins. Erak slapped Halt on the
back, sending him reeling.

"That's better," he said, and the Oberjarl growled agreement.
Halt picked himself up from the dirt.

"I'm so glad you're enjoying yourself," he said dryly. Erak
laughed, then became serious as he nodded his head toward the

right flank and the small group of archers, still pouring steady fire into the attackers.

"The boy has done well," he said. Halt was surprised to hear there was a note of pride in his voice.

"I knew he would," he replied quietly, then turned as Ragnak dropped a ponderous arm around his shoulders. He wished the Skandians didn't have to be quite so touchy-feely in expressing their feelings. Built the way they were, they put normal people at risk of serious damage.

"I've got to admit it, Ranger, you were right," the Oberjarl said. He swept his arm around the fortifications. "All of this, I didn't think it was necessary. But I can see now that we would never have stood a chance against those devils in an open conflict. As for your boy and his archers," he continued, gesturing toward Will's position, "I'm glad we looked after him when we first caught him."

Erak raised one eyebrow at that. It had caused him considerable anger that Will had been assigned to the freezing conditions of labor in the yard—an assignment that should have meant almost certain death. He said nothing, however. He assumed that being supreme leader gave one a license to forget uncomfortable events from the past.

Halt was studying Will's position with a critical eye. The defensive line in front of the archers was still well manned. Of all the Skandian positions, it seemed to have suffered the lowest number of casualties. Obviously, he thought, the Ulans were avoiding direct confrontation at that point. They'd seen what had happened to the troop that had charged directly at the archers.

But he knew that the Temujai general couldn't allow this situation to continue. He was losing too many men—both to the constant volleys of arrows and in the desperate hand-to-hand fighting with the Skandians. Soon, he would have to do something to nullify the unexpected problem posed by the archers.

He would have been interested, but not surprised, to know that Haz'kam's thoughts were running on pretty much the same lines.

The general cursed softly as he studied the casualty reports brought in by his staff.

He turned to Nit'zak, his deputy commander, and indicated the sheet of parchment in his hand.

"We cannot go on like this," he said softly. His deputy leaned toward him, turning the sheet of hastily scribbled casualty figures so that he could read it. He shrugged.

"It's bad," he agreed. "But not disastrous. We still have the numbers to defeat them, archers or no archers. They can't stand against us indefinitely."

But Haz'kam shook his head impatiently. Nit'zak had just confirmed what he had always suspected. His deputy was a capable leader in the field, but he lacked the overview necessary to make him a commanding general.

"Nit'zak, we've lost almost fifteen hundred men—either killed or wounded. That's nearly a quarter of our effective force. We could easily lose that many again if we keep on like this."

Nit'zak shrugged. Like most Temujai senior officers, he cared little for the size of his casualty reports, as long as he won the battle. If Temujai warriors died in battle, he thought, that was their role in life. Haz'kam saw the gesture and correctly interpreted the thinking behind it.

"We're two thousand kilometers from home," he told his deputy. "We are supposed to be subjugating this frozen little corner of hell so that we can mount an invasion of the Ara-land. How do you propose that we do that with less than half the force we started with?"

Again, Nit'zak shrugged. He really didn't see the problem. He was accustomed to victory after victory and the idea of defeat never occurred to him.

"We knew we'd take casualties here," he protested, and Haz'kam let go a string of curses in an unaccustomed display of temperament.

"We thought this would be a *skirmish*!" he spat angrily. "Not a major engagement! Think about it, Nit'zak: a victory here could cost us so much that we might not even make it home again."

That was the uncomfortable truth. The Temujai had two thousand kilometers to cover before they reached their homeland on the steppes once more. And all two thousand were across hostile, temporarily conquered territories—territories whose inhabitants might welcome the opportunity to rise up against a weakened Temujai force.

Nit'zak sat his horse in silence. He was angry at the tone of rebuke in his commander's voice, particularly in front of the other staff officers. It was a gross breach of Temujai behavior for Haz'kam to speak to him in such a fashion.

"So . . . what do you propose?" he asked finally.

For a long time, the general didn't answer. He gazed across the intervening space to the Skandian lines, looking from the command position in the center to the line of archers drawn up on his left— the Skandian right wing. Those two positions, he knew, held the key to this battle.

Finally, he turned to his deputy, his mind made up.

"Strip the first fifty Ulans of their Kaijin," he ordered. "And assemble them here as a special force. It's time we got rid of those damned archers."

36

"HERE THEY COME AGAIN," HORACE SAID, AND WILL AND
Evanlyn both turned to look toward the Temujai forces. The riders
were cantering forward again, and this time it looked like a major attack. Haz'kam had committed nearly two thousand men to a frontal
assault on the Skandian lines. They rode forward, their hoofbeats
echoing in the valley, formed in a wedge shape that was aimed at
the Skandian center and the command post where Halt, Erak and
Ragnak directed the Skandian defense.

Will and Evanlyn had taken advantage of the lull in the fighting to take a quick bite to eat, and a welcome drink of water. Will's
throat was parched, from both the tension and the nonstop shouting of orders. He guessed Evanlyn felt the same. Horace, who had
already eaten, had been keeping watch. Now, at his call, Evanlyn
slipped down into her sheltered position and the archers, who had
been sprawled comfortably against the earthworks, came to their
feet, bows in hand. The shield bearers, who had also been relaxing,
took their positions beside them.

Silently, they waited. In the lull, the arrow bin in front of each
archer had been replenished with new shafts. Even now, the women

of Hallasholm were gathered in the Great Hall, making fresh arrows for the battle.

Will studied the mass of riders. He had seventy-five archers still standing in the line, several of them lightly wounded. They had lost eleven men, killed by Temujai arrows, and a further fourteen had been wounded too seriously to continue fighting. As the Temujai force advanced, Will estimated that he could manage four volleys before they reached the Skandian line. Maybe five. That would be three hundred arrows raining down on the tightly packed mass of horsemen, and in that formation, the incidence of hits would be high. If Will aimed for the center of the mass, even his undershoots and overshoots would be effective.

"Left front, position three!" he called, and the machine swung into action again.

"Ready!" called Evanlyn.

"Draw . . . shoot!" shouted Will. He gestured for Horace not to call the shields into position. As yet, they were not under attack. The more time he had to do damage to that mass of Temujai horsemen, the better chance he would give Halt and Erak to repel the Temujai's main thrust.

"Reload!" he called, and waited for Evanlyn's call once more. When it came, he sent another volley on its way. As it started its upward trajectory, the first volley came down and he saw horsemen falling once again.

"Left half left!" he called, swinging the aiming point to match the progress of the horsemen as they moved from right to left across his front. He called the elevation again, shortening this time, then another seventy-five shafts soared away with that now-familiar slithering sound of arrows scraping across bows. Now the horsemen were galloping and he adjusted the angle once more.

"Left left! Position two," he called. Evanlyn's call told him that the men had reloaded.

"Draw . . . shoot!"

And now he heard the first sounds of close combat as the leading ranks of horsemen made contact with the Skandian lines. It would be too risky to try to shoot into the Temujai front ranks now, but he could still interdict the ranks behind them.

"Left half left!" he called, and the archers swung their aim point back to the right by twenty degrees. Then suddenly, the air around him was alive with the hissing sound of arrows and all along the line his archers were falling, some crying out in pain and shock and others, more ominously, silent.

"Shields! Shields!" Horace was yelling and the shield bearers moved into position—but not before more archers went down. Desperately, Will swung around and saw, for the first time, the smaller group that had moved forward to attack his position while he had been busy engaging the main force. There were about fifty archers, he estimated, all mounted, pouring steady, accurate shots into his position. Behind them rode another, larger group armed with lance and saber.

"Target front!" he called, and muttered an aside to Horace: "Be quick with those shields when we need them."

The warrior apprentice nodded, watching anxiously as the fifty riders continued to shoot. Now arrows were thudding into his own shield, and into the earth rampart in front of them.

"Position one!" Will called. This was straight and level—point-blank range. "Draw!"

"Ready!" he heard Evanlyn call. Then Horace yelled for the shields to open and Will, almost on top of him, called for the release.

As the volley hissed on its way, Horace was already calling for the shields to come back into position again. But even in that short time, another half dozen of their men went down to the Temujai arrows.

Now Will noticed the red insignia on the Temujai shoulders and he realized why the standard of enemy archery had picked up in accuracy and rate of fire.

"They're all Kaijin!" he said to Horace. As he spoke, he raised his own bow and, shooting rapidly, emptied three saddles before Horace dragged him behind the shelter of his shield again. Half a dozen shafts slammed into it as he did so.

"Are you mad?" Horace cried, but Will's eyes were wild with pain as he looked up at his friend.

"They're killing my men!" he replied, and went to lunge out into the open once more, obsessed with the idea of stopping the Temujai specialists from picking his men off one at a time. Horace's big hand stopped him.

"It won't help if they kill you!" he yelled and, slowly, the sense of it all sank into Will's brain.

"Ready!" called Evanlyn. He realized that it was the third time she had given the call. She was prompting him to action. Still covered by Horace's shield, he assessed the position.

The lancers and swordsmen, unhampered by any harassing fire from the archers, were already closing with the Skandians in front of his position. Hand-to-hand fighting was breaking out along the line. Farther to his left, the main body of Temujai were engaged in a savage battle with the center of the Skandian line. The position was too confused to see who was winning if, indeed, anyone was.

Meanwhile, to his front, the Temujai marksmen, gathered by Haz'kam into a special unit, were cantering parallel to the Skandian defensive line, widely dispersed so as not to offer a massed target to his volleys, and engaging his archers with accurate, aimed shots as they were exposed. He knew that if he attempted to direct another volley at the Temujai, he would lose half his men in the exchange. There was only one solution now, he realized. He leaned over his parapet, yelling to the line of archers below him—a line that was now severely depleted, he saw.

"Individual shots!" he yelled, pointing to the cantering lines of Temujai Kaijin. "Shoot whenever you're ready and aim for their bowmen!"

It was the best he could do. At least this way the Temujai would not be presented with an open line of shields as his men fired. They would have to react to individuals firing irregularly. It would give his men a better chance of survival. It would also lessen the effectiveness of their shooting, he knew. Without central direction, their accuracy would fall away.

There was, however, one more thing he could do. He glanced down to make sure that the arrow bin in front of him was fully charged and quickly plucked four shafts out, nocking one and holding the others ready between the fingers of his bow hand.

"Keep that shield up and ready," he said to Horace, and stepped forward to the parapet, still concealed by his friend's large shield. He took a deep breath, then stood clear and let the four shafts go in rapid succession, spinning back behind the cover of the shield as the first Temujai shafts whistled around their ears in reply. Horace, watching, saw two of the shooters go down to Will's arrows. A third took an arrow in the fleshy part of his calf and the fourth arrow missed entirely. He whistled in admiration. It was remarkable shooting. He was about to say something to that effect when he noticed the look of total concentration on his friend's face and decided to say nothing. Again, Will took a deep breath, nocking another arrow, then spun out into the open, loosed again and lunged back into cover.

Now Horace began to truly appreciate the uncanny accuracy that had been drilled into his friend in the woods and fields around Castle Redmont, as Will spun in and out of cover, loosing off shots—sometimes one, sometimes two or three—and hitting mark after mark. The other archers in the Skandian force added their contributions as well, but none of them possessed the speed and accuracy of the apprentice Ranger. And as more of them were struck by counterfire from the patrolling Kaijin, the survivors became more and more nervous and arrow-shy, more likely to shoot without aiming, then dive back behind cover again.

"Change sides," Will ordered him briefly, gesturing for Horace, who had been standing to his left, to step across to the right. Horace shifted the shield to his right arm and Will ducked below the breastworks level and moved to Horace's left side. He had been varying his shooting pattern, sometimes shooting just one arrow, and at others letting go a rapid volley, to keep the Temujai guessing. Now he decided that they were accustomed to seeing him appearing to the right of the big shield. He selected another four arrows and stepped to his left, shooting as he came clear. Two more saddles emptied and he darted back into cover again. The change in sides had worked for him. Not a single arrow had come near him in reply.

He stepped left again, snapped off another shot and then, not knowing what instinct prompted him do it, dropped immediately to his hands and knees behind the earthworks. A vicious hiss split the air directly above him as he did so and he felt his mouth go dry with fear. Horace, seeing him drop, thought he was hit and went to his knees beside him.

"Are you all right?" he asked urgently. Will tried a weak grin but didn't really think it came off.

"I'm fine," he managed to croak around the dryness in his mouth. "Just scared to death is all."

They stood again, sheltering behind the shield and feeling the rattle of Temujai arrows against it. Will realized that the pattern had changed once more and the majority of the Temujai archers were concentrating on his position. It was a chance for his men to release another massed volley, he realized. But if the Temujai saw or heard him preparing them for it, the element of surprise would be lost.

"Evanlyn!" he called to the girl, sheltering in her covered position below him. She glanced up at him, a question in her eyes, and he continued: "Relay my directions! We'll get in another volley!"

She waved her hand, indicating that she understood.

Unwittingly, as they had concentrated on his position, trying to hit the elusive figure who darted in and out of cover and peppered them with a deadly hail of arrows, the enemy had begun to bunch up. There had been little in the way of effective fire from the other archers for some minutes now and the Kaijin had all moved toward the command position to get a shot at Will.

"Front right!" he called softly, and heard Evanlyn relay the order. Nothing happened for a moment or so, then he heard her berating the men below her, shaming them into compliance. Gradually, one after another, they turned to face the direction she had given them.

"Ready," she called back, and he gave her the elevation: position one. The bows came up to the horizontal, then steadied.

"Draw," he said, and heard the order relayed once more. Then, taking a deep breath, he yelled: "Shields down! Shoot!"

And a fraction of a second after, as the volley was still on its way, he heard Horace call: "Shields up!"

Realizing that attention would be focused for some seconds on the line of archers, Will darted into the clear and poured arrow after arrow into the Temujai ranks. His archers' volley struck home— he had less than fifty men firing now, but still a mass of arrows slammed into the Temujai riders, sending a dozen of them sprawling into the dust. Then another five went down under the hail of arrows that Will had let loose before Horace, diving at him, dragged him below the level of the earthworks before the Temujai arrows could find him.

A storm of arrows thudded into the earthworks behind them. Horace rolled clear of his friend, dusting the dirt from his knees and elbows.

"Do you have a death wish?" he asked. Will grinned at him.

"I'm just relying on your judgment," he replied. "I can't keep track of everything in my head."

They stood behind the shield again and saw that the Kaijin, what remained of them, were edging away to longer range. They still fired at the Skandian ranks, but with far less effect than before. Will frowned as he assessed angles and positions, then pointed to the center of the Skandian line, where the main battle was still raging.

"We can start shooting volleys again," he told Horace. "If the shield bearers shift their shields to their right arms, and our archers stand to their left, they'll be covered from return shots."

Horace studied the position and nodded agreement. The remaining Kaijin were directly to their front now, so that the line of archers could shoot diagonally toward the rear of the main Skandian army without having to move from behind the cover of the shields.

Hastily, they called their idea down to Evanlyn, who relayed the directions to the men. The depleted line of archers looked at their young commander and nodded their understanding. Then a thought occurred to him.

"Evanlyn!" he called, and she looked up at him, her eyes questioning. "Once we've started, you call the volleys. Keep them at position three and just keep them shooting. I'll keep those damned Kaijin honest."

She grinned at him and waved a hand in reply. There would be no need to change angle or elevation once they began. The plunging volleys would be directed at the mass of the Temujai rear ranks. It might give Halt, Erak and Ragnak the respite they needed.

"Face half left!" called Will. "Position three!"

The forty-odd remaining men brought their bows to maximum elevation.

"Draw . . . shoot!"

He waited this time to assess the effect of the volley, making sure the men's angle and elevation were correct. He saw arrows striking the support ranks of Temujai, saw the panic caused by the suddenly renewed arrow storm.

"Keep them shooting!" he called to Evanlyn.

He turned and shot at the thin line of Temujai shooters, drawing a brisk shower of arrows in return. Behind him, he heard the thrumming noise of another volley arcing away toward the main battle. He shot again, picking a target and seeing him fall. Then he felt a surge of excitement in his chest as the small group of riders began to move.

"Horace! They're pulling back!" he yelled excitedly. He pointed wildly to the line of shooters. Less than twenty of them remained and they were gradually falling back from their exposed position. Gradually at first, anyway—as they moved farther, they moved faster and faster, none of them wanting to be the last one exposed to the accurate shots from the Skandian lines.

He gripped his big friend's arm and shook him with excitement. "They're turning it in!" he yelled. Horace nodded soberly, jerking his thumb toward the hard-pressed line of Skandian defenders below them.

"Just as well they are," he said. "Because these ones aren't."

Below them, the Temujai swordsmen, dismounted now, were pouring through a gap they had forced in the Skandian lines.

37

Nit'zak, field commander of the Temujai force attacking Will's position, had poured his men into the attack with reckless disregard. As the Kaijin engaged the archers, his lancers and swordsmen hurled themselves against the line of Skandian axmen protecting them.

Nit'zak had sensed that this attack was a final throw of the dice for his commander. If they couldn't break through this time, he knew Haz'kam would order a general withdrawal, unwilling to take further casualties in this campaign. The thought of withdrawal, of failure, was anathema to Nit'zak. He urged his men on now, willing them to break through the Skandian line and destroy the small but highly effective force of archers who sheltered behind it.

The ground in front of the Skandian defenses was littered with the bodies of his men and horses. But gradually, they were driving the wild northerners back as their numbers were depleted and the defensive line became more fragile. Dismounted now, the Temujai swarmed up the earth slope, slashing and stabbing with their long-bladed sabers. Grimly, the Skandians fought back.

"General!" One of his staff grabbed his arm and pointed to a small group of riders angling away from the battle. "The Kaijin are withdrawing."

Nit'zak cursed them as they rode away. Pampered and privileged, he thought. He knew they regarded themselves as elite members of the Temujai force. Kaijin shooters were excused the dangers of direct combat so they could sit back and pick off enemy commanders in relative safety. Now, faced with accurate and deadly return shooting for the first time in their lives, they had broken and deserted him. He made a vow that he would see them all die for their cowardice.

But that would have to wait. Now, he realized, the Skandian archers were launching flight after flight of arrows into the rear ranks of the main attack once more. They had to be stopped. The sudden resumption of the deadly volleys could well tip the balance of the battle.

Haz'kam had remarked that his deputy had no sense of the bigger picture when it came to warfare. But Nit'zak had an ability that made him a superb tactical commander. He could sense the crucial moment in a battle—the moment when everything hung in the balance and a determined effort from either side could make the difference between victory and defeat. He sensed such a moment now, watching his men struggling with the Skandians, seeing, for the first time, an element of uncertainty in the enemy. He drew his saber from its scabbard and turned to his own personal bodyguard, a half-Ulan of thirty seasoned troopers.

"Come on!" he yelled, and led them in a charge toward the Skandian line.

Nit'zak's instincts were accurate. The Skandians, exhausted and bleeding, their numbers depleted, were hanging on with their last reserves of strength and will. The Temujai numbers seemed neverending. For every one who fell before the Skandian axes, it seemed another two rushed to fill his place, screaming their war cries and slashing and stabbing with their sabers. Now, as a fresh force drove into the line, dismounting and scrambling up the earth berm, the balance tipped. First one, then another Skandian gave way. Then they were retreating in groups, as the Temujai drove through the gap they had finally forced, striking down the fleeing Skandians as they tried to escape.

Nit'zak waved his saber toward the line of archers, still pouring volley after volley at the main attack.

"The archers! Kill the archers!" he ordered his men, and started toward them.

In the command position, Horace threw down the bulky, clumsy shield he had been using and grabbed up his own round buckler. His sword slid from its sheath with an expectant hiss as he swung his legs over the parapet.

"Stay here," he told Will, then headed down the slope to meet the first group of Temujai as they clambered up toward him. Now it was Will's turn to watch in awe as his friend went on the attack. His sword moved in bewildering patterns, flicking in and out, overhead, backhand, forehand, thrust, as he cut down the attackers. The first attack was driven back and now a larger group of Temujai moved toward the tall warrior. Again there was the clash of steel on steel, but now, as they threatened to encircle him, Horace was forced to give ground. Will looked down at his arrow bin. There were five arrows left and he began shooting: steady, deliberate shots to pick off the Temujai who tried to surround his friend.

He glanced toward the archers. The shield bearers had grabbed up their own weapons and were moving to protect them. In addition, some of the retreating Skandians had regrouped at the archers' position. Evanlyn was still calling the volleys, he noticed.

"Keep it up!" he yelled, and she glanced around, nodded and turned back to her task.

Horace was almost back to the elevated command position now, still fighting off the determined attacks from the Temujai. He was fighting alone, however, and vulnerable from the rear. Will, his stock of arrows finally exhausted, drew his two knives and moved to protect his friend's back.

In the center of the Skandian line, Erak sensed a similar moment of opportunity. The Temujai were fighting hard, but the savage intensity had gone from their attacks.

Weakened and demoralized by the regular downpour of arrows from the right flank, their support ranks were withdrawing, and leaving those troops engaged with the Skandian line without the regular reinforcements that they needed to maintain the rhythm of their attack.

He cut down a Temujai captain who had come screaming over the earthworks, and turned to look for Halt. The Ranger was positioned behind him, standing on a parapet and coolly picking off the Temujai as they came forward.

Haz'kam's tactic of stripping his Ulans of their shooters was working against the Temujai here. For a change, it was they who were losing their commanders to accurate, aimed shots, while the Skandian leaders continued to devastate anyone who came within range of their whirling axes.

Disengaging himself, Erak vaulted up beside Halt. He gestured to the Skandian left wing, so far uncommitted.

"I'm thinking if we hit them from the flank, we might finish them," he said. Halt considered the idea for a moment. It was a risk. But battles were won by taking risks, he knew. Or lost. He came to a decision.

"Do it," he agreed, and Erak nodded. Then he looked beyond Halt and cursed. The Ranger swung around to look in the same direction and together they watched the Temujai breaking through the line below Will's position. They both knew that if the rain of arrows stopped, the Temujai rear ranks might well recover their cohesion and their moment might be lost.

Now was the time to act.

"Bring the left flank in," Halt said briefly. He grabbed up a spare quiver of arrows and started to run toward Will's command post. Erak watched him go, knowing that one man wouldn't make any difference. He looked around desperately, his gaze lighting on Ragnak, standing in the middle of a circle of fallen Temujai. The Oberjarl's eyes were wild and staring. He had discarded his shield and was swinging his massive ax two-handed. Blood streamed from half a dozen wounds on his body, but he seemed oblivious. He was on the point of berserking, Erak knew. And he also knew that one man like that might make all the difference in the world.

Erak cut his way through to the Oberjarl, winning a brief respite as the Temujai fell back from the two huge warriors. Ragnak looked up, recognized him and showed his teeth in a triumphant, savage grin.

"We're destroying them, Erak!" he yelled, his eyes still wild. Erak grabbed him by the arm, shaking him to make him focus his attention.

"I'm bringing in the left flank!" he yelled, and the Oberjarl smiled and shrugged.

"Good! Let them have some fun too!" he bellowed. Erak pointed to the battle raging on the seaward side.

"The right wing is in trouble. They've broken through. The Ranger needs help there."

It seemed odd to be giving orders to his supreme commander.

But then he realized Ragnak was incapable of directing the flank attack in this state. He was good for only one thing—a devastating, crushing attack on any enemy who stood in his way.

Now, as he heard Erak's words, Ragnak nodded repeatedly.

"That sarcastic little know-all needs help, does he? Then I'm his man!"

And with a roar, he charged off after Halt, followed by his retinue of a dozen axmen.

Erak breathed a quick prayer to the Vallas. A dozen men might not be a lot, but with Ragnak in this near-berserk mode, it could be enough. Then he shoved the troubles of the right flank to the back of his mind and began yelling for a messenger. The right flank would have to look after itself for a few more minutes. Right now, he needed the left flank to hit the enemy from the side.

38

Horace sensed the presence of someone directly behind him and pivoted rapidly, his sword swinging back, ready to cut side-handed. Seeing the slightly built form of his friend there, grimly engaging a Temujai swordsman with his two knives, he widened his stroke and laid open the Tem'uj's forehead with the point of his sword. The trooper staggered away, hands to his face, sinking to his knees.

"What do you think you're up to?" Horace yelled, in between parrying another attack from the front.

"I'm watching your back," Will told him, as he blocked a thrust from another Tem'uj trying to take Horace from the rear.

"Well, next time let me know," Horace said, grunting as he side-stepped a lance and hammered the hilt of his sword into its surprised owner's skull. "I nearly cut you in half just then!"

"There won't be a next time," Will replied. "I'm not enjoying myself here."

Horace flicked a rapid glance over his shoulder. Will was using the Ranger's double-knife defense to parry and block the Tem'uj's saber. But it wasn't a form of fighting he was particularly skilled in. Besides, it had been over a year since he and Horace had practiced the moves in the hills of Celtica. The Temujai swordsman was having the better of the exchange and in that quick glance, Horace had seen blood seeping through the left arm of Will's shirt.

"When I tell you, drop to your knees," Horace said.

"Fine," Will replied grimly. "I may even do it before you give the word."

In spite of himself, Horace grinned. Then, as he drove two attackers back, he called over his shoulder: "Now!"

He sensed that Will had dropped to the ground and, flicking the sword into a reversed grip, he thrust backward and heard a startled cry.

"You all right?" he called, reversing the sword again and deflecting that persistent lance once more. For a moment, there was no answer, and he felt a sudden jolt of fear that he had just stabbed his friend. Then Will answered him.

"Very impressive. Where did you learn that?"

"Made it up just now," Horace said, then grunted in satisfaction as the lancer stepped a little too close and took the point of his sword in the shoulder. As the man sank to the ground, Horace withdrew the sword, flicking it into a whirling overhand cut at another Tem'uj. The cavalryman's thick felt helmet saved his life as the sword crashed down on it. But there was still enough force in the blow to knock him to his knees, concussed and cross-eyed.

For a moment, they had a brief respite. Horace stepped back and studied his friend.

"Is that arm troubling you?" He nodded toward the widening seep of blood on Will's sleeve. Looking down, Will seemed to notice it for the first time.

"I didn't even feel it," he said in some surprise. Horace allowed himself a grim smile.

"You will later," he told him. Will shook his head doubtfully.

"If there is a later," he said. Then, from the lines behind them, they heard the thrum of bowstrings and the hissing flight of another volley. They looked at one another in amazement.

"It's Evanlyn," said Will. "She's still got them firing!"

Horace gestured to the swarming Temujai, surrounding the thin line of defenders who were keeping them out of the archer's redoubt.

"She won't for much longer," he said. The Skandian line was already beginning to buckle. "Come on! Watch my back and yell if you get in trouble." And with that, he bounded down the slope, his sword rising and falling as he drove his attack into the rear of the Temujai. Startled at the ferocity of his assault, they gave ground for a few seconds. Then, seeing that the new assault consisted of only two men—one of them armed only with knives and small enough to be a boy—they rallied and drove forward again.

Horace fought grimly, gathering the few remaining defenders around him. But the enemy numbers were beginning to tell and now individual Temujai were bypassing the small knot of defenders and dropping into the trench itself, where the archers were still sending their volleys into the main Temujai force.

The two boys heard Evanlyn's voice raised in urgent tones as she directed some of the archers to fire point-blank at the attackers. They knew it was a matter of minutes before the Temujai overran the trench and killed everyone in it.

"Come on!" said Will, leading the way toward the trench. Horace followed close behind him.

A Temujai warrior barred his way and he struck at the man with his saxe knife, feeling the blow jar all the way up his arm as it struck home. A warning cry from Horace alerted him to danger and he turned just in time to block a savage saber cut with his crossed knives. Then Horace was by his side, slashing at the man who had attacked him, and the three others with him. The two friends fought side by side, but there were too many of the Temujai. Will's heart sank as he realized that they were not going to reach the trench in time. He could see Evanlyn, not twenty meters away, with a group of archers around her, facing a still larger group of Temujai as they advanced up the trench—moving slowly, held back only by the threat of the bows.

"Look out, Will!" It was Horace again, and once more they were fighting for their lives as more of the Temujai swarmed toward them.

Nit'zak led a party of men into the trenches that had sheltered the Skandian archers. His other men could take care of the two young warriors who had counterattacked so effectively. His task was to silence the archers once and for all.

His men poured into the trench behind him, striking out at the unarmored, virtually unarmed bowmen. They retreated down the line of the earthworks, some of them scrambling up and over and running to the rear. Grimly, Nit'zak followed until, rounding an angle in the trench, he stopped in surprise.

There was a young girl facing him, a long dagger in her hand and a look of total defiance in her eyes. The remaining archers gathered protectively around her. Then, on her command, they brought their bows up to the present position.

The two groups faced each other. There were at least ten bows aimed at him, Nit'zak saw—at a range of barely ten meters. If the girl gave the order, there was no way the archers could miss. Yet, once that first volley was released, the girl and her archers would be helpless.

He flicked his eyes sideways. His men were level with him, and there were more behind. He had no intention of dying under the

Skandian volley. If it might serve a purpose, he would do so willingly. But he had a job to do and he didn't have the right to die until that job was done. On the other hand, he had no qualms about sacrificing ten or twelve of his own men, if necessary, to get that job done. He gestured them forward.

"Attack," he said calmly, and his men surged forward in the constricted space of the trench.

There was a second's hesitation, then he heard the girl's command to shoot and the instant thrum of the bowstrings. The arrows tore into his men, killing or wounding seven of them. But the others kept on, joined by more men from behind him, and the archers broke and ran, leaving only the girl to face him. Nit'zak stepped forward, raising the saber in both hands. Curious, he studied her eyes for some sign of fear and saw none there. It would be almost a shame to kill one so brave, he thought.

Off to one side, he heard an agonized cry—a young man's voice that broke with fear and pain.

"Evanlyn!"

He assumed it must be the girl's name. He saw her eyes flick away from his, and then she smiled sadly at someone out of his view. It was a smile of farewell.

Will had witnessed it all. Helpless to intervene, fighting desperately to protect Horace's back and his own life, he had seen the Temujai move up the trench, saw the archers threaten them with a point-blank volley, and then watched, horrified, as the Temujai calmly moved forward once more, oblivious to the danger. The final volley stopped them for a second or two, then they charged, sweeping the archers away before them.

Horace's urgent warning brought him back to his own situation and he darted sideways to avoid a saber, jabbing with the saxe to drive the off-balance Tem'uj back a few paces. He turned to look again and saw a Temujai officer poised over Evanlyn, his sword held in two hands as he raised it.

"Evanlyn!" he cried in torment. And, hearing him, she turned, met his agonized gaze and smiled at him—a smile that remembered all they had been through together in the past eleven months.

A smile that remembered all they had ever meant to each other.

And in that moment, he knew he couldn't let her die. He spun the saxe knife in his hand, catching it by the point and feeling the balance, then brought his arm back, then forward in one fluid movement.

The big knife took Nit'zak under the left arm just before he began his downward cut.

His eyes glazed and he crumpled slowly to one side, lurching against the earth wall of the trench, then sliding down to the hard-packed earthen floor. The saber fell from his hands and he plucked with weakened fingers at the heavy knife in his side. His last thought was that now Haz'kam would probably abandon the invasion after all, and he was angry about that.

Will, now unarmed except for his small throwing knife, was under attack once more. He leapt forward to grapple with a Tem'uj and they rolled down the earthen slope together, with Will clinging desperately to the man's sword arm, while he, in his turn, tried to avoid the ineffectual slashing attacks Will made with the small knife.

He saw Horace overwhelmed by four warriors attacking him at once and he realized that, finally, it was all over.

And then he heard a blood-chilling roar and a huge figure was standing over him, literally plucking his adversary from the ground and throwing him a dozen meters down the slope, to send another three men sprawling under the impact.

It was Ragnak, terrifying in his berserker rage. His shirt had been torn to ribbons and he wore no armor save his massive horned helmet. The horrifying roaring noise came constantly from his throat as he plunged into the midst of the Temujai attackers, the huge double-bladed ax whirling in giant circles as he struck his enemies down on either side.

He made no effort to protect himself and he was cut and wounded over and again. He simply ignored the fact and cut and hacked and beat at the men who had invaded his country—who had dared to awaken the berserker rage in his blood.

His personal guard followed him, each man in the same awful killing rage. They drove a wedge into the Temujai force, implacable, irresistible. A dozen men who didn't care if they lived or died. Who cared about one thing and one thing only: getting close to their enemies and killing them. As many as possible. As quickly as possible.

"Horace!" Will croaked, and tried to scramble to his feet, remembering that last image of Horace desperately holding off four attackers. And then he heard another sound—a familiar one this time. It was the deep-throated thrum of a longbow. As he watched, Horace's attackers seemed to fade away like snow in the sunshine, and he knew that Halt had arrived.

On a knoll a kilometer away, Haz'kam, general of the army and Shan of the People, watched his attack fail. The enemy's left flank had curled around to crash into his main force, buckling them and driving them back, causing severe losses. On the enemy's right flank, Nit'zak and his men had finally managed to silence the Skandian archers. In his heart, he had always known that his old friend would succeed in the task.

But he had taken too long over it. The success had come too late, after his main force had been demoralized and disorganized by the constant hail of arrows. After they had been driven back in confusion by that flanking attack.

It was just one failed attack, of course, and he knew he could still win this battle, if he chose to. He could regroup his Ulans, commit his fresh reserves to drive these damned Skandians out from behind their defenses and send them scattering into the hills and the trees. For a moment, he was tempted to do it—to have a savage revenge on these people who had thwarted his plans.

But the cost would be too high. He had lost thousands of men already and another attack, even a successful one, would cost him more than he could afford. He turned in his saddle and beckoned the bugler forward.

"Sound the general withdrawal," he said calmly. His face gave no hint of the seething fury, the bitter rage of failure that burned in his heart.

It was not polite for a Temujai general to allow his emotions to show.

39

Ragnak's body was cremated the day after the battle. The Oberjarl had died in the final moments, before the Temujai had begun their withdrawal. He had died battling a group of eighteen Temujai warriors. Two of them survived—so badly injured they could barely crawl away from the terrifying figure of the Skandian leader.

There was no way of knowing who had struck the fatal blow, if, indeed, there had been one. They counted over fifty separate wounds on the Oberjarl, half a dozen of which could have caused death under ordinary conditions. As was the Skandian custom, the body was laid on his cremation pyre as it was—without any attempt to clean away the blood or the mire of battle.

The four Araluens were invited to pay their last respects to the dead Oberjarl and they stood silently for a few moments before the massive pile of pitch-soaked pine logs, gazing up at the still figure. Then, politely but firmly, they were informed that the funeral of an Oberjarl, and the subsequent election of his successor, was a matter for Skandians only and they returned to Halt's apartment to await events.

The funeral rituals went on for three days. This was a tradition that had been established to allow jarls from outlying settlements time to reach Hallasholm and participate in the election of the next Oberjarl. Obviously, there were few jarls expected from the areas that the Temujai had already passed through, and the majority of the others had already been summoned to repel the invasion. But tradition called for a three-day period of mourning—which, in Skandia, took the form of a lot of drinking and much enthusiastic recounting of the deceased's prowess in battle.

And tradition, of course, was sacred to the Skandians—particularly tradition that involved a lot of drinking and carousing late into the night. It was noticeable that the amount of liquor consumed and the degree of enthusiasm in the recounting of Ragnak's prowess seemed to be in direct correlation.

On the second night, Evanlyn frowned at the sound of drunken voices raised in song, counterpointed by the splintering sounds of furniture breaking as a fight got under way.

"They don't seem very sad about it," she pointed out, and Halt merely shrugged.

"It's their way," he said. "Besides, Ragnak died in battle, as a berserker, and that's a fate that every true Skandian would envy. It gains him instant entry to the highest level of their version of heaven."

Evanlyn twisted her mouth in a disapproving pout. "Still," she said, "it seems so disrespectful. And he did save our lives, after all."

There was an awkward silence in the room. None of the other three could think of a tactful way of pointing out that had Ragnak survived, he was sworn to kill Evanlyn.

Finally, the period of mourning was over, and the senior jarls gathered in the Great Hall to elect their new Oberjarl. Will said hopefully, "Do you think Erak has a chance?" But Halt shook his head.

"He's a popular war leader, but he's only one of four or five. Add to that the fact that he's no administrator. And he's certainly no diplomat either," he added with some feeling.

"Is that important?" Horace asked. "From what I've seen, diplomacy is very low on the list of required skills in this country."

Halt acknowledged the point with a nod. "True," he admitted. "But a certain amount of buttering up is necessary when there's an election among peers like this. Nobody gives their vote because you're the best candidate. They vote for you because you can do something for them."

"I guess the fact that Erak's spent the last few years as Ragnak's chief tax collector isn't going to help either," Will chipped in. "After all, a lot of the people voting are the ones he's threatened to brain with an ax."

Again Halt nodded. "Not a good career move if you hope to be Oberjarl one day."

In truth, the Ranger was indulging in a mild form of personal superstition by talking down Erak's chances in the election. There were still issues to be settled between Skandia and Araluen and he would have preferred to be settling them with Erak as the Skandian supreme leader. Still, the more they talked, the slimmer Erak's chances became. He hadn't known about the tax collecting until Will mentioned it. That would seem to put the final stopper on the jarl's chances.

"He probably wouldn't make a good Oberjarl anyway," Horace decided. "What he really wants to do is get back to sea in his wolfship and go raiding somewhere."

The others agreed with this statement. It was reasonable and logical.

But reason and logic have little to do with politics. On the fifth day, a stunned-looking Erak stepped into Halt's apartment. He looked around at the four expectant faces and said:

"I'm the new Oberjarl."

"I knew it," said Halt instantly, and the other three looked at him, totally scandalized.

"You did?" Erak asked, his voice hollow, his eyes still showing the shock of his sudden elevation to the highest office in Skandia.

"Of course," said the Ranger, shrugging. "You're big, mean and ugly and those seem to be the qualities Skandians value most."

Erak drew himself up to his full height, trying to muster the sort of dignity that he felt an Oberjarl should assume.

"Is that how you Araluens speak to an Oberjarl?" he asked, and Halt finally grinned.

"No. That's how we speak to a friend. Come in and have a drink."

Over the next few days, it began to appear as if the council of jarls had chosen wisely. Erak quickly moved to end old feuds with other jarls, particularly those he had visited in his role as tax collector. And, surprisingly, he kept Borsa in the role of hilfmann.

"I thought he couldn't stand Borsa," Will said, puzzled. But Halt merely nodded his head in acknowledgment of Erak's choice.

"Borsa's a good administrator, and that's what Erak's going to need. A good leader is someone who knows what he's bad at, and hires someone who's good at it to take care of it for him."

Will, Horace and Evanlyn had to think that through for a few seconds before they saw the logic in it. Horace, in fact, was still pondering it some time after the others had nodded and moved on to discuss other matters.

As Oberjarl, Erak would no longer be able to go on his annual raiding cruises at the helm of *Wolfwind*, and that fact tinged his sudden elevation with a certain amount of regret. But he announced that he would be making one last voyage before he handed the ship over to the care of Svengal, his longtime first mate.

"I'll be taking you lot back to Araluen," he announced. "Seems only fair, since I was the one responsible for your being here in the first place."

Will was quietly pleased with the news. Now that the time was almost here to return home, he realized that he would be sad to fare-well the big, boisterous pirate. With some surprise, he recognized the fact that he had come to regard Erak as a good friend. Anything that delayed the moment of parting found favor in his eyes.

Spring had come, the geese were returning from the south and there were deer back in the hills, so there was plenty of fresh meat in place of the dried and salted provisions that had formed the bulk of the winter fare in Hallasholm.

When he saw the first hunting parties returning from the high reaches inland of the Skandian capital, Will remembered one debt he still owed. Early one morning, he slipped quietly away on Tug and headed up the trail that he and Evanlyn had followed so many months ago, in a freezing blizzard.

At the little cabin where they had sheltered through the winter, he found the uncomplaining, shaggy little pony who had saved his life. The patient creature had broken the light tether holding him in the lean-to stable behind the cabin, and was quietly cropping the new season's grass in the clearing when Will arrived.

Tug looked a little askance at his master when Will unfastened a small sack of oats, indicating that it was for the pony alone. Will consoled his horse with a quiet pat on the muzzle.

"He's earned it," he told Tug, and the Ranger horse shrugged—insofar as any horse is capable of shrugging. The nondescript pony may well have earned the sack of oats, but that didn't stop Tug's mouth from salivating at the sight and smell of them. When the pony had finished the oats, Will remounted Tug and, holding on to the lead rein, rode back down to Hallasholm, where he quietly returned the pony to Erak's stable.

The night before they were due to leave, Erak threw a farewell banquet in their honor. The Skandians were eager to show their appreciation of the efforts of the four Araluens in defending their land against the invaders. And with the shadow of the Vallasvow lifted from Evanlyn, they paid particular attention to her—repeatedly toasting her bravery and resourcefulness in continuing to direct the fire of the archers as their position was being overrun.

Halt, Borsa and Erak sat in a quiet huddle at the head table, discussing outstanding matters such as the repatriation of the slaves who had served in the archers' corps. Sadly, many of them hadn't survived the battle, but the promise of freedom had been made to their dependants as well, and the details had to be thrashed out. When the subject was finally closed, Halt judged the moment right and said quietly:

"So what will you do when the Temujai come back?"

There was a deafening moment of silence at the head table. Erak pushed his bench back and stared at the small, grim-faced man next to him.

"Come back? Why should they come back? We beat them, didn't we?"

But Halt shook his head slowly. "As a matter of fact," he said, "we didn't. We simply made it too costly for them to continue—this time."

Erak thought about what he had said and glanced at Borsa for his opinion. The hilfmann nodded, a little reluctantly.

"I think the Ranger is right, Oberjarl," he admitted. "We couldn't have held out much longer." Then he shifted his eyes to Halt's and asked him: "But why should they come back?"

Halt took a sip of the rich Skandian beer before he answered. "Because it's their way," he answered simply. "The Temujai don't think in terms of this season or this year, or next year. They think of the next ten or twenty years and they have a long-term plan to dominate this part of the world. They need your ships. So they'll be back."

Erak considered the point, twisting one end of his mustache in his fingers. "Then we'll beat them off again," he said.

"Without archers?" Halt asked quietly. "And without the element of surprise next time?"

Again there was a silence. Then Erak said, half hopefully, "You could help us train archers. You and the boy?" But Halt shook his head immediately. And very definitely.

"I'm not prepared to provide Skandia with such a potent weapon," he said. "Once you learned those skills, I'd never know when they might be turned against us in the future."

Erak had to admit the logic in the Ranger's statement. Skandia and Araluen were traditional enemies, after all. But Borsa, with his negotiator's ear, had caught an overtone in Halt's refusal.

"But you do have a suggestion?" he said keenly, and Halt almost smiled at him. He'd hoped the hilfmann would see where he was heading.

"I was thinking," he said, "that a force of, say, three hundred trained archers might be stationed here on a regular basis. They could spend the months of spring and summer here, then be rotated back home during the winter."

"Araluens?" Erak said, beginning to catch on. Halt nodded.

"We could supply you with an archery force that way. But if it

ever came to hostilities between our countries, I'd feel a lot more secure knowing you wouldn't be turning them against us. We'd need
to stipulate that in the treaty," he added casually.

Erak looked cautiously at his hilfmann now. The word *treaty*
seemed to have appeared on the table in front of them without his
seeing it arriving. Borsa caught his eye and shrugged thoughtfully.

"I'm proposing that we have a mutual defense treaty for a period
of . . ." Halt seemed to think and Erak suddenly had the distinct impression that he had weighed every word he was going to say well in
advance of this moment. "Five years, let's say. You get a viable force
of archers—"

Erak decided it was time that someone else made the running.
"And you get what?" he asked abruptly.

Halt smiled at him. "We get a peace treaty that says Skandia
won't be launching any surprise attacks on our country during that
period. And that in the event that hostilities become inevitable, our
archers would be allowed free passage back home."

Erak shook his head abruptly. "I'll never convince my men not
to raid," he said indignantly. "I'd be thrown out on my ear if I pro-
posed that." But Halt held up a hand to calm him down.

"I'm not talking about individual raids," he said. "We can cope
with them. I'm saying no more massed attacks, like the one with
Morgarath."

There was another long pause while Erak considered the offer.
The more he thought about it, the more attractive the idea seemed.
As well as any of them, he knew how close they had come to being
overwhelmed by the Temujai. Three hundred trained archers would
provide a powerful defensive force to Skandia, particularly if they
were deployed in the narrow passes and twisting defiles at the border. He realized, with a shock, that he was beginning to think like

a tactician. Maybe he'd been spending too much time around the Ranger, he thought.

"You have the authority to sign a treaty like that?" he asked, and for the first time, Halt hesitated. In fact, he had no authority at all. As a member of the Rangers, he would have been empowered to sign, but he had been dismissed from the Corps when Duncan had banished him. He could brazen it out now, of course. He was reasonably sure that Crowley or Duncan himself would ratify such a treaty. But when that happened, Erak would know that he had acted falsely and he didn't think that was a good start to any relationship.

"I have," said a quiet voice from behind him, and the three men looked up in some surprise. Evanlyn, slipping away from the enthusiastic toasting and tributes, had been an interested audience to their conversation for the past few minutes.

"As Princess Royal of Araluen, I have authority to sign on my father's behalf," she told them, and Halt heaved an unseen sigh of relief.

"I think it's best if we do it that way," he said. "After all, the princess does outrank me, just a little."

40

~~~~~~~~~~~~~~~~~~~~~

WOLFWIND FOLLOWED THE RIVER SEMATH ALL THE WAY FROM the Narrow Sea to Castle Araluen itself. It was an astounding sight for the locals, to see a wolfship gliding, unmolested and peaceful, past their fields and villages, so far inland. The many river forts and strongpoints, which would normally have denied such progress to a Skandian ship, now deferred to the fact that Princess Cassandra's personal standard, a stooping red hawk, flew from the masthead. A message had been sent ahead of the wolfship's progress to make sure that local commanders recognized the standard and the fact that the voyagers traveled upriver in peace.

It was also something of a novelty for Erak and his crew.

Finally, they rounded the last bend in the river and there before them were the soaring spires and turrets of Castle Araluen. Erak drew breath in wonder at the sight of it. Halt, watching him, was sure that, as well as the sheer admiration the castle inspired, Erak's old plundering instincts were at work, estimating just how much treasure the castle could contain. He stepped close to the Oberjarl and said softly:

"You'd never make it past the moat."

Erak started in surprise and looked at the Ranger.

"How did you know what I was thinking?" he asked. Halt raised an eyebrow.

"You're a Skandian," he said.

There was a landing stage jutting out into the river, bedecked with flags and bunting. And a large crowd was awaiting their arrival. At the sight of the wolfship, they began sounding horns and cheering.

"That's a first," Erak said mildly, bringing a grin to Halt's face.

"And there's another," he said, pointing discreetly to a tall, bearded figure standing a little way back from the landing stage, surrounded by an expensively dressed retinue of knights and ladies. "That's the King himself, come down to welcome you, Erak."

"More likely he's here for his daughter," the Skandian replied. But Halt noticed that he did look a little pleased with himself.

Evanlyn had seen the tall man now and was standing in the prow of the wolfship, waving excitedly. The cheers from the shore redoubled at the sight of her and now Duncan was leading the way down the landing stage, lengthening his stride so that he was almost running, not content to stand back and preserve his royal dignity.

"Oars!" called Erak, and the rowers raised their oars, dripping, from the water as the wolfship glided smoothly alongside the landing stage.

The Skandian crew passed mooring lines to those on shore, the two parties regarding each other with deep interest. It was the first time in memory that Araluens and Skandians had been face-to-face without weapons in their hands. Will, his face alight with the joy of the moment, leapt onto the wolfship's railing as Evanlyn hurried to the entry port in the ship's waist. She and her father, their hearts too full for words, simply smiled at each other over the decreasing gap as the line handlers hauled the ship in to the landing stage. Then the wickerwork fenders bumped and groaned and the ship was fast alongside. Svengal, grinning broadly at her, unlatched the entry port in the ship's rail and she leapt into her father's arms, burying her face in his chest.

"Dad!" she cried once, her voice muffled by his shirt and by the sobs that welled up in her throat.

"Cassie!" he murmured—his pet name for her from when she was a toddler—and the cheering intensified. Duncan was a popular king and the people knew how much pain the loss of his daughter had caused him. Even the Skandians were grinning at the scene.

In the midst of all that joy and celebration, only Halt stood apart. His face was a mask of pain and misery and he remained unobtrusively by the steering oar at the stern of the ship as the others surged forward to the waist.

Duncan and Evanlyn—or Cassandra, as her father knew her—stood in each other's embrace, oblivious to those around them. Will, scanning the crowd, saw a heavily built form in the ranks behind the King: a middle-aged man who was waving enthusiastically at him, shouting his name.

"Will! Welcome home, boy! Welcome home!"

For a moment, Will was puzzled, then he recognized Baron Arald—a man who for years had been a stern-faced figure of authority. Now here he was, waving and yelling like a schoolboy on holiday. Will dropped lightly to the planks of the landing stage and made his way through the crowds of well-wishers to the Baron. He began to make a formal bow when the Baron grabbed his hand and started pumping it enthusiastically.

"Never mind that! Welcome home, lad! And well done! Well done! My god, I thought we'd never see you again! Wasn't that right, Rodney?"

He spoke this last to the mail-clad knight beside him and Will recognized Sir Rodney, head of the Battleschool at Castle Redmont.

He realized that the knight was anxiously scanning the faces on the deck of the wolfship.

"Yes, yes, my lord," he agreed distractedly. Then he seized Will's other arm and said urgently, "Will, I thought Horace was with you. Don't tell me something's happened to him?"

Puzzled, Will looked to where Horace was shaking hands with the Skandian crew, farewelling friends among them before he came ashore.

"That's him there." He pointed Horace out for Sir Rodney, and had the satisfaction of seeing the knight's jaw drop in surprise.

"My god! He's turned into a giant!" he gasped. Then Horace recognized his mentor and marched briskly through the crowd, coming to attention and saluting, his fist to his right breast.

"Apprentice Horace reporting, Battlemaster. Permission to return to duty, sir?" he said crisply.

Coming to attention himself, Rodney returned the salute.

"Permission granted, apprentice."

Then, formalities over, he seized the muscular apprentice in a bear hug and danced him around a few undignified steps, all the while crying:

"Damn me, boy, but you've done us all proud! And when the devil did you get so tall?"

Once again, the crowd cheered with delight. Then, all at once, a silence fell over them and Will turned to see the reason. Erak Starfollower, Oberjarl of the Skandians, was stepping ashore.

Instinctively, those nearest him drew back a little. Old habits died hard. Will, not wishing to see his friend insulted, started forward impulsively, but there was one other in the crowd who was quicker off the mark. Duncan, King of Araluen, stepped forward to greet his Skandian counterpart, his hand extended in friendship.

"Welcome to Araluen, Oberjarl," he said. "And thank you for

bringing my daughter safely home." And with that, the two leaders shook hands.

Then the cheering started again, this time for Erak and his crew so that the Skandians looked about them with delight. And that, thought Will, was going to make it a little harder for them to raid here again in the years to come. Duncan let the cheering go on for a little while, then held up his hand for silence. He scanned the faces on the dock. Then, not seeing the one he looked for, he let his gaze switch to the wolfship.

"Halt," he said softly, finally seeing him, wrapped as ever in his Ranger's cloak and standing alone by the great steering oar. The King held out a hand and gestured to the dock.

"Come ashore, Halt. You're home."

But Halt stood awkwardly, unable to mask the sadness that he felt. His voice broke as he began to speak, and he gathered himself and started again.

"Your ... your majesty, the year of banishment still has three weeks to run," he said at last.

A low buzz of comment ran through the crowd. Will, unable to restrain himself, reacted in total surprise.

"Banishment? You were banished?" he said incredulously. "Why?" he said. The word hung in the air. Duncan shook his head, dismissing the matter.

"A few incautious words, that was all. He was drunk and we've all forgotten what he said and I forgive him, so for god's sake, man, come ashore."

But Halt remained where he was. "Your majesty, nothing would make me happier. But you must uphold the law," he said in a low voice. Then another speaker chimed in: Lord Anthony, the King's chamberlain.

"Halt is right, your majesty," he said. Anthony was a well-meaning man, but he tended to be a little pedantic when it came to interpreting the law. "After all, he did say you were the issue of an encounter between your father and a traveling hatcha-hatcha dancer."

There was a gasp of horror from the crowd.

Duncan, smiling thinly, said through gritted teeth: "Thank you for reminding us all, Anthony."

But then a peal of helpless laughter rang out and Princess Cassandra doubled over, hooting in a most unroyal fashion. Every eye turned to her, and slowly, she recovered enough to speak.

"I'm so sorry, everyone. But if you ever knew my grandmother, you'd understand why my grandfather might have been tempted! Grandma had a face like a robber's dog—and a temperament to match it!"

"Cassie!" her father said in his most disapproving tone, but she was holding her sides and laughing again and he couldn't keep a smile from forming at his lips. Then he felt Lord Anthony's disapproving stare on him and he recovered, nudging Cassandra until her laughter subsided into a series of choked snuffles and snorts. The laughter had been infectious, however, and it took a while for the assembled crowd to come to order. Throughout all this, Halt remained standing stiffly on the deck of the wolfship.

Duncan turned to his chamberlain and said, in his most reasoning tone: "Surely, Anthony, it's within my powers to pardon Halt for the last three weeks of his sentence?"

But Anthony frowned and shook his head. "It would be most irregular, your majesty," he said heavily. "Such a thing would set unfortunate precedents in law."

"King Duncan!" boomed Erak, and instantly he had the attention of everyone there. He realized he'd spoken a little more forcibly than he'd intended—he was still getting the hang of these formal occasions. Now he continued at a more moderate level.

"Perhaps I could request that you grant this pardon—as a gesture of goodwill to seal the treaty between our two countries?"

"Good thinking!" muttered Duncan. He turned quickly to Lord Anthony. "Well?" he said. The chamberlain pursed his lips thoughtfully. It was never his wish to deny the King what he wanted. He merely tried to do his duty and uphold the law. Now he saw a loophole and seized upon it gratefully.

"Such a request wouldn't set any precedents, your majesty," he said. "And this is a very special occasion, after all."

"So be it!" said Duncan quickly, and turned to face the figure on the wolfship. "All right, Halt, you're pardoned—so for god's sake, come ashore and let's have a drink to celebrate!"

Halt, tears in his eyes, set foot on Araluen soil once more, after eleven months and five days of banishment. As he came ashore to the renewed cheers of the crowd, those around him saw another man dressed in a gray-green cloak, who slipped forward and pressed something into his hand.

"You might be needing this again," said Crowley, Commandant of the Ranger Corps.

And when Halt looked down, he saw a thin chain in his hand, with a silver oakleaf insignia on it.

And then he knew he was really home.

Something was afoot, Will knew. After the first round of celebrations, and after Erak and his crew had set sail once more for Skandia, with the administrative details of the Araluen archery force deployment agreed for the following spring, there had been much consultation and discussion between the King and his advisers, including Halt, Crowley, Baron Arald and Sir Rodney.

During this period, Will and Horace were left pretty much at a loose end, although there was no shortage of admirers who would greet them as friends and sit spellbound as they told the story of their time in Skandia and their fierce battle against the Temujai. But even such adulation palled after a while.

Horace, now that his adventures as the Oakleaf Knight were over, had reverted to the plain white surcoat of a warrior apprentice.

Evanlyn, of course, had reverted to her true identity as Princess Cassandra. She was whisked away to the royal family's apartments in one of the towers of Castle Araluen, and whenever Will saw her, she was surrounded by a retinue of knights and ladies-in-waiting. She was also, he realized, a beautiful young woman, immaculately dressed and at ease among the young nobles and ladies who surrounded her.

Saddened, he felt the distance between them growing wider as he came to terms with the fact that his companion through so many adventures and dangers was, in reality, the highest-born woman in the kingdom, whereas he was the orphan child of a sergeant in the army and his farm girl wife. On those increasingly rare occasions when he did speak to Cassandra, he became awkward and stilted. He was tongue-tied in her presence and tended to mumble formulaic replies to her attempts at conversation.

His reaction frustrated and infuriated Cassandra. She was making a genuine attempt to restore their friendship to its former basis, but she was too young to realize that all the trappings of royalty and wealth, things she took for granted and gave no account to, could only serve to distance Will from her.

"Doesn't he see that I'm the same person I always was?" she asked her mirror in frustration. But, in fact, she wasn't. Evanlyn had been a frightened girl, her life at constant risk, reliant for months on the wits and courage of her young companion to keep her safe. Then she in turn had become the savior, the one who nursed a confused, frightened boy back to health.

Cassandra, on the other hand, was a beautiful, perfectly groomed princess, whose station in life was so far above Will's as to be unattainable. One day, he realized, she would rule as Queen, in her father's place. It wasn't her personality that had changed. It was her position. And both she and Will were too young and inexperienced to overcome the inevitable strain that such a social gulf put upon their relationship.

Oddly enough, at the same time, she found herself becoming more closely aligned to Horace. Accustomed to the formality of life as an apprentice knight and the strictures and protocols of court life at Castle Redmont, Horace was unfazed by Cassandra's rank. Of course, he deferred to her and treated her with respect. But then, he always had done so. Horace's simplistic and uncomplicated approach to life led him to accept things as they were and not seek complications. Evanlyn had been his friend. Now, Princess Cassandra was too. There were certain differences in the way he might be expected to approach her and address her, but this sort of formality had been part of his training.

When she finally broached the subject of the widening gap between herself and Will, Horace merely counseled patience.

"He'll get used to the way things are," he told her. "He's a Ranger, after all, and they're sort of . . . different . . . in their ways. Give him time to adjust."

So Cassandra bided her time. But Horace's comment about Rangers stayed with her and she determined to do something about that situation.

And there was, she knew, a perfect opportunity for that in the very near future.

Duncan had declared a formal banquet to celebrate the safe return of his only daughter, and invitations had been carried to the fifty baronies in the kingdom. It would be a massive event.

It took a month for the invited guests to assemble, and then the immense dining hall in Castle Araluen saw an evening unrivaled since Duncan's coronation, twenty years prior.

The feasting went on for hours, with the castle servants laboring under trays of roasted meat, huge savory pastries, steaming fresh vegetables and confectioneries designed to dazzle the eyes as much as the taste. Master Chubb, the Kitchenmaster at Castle Redmont and one of the finest chefs in the kingdom, had traveled to the capital to oversee the affair. He stood in the kitchen doorway, watching in satisfaction as the nobles and their ladies devoured and destroyed the fruits of the kitchen staff's labors for the past week, and idly cracking his ladle on the head of any unwary waiter or kitchen worker who came within reach.

"Not bad, not bad," he muttered to himself, then directed another servant to take yet another special dish for the enjoyment of "young Ranger Will," as he termed him.

Eventually, the massive feast was over and the entertainment was due to begin. The King's harper was nervously tuning his strings—the heat of the packed dining hall had caused them to stretch unevenly—and mentally reviewing the lyrics to the heroic ode he had written, celebrating the rescue of the Princess Royal from the jaws of death by three of the kingdom's worthiest heroes. He was still wishing that he had managed a better rhyme for "Halt." The best he had come up with so far was to affirm that he was a man "well worth his salt," which seemed, in the face of things, to be underselling the value of the legendary Ranger.

Before he was called upon, however, King Duncan rose from his seat to address the huge crowd. As ever, the vigilant Lord Anthony was on hand, and at his monarch's signal, he pounded his steel-shod staff on the flagstones of the dining hall.

"Silence before the King!" he bellowed, and instantly, the babble of talk and laughter in the huge room fell away to nothing. All eyes turned expectantly to the top table.

"My lords and ladies," Duncan began, his deep voice carrying seemingly without effort to every corner of the hall, "this occasion is one of great pleasure for me. For a start, we are here to celebrate the safe return of my daughter, Princess Cassandra—an eventuality that brings me more joy than you could possibly comprehend."

The hall rang with cries of "Hear! Hear!" and enthusiastic applause.

"The other source of pleasure to me tonight is the opportunity to reward those who were responsible for her safe return."

This time, the applause was louder and more prolonged. The audience was delighted to see Cassandra safely back with her father. But they knew the main business of the evening was the rewarding of the three companions who had brought her there.

"First," said Duncan, "would the Ranger Halt please step forward."

There was a murmur of interest in the crowd as the slightly built figure, for once without the anonymity of his gray-and-green cloak, stood before the King. Several of those at the rear of the hall stood to get a better view. Halt's reputation was known throughout the kingdom, but relatively few of those present had ever seen him in the flesh. That was due in no small part to the Ranger predilection for secrecy, of course. Now there were more than a few expressions of surprise at the legendary Ranger's diminutive size. Most of those present had formed a mental picture of a longbow-wielding hero of majestic build who stood just under two meters high.

Now, he bowed his head to the King. Not for the first time, Duncan found himself studying the Ranger's shaggy, uneven haircut. It had obviously been recently trimmed in honor of the event, but Duncan couldn't help grinning. Halt had been at Castle Araluen for over a month, surrounded by servants, valets and, above all, skilled barbers. Yet apparently, he still chose to cut his own hair with his saxe knife. Duncan realized the crowd was waiting while he appraised Halt's tonsorial efforts. He gathered his thoughts and continued.

"Halt has already stated that his restoration to the ranks of the Ranger Corps is sufficient reward," Duncan said, and once again there was a murmur of surprise.

"As on so many occasions before this, I stand in debt of one of my most loyal officers and I accede to his wishes in this matter. Halt, I owe you more than any King ever owed a man. I will never forget all you have done."

And at that, Halt inclined his head once more and slipped back to his seat, moving so quickly and unobtrusively that most of those present didn't realize he was gone, and their startled applause died stillborn.

"Next," Duncan said, raising his voice slightly to still the buzz of conversation that had broken out, "let the warrior apprentice Horace stand forward."

Will slapped his friend on the back as Horace, an apprehensive look on his face, rose from his seat and moved forward to stand at attention before the King. The crowd waited expectantly.

"Horace," Duncan began, straight-faced but with a hint of laughter in his eyes, "it has come to our attention that you traveled

throughout Gallica in the guise of a fully qualified knight . . ." He
made a show of consulting a note on the table before him, then
added, "The *Chevalier de Feuille du Chêne*—the Oakleaf Knight."

Horace gulped nervously. He knew, of course, that the tale of
his exploits had been told. But he had hoped that officialdom would
turn a blind eye to the fact that he had no right to pose as a knight.

"Your majesty, I'm sorry . . . I sort of felt that it was necessary
at the . . ."

He realized that Duncan was eyeing him coolly, one eyebrow
raised, and then it dawned on him that he had committed a grave
breach of etiquette by interrupting the King. Belatedly, he stopped,
and came to attention once more as the King resumed.

"As you know, I'm sure, it is highly irregular for an apprentice
to bear an insignia or to pose as a knight, so now it is necessary that
we rectify this irregularity." He paused.

Horace was about to say, "Yes sir," then realized he'd be interrupting again and said nothing.

Duncan continued. "I've conferred with your Baron, your
Battlemaster and the Ranger Halt, and we all agree that the best
solution is to regularize the situation."

Horace wasn't sure what that meant, but it didn't sound good.
Duncan made a signal and Horace heard heavy footsteps approaching from behind. Glancing sideways, he saw Battlemaster Rodney
coming to a stop beside him, holding a sword and shield before him.
In a daze, Horace saw the device on the shield—a green oakleaf on
a field of white. He watched in awe as Duncan stepped down from
his dais, took the sword and touched him lightly on the shoulder
with it.

"Kneel," Rodney hissed out of the corner of his mouth, and
Horace did so, then heard the next words ringing in his ears.

"Arise, Sir Horace, Knight of the Oakleaf, and ensign in the Royal Guard of Araluen."

This caused bedlam in the crowd. It was virtually unheard of for an apprentice to be knighted in his second year and then to be appointed as an officer in the Royal Guard—the elite force who garrisoned Castle Araluen. The nobles and their ladies went wild with delight.

"Get up," Rodney hissed again. Slowly, a huge grin spreading over his face, Horace rose and took the sword from the King's hand.

"Well done, Horace," the King said quietly. "You've more than earned it."

Then he shook the hand of his newest knight and indicated that he might return to his seat. Horace did so, the faces around him in a blur. He saw only the huge, delighted grin on Will's face as his friend pounded him on the back in congratulation. Then the crowd was hushed again and this time both boys heard the King's voice:

"Would the Ranger apprentice Will stand forward."

Even though he had assumed that such a thing might happen, Will was caught unprepared. He hurried from his seat, stumbling as he went, and finally regained his balance to stand before the King.

"Will, your Ranger Corps have their own ways and their own regulations. I've spoken to your mentor, Halt, and to the Corps Commandant, and unfortunately it's beyond my power to rescind your period of training and declare you a fully qualified Ranger. Halt and Crowley insist that you must complete your full period of training and assessment."

Will swallowed nervously and nodded. He knew that. There was still so much he had to learn about his craft, so many skills he had to develop. Horace's natural talent was sufficient for the King to waive his further training. But Will knew that could never be the case for him.

"However," Duncan continued, "I can offer an alternative. It is within my power to appoint you as a lieutenant in the Royal Scouts. Your masters have agreed that you are totally qualified for such an appointment and will release you from your apprenticeship if that is your wish."

The assembled people gave one concerted gasp of surprise. Will was speechless. The Royal Scouts were an elite force of light cavalry, tasked with the responsibility of training the kingdom's archers and scouting ahead of the King's army in battle. Scout officers and recruits generally came from the ranks of the nobility and the appointment was virtually the equivalent of a knighthood.

It meant honor, prestige, rank and recognition, compared to another three years of grinding study and application as an apprentice.

And yet . . .

In his heart of hearts, Will knew it was not for him. It was tempting, to be sure. But he thought of the freedom of the green forests, of the days spent with Tug and Halt and Abelard, of the fascination of learning and perfecting new skills and the intrigue of always being at the heart of events. That was a Ranger's life, and when he compared it with the protocol and etiquette, the formality and restrictions of life in Castle Araluen, he knew, for the second time in the space of a few years, what he really wanted.

He turned to look for some hint of advice from Halt, but his master was sitting, eyes cast down to the table, as was Crowley, a few places away. Then, his voice seeming unnaturally loud in the expectant silence of the room, he replied:

"You do me great honor, your majesty. But my wish is to continue my training as an apprentice."

And now the babble of surprise rose to fever pitch in the room. Rangers were, as everyone agreed, different. And most people present simply could not understand Will's choice. Duncan, however, could. He gripped Will's shoulder and spoke to him alone.

"For what it's worth, Will, I think you've chosen wisely. And for your ears alone, your Craftmasters tell me that they believe you will be one of the greatest of the Rangers in the years to come."

Will's eyes widened. To him, that knowledge was sufficient reward. He shook his head.

"Not as great as Halt, surely, your majesty?"

The King smiled. "I'm not sure anyone could be that great, wouldn't you agree?"

And with his hand still on his shoulder, he turned the lad around, to where Crowley and Halt were smiling warmly at him, making a space between them for him. The applause as he sat down was polite but a little confused. Nobody could really understand Rangers, after all.

There was one small pang of sadness in Duncan's heart as he turned toward the place where his daughter was sitting. His lips were already forming the words "I tried," but when he looked, Cassandra was gone from the room.

Two days later, Will and Halt rode out from Castle Araluen, heading for the cottage by Castle Redmont. From time to time, Halt glanced fondly at his young friend. He knew Will had made a big decision and he knew his mind was troubled. He suspected it was to do with the Princess. Since the banquet, Will had tried to see her several times, to explain his decision. But she had been unavailable.

He sensed that Will wanted to be alone with his thoughts as they rode to the southwest, so he kept his peace, resolving to plunge the boy into a regimen of unremitting hard work and training that would give him no time to ponder his heartbreak.

Behind the riders, two figures on a terrace of the huge castle stood watching, dwarfed by the soaring turrets and buttresses. Evanlyn raised a hand in farewell and Horace put a comforting arm around her shoulders.

"He's a Ranger," the newly made knight told her sympathetically. "And people like us can never understand Rangers. There's always a part of them they keep to themselves."

She nodded, unable to speak. The early-morning mist that was cloaking the riders seemed to be thickening for a moment, then she blinked rapidly, and realized that it was tears misting her eyes. As they watched, the sun finally broke through and washed Castle Araluen in a pale golden light.

But Will was riding to the south, and he didn't notice.

Turn the page for a preview of

RANGER'S
APPRENTICE

BOOK FIVE: THE SORCERER OF THE NORTH

1

In the north, he knew, the early winter gales, driving the rain before them, would send the sea crashing against the shore, causing white clouds of spray to burst high into the air.

Here, in the southeastern corner of the kingdom, the only signs of approaching winter were the gentle puffs of steam that marked the breath of his two horses. The sky was clear blue, almost painfully so, and the sun was warm on his shoulders. He could have dozed off in the saddle, leaving Tug to pick his way along the road, but the years he had spent training and conditioning in a hard and unforgiving discipline would never allow such an indulgence.

Will's eyes moved constantly, searching left to right, right to left, close in and far ahead. An observer might never notice this constant movement—his head remained still. Again, that was his training: to see without being seen; to notice without being noticed. He knew this part of the kingdom was relatively untroubled. That was why he had been assigned to the Fief of Seacliff. After all, a brand-new, just-commissioned

Ranger was hardly going to be handed one of the kingdom's trouble spots. He smiled idly at the thought. The prospect of taking up his first solo posting was daunting enough without having to worry about invasion or insurrection. He would be content to find his feet here in this peaceful backwater.

The smile died on Will's lips as his keen eyes saw something in the middle distance, almost concealed by the long grass beside the road.

His outward bearing gave no sign that he had noticed anything out of the ordinary. He didn't stiffen in his seat or rise in the stirrups to look more closely, as the majority of people might have done. On the contrary, he appeared to slouch a little more in the saddle as he rode—seemingly disinterested in the world around him. But his eyes, hidden in the deep shadow under the hood of his cloak, probed urgently. Something had moved, he was sure. And now, in the long grass to one side of the road, he thought he could see a trace of black and white—colors that were totally out of place in the fading greens and new russets of autumn.

Nor was he the only one to sense something out of place. Tug's ears twitched once and he tossed his head, shaking his mane and letting loose a rumbling neigh that Will felt in the barrel-like chest as much as heard.

"I see it," he said quietly, letting the horse know that the warning was registered. Reassured by Will's low voice, Tug quieted, though his ears were still pricked and alert. The packhorse, ambling contentedly beside and behind them, showed no interest. But it was a transport animal pure and simple, not a Ranger-trained horse like Tug.

The long grass shivered once more. It was only a faint movement but there was no wind to cause it—as the hanging clouds of steam from the horses' breath clearly showed. Will shrugged his shoulders slightly, ensuring that his quiver was clear. His massive longbow lay across his knees, already strung. Rangers didn't travel with their bows slung across their shoulders. They carried them ready for instant use. Always.

His heart was beating slightly faster than normal. The movement in the grass was barely thirty meters away by now. He recalled Halt's teaching: Don't concentrate on the obvious. They may want you to miss something else.

He realized that his total attention had become focused on the long grass beside the road. Quickly, his eyes scanned left and right again, reaching out to the tree line some forty meters back from the road on either side. Perhaps there were men hiding in the shadows, ready to charge out while his attention was distracted by whatever it was that was lying in the grass at the road's edge. Robbers, outlaws, mercenaries, who knew?

But he could see no sign of men in the trees. He touched Tug with his knee and the horse stopped, the packhorse continuing a few paces before it followed suit. His right hand went unerringly to the quiver, selected an arrow and laid it on the bowstring in less than a second. He shrugged back the hood so that his head was bare. The longbow, the small

shaggy horse and the distinctive gray and green mottled cloak
would identify him as a Ranger to any observer, he knew.

"Who's there?" he called, raising the bow slightly, the
arrow nocked and ready. He didn't draw back yet. If there
was anyone skulking in the grass, they'd know that a Ranger
could draw, fire and hit his mark before they had gone two
paces.

No answer. Tug stood still, trained to be rock steady in
case his master had to shoot.

"Show yourself," Will called. "You in the black and white.
Show yourself."

The stray thought crossed his mind that only a few moments ago he had been daydreaming about this being a peaceful backwater. Now he was facing a possible ambush by an
unknown enemy.

"Last chance," he called. "Show yourself or I'll send an
arrow in your direction."

And then he heard it, possibly in response to his voice.
A low whimpering sound: the sound of a dog in pain. Tug
heard it too. His ears flicked back and forth and he snorted
uncertainly.

A dog? Will thought. A wild dog, perhaps, lying in wait
to attack? He discarded the idea almost as soon as it formed
in his mind. A wild dog wouldn't have made any sound to
warn him. Besides, the sound he had heard had been one of
pain, not a snarl or a warning growl of anger. It had been a
whimper. He came to a decision.

In one fluid movement, he removed his left foot from the stirrup, crossed his right leg over the saddle pommel and dropped lightly to the ground. Dismounting in that fashion, he remained at all times facing the direction of possible danger, with both hands free to shoot. Had the need arisen, he could have loosed his first shot as soon as his feet touched the ground.

Tug snorted again. In moments of uncertainty like this, Tug preferred to have Will safely in the saddle, where the little horse's quick reflexes and nimble feet could take him quickly out of danger.

"It's all right," Will told the horse briefly, and walked quietly forward, bow at the ready.

Ten meters. Eight. Five . . . he could see the black and white clearly now through the dry grass. And now, as he was closer, he saw something else in the black and white: the matted brown of dried blood and the rich red of fresh blood. The whimper came again and finally Will saw clearly what it was that had stopped them.

He turned and gave the "safe" hand signal to Tug, and the horse responded by trotting forward to join him. Then, setting the bow aside, Will knelt beside the wounded dog lying in the grass.

"What is it, boy?" he said gently. The dog turned its head at the sound of the voice, then whimpered again as Will touched it gently, his eyes running over the long, bleeding gash in its side, stretching from behind the right shoulder back to the rear haunch. As the animal moved, more fresh blood welled out of the wound. Will could see one eye as the dog lay, apparently exhausted, on its side. It was filled with pain.

It was a border shepherd, he realized, one of the sheepdogs bred in the northern border region, and known for their intelligence and loyalty. The body was black, with a pure white ruff at the throat and chest and a white tip to the bushy tail. The legs were white and the black fur repeated again at the dog's head, as if a cowl had been placed over it, so that the ears were black, while a white blaze ran up the muzzle and between the eyes.

The gash in the dog's side didn't appear to be too deep and the chances were that the ribcage had protected the dog's vital organs. But it was fearfully long and the wide-gaping edges were even, as if they had been cut by a blade. And it had bled a lot. That, he realized, would be the biggest problem. The dog was weak. It had lost a lot of blood. Perhaps too much.

Will rose and moved to his saddlebags, untying the medical kit that all Rangers carried. Tug eyed him curiously, satisfied now that the dog represented no threat. Will shrugged and gestured to the medical kit.

"It works for people," he said. "It should be all right for a dog."

He returned to the injured animal, touching its head softly. The dog tried to raise its head but he gently held it down, crooning encouraging words to it as he opened the medical pack with his free hand.

"Now let's take a look at what they've done to you, boy," he said.

The fur around the wound was matted with blood and he cleaned it as best he could with water from his canteen. Then he opened a small container and carefully smeared the paste it contained along the edges of the gash. The salve was a painkiller that would numb the wound so that he could clean it and bandage it without causing more pain to the dog.

He allowed a few minutes for the salve to take effect, then began applying an herbal preparation that would prevent infection from setting in and help the wound heal. The painkiller was working well and his ministrations seemed to be causing no problem for the dog, so he used it liberally. As he worked, he saw that he had misnamed the dog by calling it "boy." It was a female.

The border shepherd, sensing that Will was helping, lay still. Occasionally, she whimpered again. But not in pain. The sound was more a sound of gratitude. Will sat back on his haunches, head to one side as he surveyed the now cleaned injury. Fresh blood still seeped from the gash and he knew he would have to close it. Bandaging was hardly practical, however, with the thick fur of the dog and the awkward position of the gash. He shrugged, realizing that he would have to stitch it.

"Might as well get on with it while the salve's still working," he told the animal. She lay with her head on the ground, but one eye swiveled around to watch him as he worked.

The shepherd obviously felt the sensation of the needle as he quickly put in a dozen stitches of fine silk thread and drew the lips of the wound together. But there seemed to be no pain and, after an initial flinching reaction, she lay still and allowed him to continue.

Finished, Will rested one hand gently on the black-and-white head, feeling the softness of the thick fur. He had done his job well but it was obvious that the dog would be unable to walk.

"Stay here," he said softly. "Stay."

The dog lay obediently as he moved to the packhorse and began rearranging its load.

There were two long satchels, holding books and personal effects, on either side of the packsaddle. They left a depression between them and he found a spare cloak and several blankets to line the space until he had a soft, comfortable nest in which the dog could lie—with enough space for her to move a little, but snug enough to hold her securely in place.

Crossing back to where she lay, he slid his arms under the warm body and gently lifted her, talking all the time in a low crooning voice. The salve was effective but it didn't last long and he knew she would be hurting again soon. The dog whimpered once, then held her peace as he lifted her into position in the space he had prepared. Again, he fondled her head, scratching the ears gently. She moved her head slightly to lick his hand. The small movement seemed to exhaust her. He noted with interest that her eyes were two different colors.

Till this moment, he had seen only the left eye, the brown one, as the dog lay on her side. Now, as he moved her, he could see that the right eye was blue. It gave her a raffish, mischievous look, he thought, even in her current low condition.

"Good girl," he told her. Then, as he turned back to Tug, he realized that the little horse was eyeing him curiously.

"We've got a dog," he said. Tug shook his head and snorted, Why?